Josephine Woempner Clifford McCrackin

Another Juanita

And other stories

Josephine Woempner Clifford McCrackin

Another Juanita
And other stories

ISBN/EAN: 9783744754965

Printed in Europe, USA, Canada, Australia, Japan

Cover: Foto ©Andreas Hilbeck / pixelio.de

More available books at **www.hansebooks.com**

"ANOTHER JUANITA"

AND OTHER STORIES

BY

JOSEPHINE CLIFFORD

BUFFALO
CHARLES WELLS MOULTON
1893

PREFACE AND DEDICATION.

YEARS have passed since the first of the sketches contained in this volume were written, and so many of the Army people of my day have crossed the River before me, that I stand waiting on this shore, almost alone. To those living, whether grey in honors when the chief drama of my life was enacted, or yet cadets at West Point, and whose friends were my friends, this book is inscribed, with a thousand remembrances of acts of courtesy and chivalrous protection granted.

To California, which gave me welcome and a home when my Army life was over, I have endeavored to become a daughter worthy of the fair land and the generous, great-hearted people who live in it.

May their kindness to me never grow less.

JOSEPHINE CLIFFORD McCRACKIN.

Monte Paraiso Rancho, Santa Cruz Mountains, Cal.,
September 15, 1892.

CONTENTS.

"ANOTHER JUANITA."

"ANOTHER JUANITA."

It was years ago, before railroads or street cars were even dreamed of in Albuquerque, and the arrival of a military outfit, however large or limited, was always an event of some importance, furnishing entertainment for the unclothed and unkempt youth of this ancient town, as well as change and excitement for the troops garrisoned there.

The cavalcade approaching now consisted of half a dozen men, and sergeant of Co. N., 105th United States cavalry, and a dozen or so of recruits for Co. O, of the same regiment, stationed at Fort Craig, the entire outfit serving as escort to Captain Dunwood, who was coming to take command of his company and the fort, after having passed what he considered a very unprofitable winter in Washington, on staff duty.

"So Dunwood is coming," had been the comment of Lieutenant Crane, class-mate and best friend of his captain, and whose ruling passion it was to pose as a cynic. "Why in the name of all that's sensible, didn't he stay where he was well off, and where his military services were needed, as leader of the German at evening parties, and martial lay-figure at presidential receptions. But he was always one of the kind who wanted to go where duty called him, and he will find this, I venture to say, just the field to practice it."

The younger lieutenant, to whom these remarks were

addressed, reminded his senior how he himself had assured him frequently that everybody liked Captain Dunwood in spite of his perfections; to which the elder laughingly assented, adding with a cynical smile, "but that was before he had spent the winter on staff-duty in Washington."

In the meantime the captain was slowly nearing his destination. His tired horse's hoofs pressed on hot sand, and the dreary mound, rising just ahead of horse and rider, seemed entirely composed of this same material, looking exactly as dull yellow, as dry and as hot as the sand under the horse's feet. He threw rather a disconsolate look upon this mound, but would have relapsed into his former train of thought, had not a movement among his men attracted his attention.

"Albuquerque!" he heard some one say, and after a little he descried the low, flat-roofed houses, singly or in clumps of two and three, scattered, without order or system, in among the sand. On closer approach he could see where the flag waved above the military quarters, and the Rio Grande, where it wound its muddy way along. The weary horses seemed to understand that the end of the long tedious march was near; their riders knew what they owed to themselves and their position, and by the time the little half-nude street gamins had heralded the coming of a soldier's train to the rest of the population, it was quite like a band of conquering heroes that Captain Dunwood's escort arrived at the adobe buildings representing the barracks at Albuquerque.

Amidst much clatter and stamping of hores's feet,

clinking of arms and shouting of orders, the captain and his friend clasped hands and exchanged cordial greetings, while the salutation of the junior, an exchange from another regiment, and who had lately joined, was more ceremonious and official, but returned not less heartily on the captain's part.

The sun had set long before the din and confusion common to such occasions had quite subsided; indeed it was not until after roll-call and retreat that the troopers seemed to have fitted themselves to their new quarters, and not until after "taps" that the captain and his first lieutenant were allowed the luxury of a conversation strictly tête à tête, Lieutenant Howard wearing the sash as officer of the day being necessarily detained outside, by his duties. Many a peal of laughter reached his ears, however, making him feel lonely and isolated, though he knew it was childish to harbor the little jealous pang that tried to steal into his heart. But it was not entirely a discussion of social affairs, or the Colonel's last *mot*, that filled up the hours intervening between taps and midnight; for by the time the sentinel called out this hour of ghosts and goblins on his short and beaten way, Captain Dunwood had made himself *au fait* in regard to everything concerning his company from which he had been separated for over a year, as well as the people, so far as necessary, and the conditions of the place where he was to command post.

After guard-mount, the next morning, Lieutenant Crane's horse was led out for Captain Dunwood, as he had decided to visit the commissary quarters at once, partly to make an inspection of the buildings with a view to extending them, partly to see what portion of its contents might be found available for his own larder. The orderly who held the horse, and was to escort the captain, seemed to have some trouble in keeping the animal quiet, and with the instinct of a cavalry man, Captain Dunwood's attention was immediately fixed upon the handsome black, whose bridle he had taken from the man's hand. Stepping back a few paces for better scrutiny, he soon satisfied himself that the horse was only impatient to be off, and turned to mount the animal.

The space in front of the quarters was ample enough in dimension to be called "plaza" by the natives, parade ground by the soldiers. An old church, built of adobe, but Moorish in architecture, straggled into the street that ran past the square; and while the captain's back was turned, two figures had come in sight on this street, both females, one dressed in the conventional limp black skirts of the Mexican woman, with a coarse *rebozo* over her head, the other, the mistress, evidently, arrayed also in black, though dress and *rebozo* were finer, and different in make. A lithe, slender figure this, that moved along with the half languid grace, which only the Spanish women seem to possess, a little ahead of her companion. The servant had long since passed the last milestone of youth, while the mistress still stood upon its threshold. From the folds of the *rebozo* over the old woman's head, but one eye gleamed out with watchful fire. The face of the young lady was hardly more than half covered; her eyes, lustrous, soft and black, looked timidly and a little startled at horse and man, and the straight line of a delicate nose, with thin, sensitive nostrils, was left uncovered. Only one moment, however; the next a narrow, wax-white hand drew the screen closer, and head and face were both averted, leaving nothing but the other hand exposed to view; this hand, as the captain, recovering himself with an effort, and quickly mounting his horse, could not but observe, held a little, shabby prayer-book, and wrapped around it a rosary, composed of some blood-red bead or berry, such as natives of tropic countries love to shape into strands for this pious purpose.

The women passed to the right of him, while Captain Dunwood proceeded slowly on his way by the old church, from which they had probably emerged. Not that he allowed himself to speculate upon anything of the kind; what concern of his was it where two women had come from or where they were going to? He did not even cast a look at the church, as he would have done, probably, under other circumstances; but looked straight ahead, so as not to miss the street he was to turn into, in order to reach the commissary. Street, he said to himself, was too dignified a name to bestow upon these mud-baked thoroughfares, running this way and that, accommodating themselves to the mud-baked houses, that stood wherever their builder had seen fit to put them. The window in these buildings was merely a square hole let into the mud wall, high up in some corner; but wherever there was a door, it stood hospitably open, and if there were inmates, they were sure to come out and give pleasant greeting to the stranger.

Captain Dunwood's severely classic features softened, and

a little later on, when he came to a more pretentious place, where an adobe wall enclosed a garden with peach trees and grape vines, to say nothing of the broad, cool-looking, though rough-built *casa*, he said to himself: "It is not so bad, after all; a polite, good-natured people, and among the better classes no doubt there is refinement, and probably great comfort in the homes of the wealthy. I wonder—" he checked himself, but blushing like a girl, at his own hypocrisy, he continued, "yes, I wonder what those blood-red berries were, in the rosary."

At noon they had a cheerful dinner together, the three officers, and in the course of the afternoon Lieutenant Howard declared to his friend Crane that he too liked Captain Dunwood in spite of his perfections.

Toward sunset, just before retreat was sounded, and while Lieutenant Crane was re-adjusting his sash, as officer of the day, there was borne on the light breeze that wandered in at the window, a sound that startled Captain Dunwood more thoroughly than the firing of cannon would have done; the tones of a woman's voice in song, soft, sweet and expressive, but without great depth or power.

"What is that?" he asked turning to his friend, surprised and paralyzed at the perfect equanimity with which his second in command continued to spread the sash across his breast.

"That?" he asked in return. "Ah, that is Juanita," and as the orderly appeared at the door just then, he called out some direction to him, following the man immediately so that the captain was left alone in the room,

" Juanita," he repeated, " as if everybody didn't know 'Juanita' as well as they know their A B C's; but—" and again a blush came to his face as his thoughts ran back swiftly to that morning's meeting, and he found himself wondering in which direction the two forms had vanished after passing him. All this time the tones of the voice still came floating in, nearer now, and more distinct since he was entirely alone; both verses of the old Spanish love-song were sung, though he could not catch the words at this distance. It was not till the last note had died away that he became aware how absorbed he had been; he roused himself with a guilty start when he found that the tramp of the soldiers, the loud voice of the sergeant, even the call of the bugle on the outside, had been completely unheard by him.

Not another word of information was volunteered by his lieutenant, and no siren's voice could have wooed the captain into compromising his dignity by asking further questions. Next morning, at guard-mount, he observed for the first time, a heavy adobe wall, running around what seemed a fair-sized garden, with the house standing close to the wall next the quarters. Only a narrow street, or lane, divided it from the barracks, and high up in the corner of the house facing the lane, was one of the small, square windows he had noticed everywhere, latticed here, and giving a decidedly Spanish look to the whole place.

During the day, it must be confessed, the captain's eyes traveled more than once in the direction of the lattice, and he listened, involuntarily, for a sound of the voice he had heard on the previous evening. But the day passed, somewhat tediously; the fatigue of the long march was still upon him, he thought, making him *distrait* and averse to earnest application. To-morrow that should be remedied, he resolved; he would take up the duties for which he had left the gay life at the Capitol, and nothing should make him swerve from his self-chosen path. To be sure it did not run among flowers nor along green fields; it had turned into a dry and barren land, without freshness or beauty, unless it were such stray bits as he raised his eyes to now, where he stood in front of the quarters and looked afar off to the mountain-range that bordered the horizon. The sun was just setting, and as it bathed the lower hills in pale rose and dim yellow, the higher and more distant peaks and mountain-tops were transformed into domes and spires, flushed with deep red and royal purple, save where a cool silver hue marked some pinnacle more lofty than the rest.

With rapt attention he watched the glorious sight, his deep, earnest eyes full of a warm light, though his form stood erect and unbending, as if ready to give the word of command. Suddenly, and almost beside him, he fancied, the notes of the song he had heard the day before rang out again, coming, as he could not doubt, through the lattice-work of the window high up in the *casa* on the other side of the lane. Not a soul was in sight, though within the barracks he heard the sounds of preparation for roll-call and retreat, and that, perhaps, was the reason why neither Crane nor Howard was here to listen to the voice that came so clear and sweet from the throat of the singer.

But the next moment, with bent brows and an impatient pull at his moustache, Captain Dunwood turned away and entered his quarters. What had he to do with golden sunsets, or the romance to be woven out of a Spanish love-song, and the woman who sang it behind her latticed window?

On the Sunday following, before inspection and dress-parade, the captain and his two subalterns, one acting as adjutant, were assembled in front of the quarters, waiting for the Padre to dismiss his scant congregation from the church, so that the clash of arms and the blare of trumpets might not interfere with the devotions of the little flock. Soon they emerged, passing, for the most part, down the street in an opposite direction to the open square; only three figures turned and came toward where our friends stood. It was impossible for Captain Dunwood to change his position, as the good Padre Carmelo was evidently bent on saluting him, and while he waited for the priest to approach, his eyes scanned the other two figures. To-day the younger, though again clad in the sombre black which the Spanish women so love, was not shrouded in the *rebozo;* a lace mantilla, while it draped the form, was thrown over the head so as to cover only the heavy braids of hair, leaving the face and a part of the slender throat entirely uncovered. The same shabby little prayer-book was in her hands, and the rosary of blood-red beads; but the slim hands were gloved to-day, and their waxen whiteness hidden. The old woman behind her was dressed as usual, but dress and *rebozo* were of a more glossy black.

Only a moment his eyes had rested on her, our friend thought; he had had time, however, to see that her throat was white as any swan's, and that her lips were not as bright red as some would suppose a Spanish girl's lips ought to be. But the Padre was already shaking him by the hand, and in his stiff and not always correct English, was expressing his acknowledgements of Captain Dunwood's kindness, branching out into profuse praise of the younger officers and the soldiery in general. These two younger officers, in the meantime, were exchanging brief but significant remarks and observations.

"She never looked like that at either of us," said the adjutant, and his friend Crane seemed to know at once whom the young man meant, for he replied:

"Poor thing; but she might as well strangle her young affections. Dunwood is not given to flirtation, and would in cold blood order any man to be shot, if he could, who cast his eye on a female whom he could not, or would not, make his wife. Somerville, of the 12th, wrote and said that the women in Washington were too much for our brave captain; he did not capitulate, he simply ran.

"He *is* a handsome fellow," the other admitted, "though rather stern-looking for a lady-killer."

"Does not the greatest glory attach to the taking of the most forbidding fortress? However, Herbert can be as gay as a lark, and we all know how good and gentle he is at heart."

"Indeed he is," was the younger lieutenant's ready acknowledgement, though his face blushed at the remembrance of the little short-comings, the kindly setting aright of which had made him so enthusiastic in his captain's praise. "A very 'Knight Bayard.' When I had first left the Academy and was in the other regiment, the fellows used to say of him that he would kill his enemy in the field without compunction, but would die of remorse if he thought he had taken unfair advantage of him, or hurt his feelings before he cut him down."

At this point the interview between Father Carmelo and the post-commander came to an end, as the ceremonious salutations from both sides showed, and the tramp of horses and shouts of sergeant and corporal put every thought, not connected with the service, to flight.

A soldier's duties do not relax on Sunday, and a commander must be ever at his post, so that he could not have escaped the tones of the voice that sang "Juanita" in the old *casa* next to him, if he had wanted to. But he did not want to; he listened and wondered; wondered how the low, sweet voice that seemed so well fitted to sing

> " Soft o'er the fountain,
> Lingering falls the southern moon "

could rise to the force and the passion of the love-glowing refrain:

> " Nita! Juanita!
> Ask thy soul if we should part."

It was the first time, perhaps, that he had listened with a critic's ear, and he could hear no change of expression in the singer's voice; throughout the song it was pleading, entreating, beseeching, but there was neither longing nor passion in the tones. If he had examined the inmost recesses of his heart he would have discovered that the face of the girl whom he took to be the singer, had been present with him all day; the face was so pure, the eyes so soft, and the lips, the lips were not the color that always accompany black eyes and ebony hair. They were full and perfect in mold, but the color was pale red, much better suited to the expression of her eyes, he thought, than to the words of that song she was always singing. He arose and left his room before the clang of the bugle sounding roll-call could break into the last faint strains that came from the latticed window.

In the course of the week Captain Dunwood had occasion to visit what was termed "the pasture," a piece of land close by the river, where a number of cottonwood trees flourished, and underneath, in clumps, grew coarse, wiry grass of some kind. The Mexicans grandly called it a *bosque*, for in their eyes, in this tree-barren land, it represented quite a little forest, but had been made use of, by that cynical individual, the *teniente* Crane, to turn any horse into, that had in any manner become temporarily unfit for service. The captain was on foot, and as the nearest way led directly past the front of the garden-wall enclosing the *casa* with the latticed window, he felt no hesitation in looking in at the open gate, and, as the door was just opposite, and it open too, he could see through the hall of the house, and into the little court-yard it enclosed. The sun lay warm and golden on the flags with which it was paved, and drew heavy perfume from the tuberoses and white

Annunciation lilies with which the round beds, raised several feet above the ground and neatly walled in with white slabs, were filled. A Castilian rose covered one side of the house, the foliage fresh and green, a joy to the eye, huge bunches of its sweet-smelling blossoms making the picture perfect in its way. Outside there was not a blade of grass, not the tiniest spot of green to be seen, but the gurgle and drips of water inside the garden, explained the secret of the wealth of bloom; it drew its supply from the chief *acequia* leading from the Rio Grande, and the owner of the *casa* unquestionably belonged to the *gente finos* of Albuquerque.

Captain Dunwood's horse had been turned into the pasture after the march out from Fort Riley, and the faithful animal came running up with a glad whinny, when he heard the whistle with which his master had been wont to call him. He was so overjoyed to see his master again, that he seemed broken-hearted when the captain turned to go and leave him behind, and determining to send his orderly for him at once, Captain Dunwood retraced his steps quickly, to have the horse brought in before stable-call. As he neared his neighbor's house he became aware of a sound of chatting and laughter, and looking up saw a number of young ladies approaching, a sight rare enough in the dreary streets of Alberquerque. It was plain that they were coming toward the house, and that he would meet them almost in front of the gate; but he could neither turn, nor accelerate his already swift pace, so he raised his hat to the whole bevy, among whom he recognized two of the daughters of the renowned Mexican,

General Armigo, of Santa Ana fame, and, as centre of the group, the face and form of her who had been present to his thoughts more than he liked to own to himself. She alone was not laughing; indeed there was something inexpressibly sad in the eyes that were raised to his, though she did not speak when the rest gayly returned the Captain's salute. How delicate, nay, fragile, she looked beside some of the women, whose rich, dark beauty did full justice to the descriptions one reads of the star-eyed daughters of the Spanish race. One in particular, who was supporting his young neighbor, in jest, apparently, though the girl looked as if she might well need her support. He felt an impulse to fling off the arm that encircled the girl's slender waist, as if it were the grossest contamination to have it there.

" *That* one might sing 'Juanita,' and I would never wonder at it; but the little one with the pale-red lips and the flower-eyes—No," he decided, "she ought not to sing it." And he felt fairly indignant, when, just as the sun, with its last rays, clothed the distant mountains with a beauty evanescent as it was glorious, her voice floated out again, sweet and low at first, but growing almost piercing in its tones— beseeching, entreating, pleading. It irritated him so that he left his room to once more fondle his horse, who stamped impatiently for him to come.

One morning an unusual excitement stirred the pulses of the sleepy old town; *commadres* and *compadres* flitted from their own *casa* to their neighbors', and a sound of loud talking was heard on the street; the Indians had attacked a band of sheep-herders on the river-bank, some fifteen or twenty miles below, had driven off the sheep and killed one or two of the herders. This, however, was so common an occurrence, that the Mexicans would hardly have troubled themselves or the post-commander about the matter, but the sheep-herders who came in, reported an unusually large band of savages, and that they had taken the direction toward the camp of Señor Francisco Delagado, who, with his herders, was engaged in branding horses and cattle, of which he had the greater number by far, of any man in the surrounding country. It was not long till Lieutenant Crane appeared before his commander, in official attitude, to report that some of the citizens had applied for military escort and protection to reach the camp of Señor Delagado, if possible, before the Indians could commit further depredations. The report ended, the subaltern officer quickly lapsed into friend and class-mate of by-gone years.

"Let me go, Bert," he pleaded excitedly. "You know who Don Francisco is, don't you?"

"No," replied his captain, "and it makes no difference; he must have succor and protection. But, I say, Fred, let young Howard go—give him a chance to win his spurs. And by Jove! the youngster shall have my horse, his own is under the weather."

And when "boots and saddles" was sounded, there was no prouder mortal on earth than Lieutenant Charles Howard, Co. N., 105th U. S. Cavalry. Twenty men was quite a command, and the young officer felt that he would settle the vexed question of "what to do with the Indians," in very short order, before he got back. His captain made preparations, however, to send re-inforcements if it became necessary.

Late in the afternoon, just before stable call, a courier arrived at headquarters to report Señor Delagado murdered by the Indians, of whom two bands were on the war-path, slaughtering sheep and cattle, driving off horses, and killing and scalping those who tried to protect their herds. The body of the murdered man was being brought home by the herders who had escaped, but as they had saved only a few of the little *burros*, their progress was slow, having to shift the corpse from the back of one *burro* to that of another, as the animals tired down.

At the same time a number of Mexicans living in the out-skirts of the town, came trooping in, fearing that the Indians would attack their forlorn little ranchos and besiege the town, wherefore they implored the *teniente* and his *commandante* not to send any more of the troops away, but issue rations to them, the Mexicans, at once, as they had no doubt the Appaches had stolen the provisions left on their ranches already, and that it had consequently become the duty of the government to feed them.

"The blind faith these people have in their Uncle Sam's willingness and ability to take care of them, would be touching, if it were not so amusing," remarked Lieutenant Crane with his most synical smile, which died away, however, to give place to an expression of real concern, as he saw, in the fading light, the figure of the old woman from the neighboring *casa*, coming around the corner and approaching them, making her way fearlessly through horses and men, turning neither right nor left till she reached the captain and stepped in front of him. This gentleman had noticed her approach but paid no heed, as he was anxious to have Lieutenant Crane and his men on the march before nightfall, and in the confusion hardly caught the meaning of what she said. Only one word had struck his ear, but being by no means perfect in the language of the country he turned impatiently to his lieutenant.

"What does she want? Tell her not to bother us now; let her come some other time."

"Maria comes with a message from her young mistress. The Señorita Juanita wishes, nay begs, to see you at her *casa* some time this evening, as soon as you can make it possible."

"Who?" asked the captain in bewilderment so deep that his friend could scarce refrain from laughing.

"Juanita Delagado," he repeated tersely. "Did you not know it was her father whom the Indians killed?"

"I knew nothing," and he leaned against the horse of his lieutenant, so white in the face that this individual compassionately suppressed the long, low whistle, which, as a cynic, he felt that he ought to give vent to.

"But Juanita, she says," continued Lieutenant Crane, interpreting, "knows nothing of her father's death as yet, and Maria says that you must not allude to it when you call on her. She is frail and delicate, and they want time to prepare her for the shock."

"I can't go, Crane; not to-night. Tell her so," said the captain desperately; then casting his eyes around, "how can I?   Don't you see, it will be my duty to stay right here, after you go?"

Lieutenant Crane's good-nature seemed suddenly to leave him, and he showed decided symptoms of mutiny, as he turned to go, muttering something about "martinet-ism" under his breath.

"No, no, Fred, don't say that!" the great, tall man called after him in piteous tones, and his friend Crane never forgot the look of pain on his face, and never forgave himself for having brought it there.

He dismissed the old woman with the assurance that if Captain Dunwood could not come that night, he would do himself the honor to call upon the señorita at the earliest possible moment the next morning, and the old servant, mourning bitterly the loss of her master, expressed her gratification at seeing all these soldiers going forth to punish his murderers.

During the night Lieutenant Crane with his men returned, having met old Arrogo, the guide, whom Lieutenant Howard had sent as avant-courier with the message that the Indians had fled to the mountains, after a short, sharp encounter, which had cost one horse and the wounding of two men.   As these could be transported but slowly on improvised litters swung between two horses, the herders bearing the body of Señor Delagado, had attached themselves to the command, by the *teniente* Howard's permission, and the whole train would arrive probably sometime before noon on the morrow.

In the morning, directly after guard-mount, Captain

Dunwood stood irresolute in front of the quarters, with brows contracted, an anxious, troubled look on his face, not aware that the look was reflected on another face, brought close to the window, inside the quarters. For once Lieutenant Crane seemed to have forgotten that a true cynic knows neither pity nor feels concern, for his eyes were full of a compassion for which there was no apparent cause, as he watched the tall figure, standing idly and with an air of indecision entirely foreign to his usually quiet, determined manner.

At this moment old Maria came in sight, evidently on her way from the Delagado *casa* to the church, and Dunwood at once moved forward, so that he intercepted the woman half way between the two places. The little plaza was deserted, as were the streets and winding ways that ran into it, but Maria took no notice of the captain's approach; when he stood before her she stopped, and after some little difficulty he made her understand his wish to be led to her mistress, the Señorita Juanita. The old woman looked up at him with dim, lustreless eye.

"You wish to see my mistress?" she asked in low, hushed tones; "Come, then, with me, and you shall see Juanita," and she continued on her way to the church, beckoning him on when she noticed him hesitate and stop. Seeing her motion to him, he followed her, as in a dream, till they reached the narrow little vestibule of the church, the inside of which he saw to-day for the first time. Only once, passing just as the congregation was dismissed, and both inside doors open, he had observed, half unconsciously, that as in all the old Catholic churches in the Territory, there were neither seats nor benches through the entire body of the church, the pious worshippers kneeling during mass and vespers.

As the door swung back, the old servant, with a deft motion of the hand, threw a thin spray of the blessed water on the heretic whom she was admitting into the sanctuary, ere she took him by the hand and led him toward the altar. . Tall tapers were burning here, shedding a subdued light on the emblems of faith adorning it; but, strange to say there were no flowers there, and the balustrade, running around the raised dais, was shrouded in black. When he grew accustomed to the half darkness, after the glaring light outside, he saw that the church was empty; no worshippers were there, only he and the old servant, and directly in front of them, at the foot of the altar, a bier, upon which lay stretched a figure that might have been molded in wax, or cut out of marble. Snowy draperies enshrouded it, and a filmy, spotless veil was thrown over glossy braids of darkest hair. The face, so fair and sweet to look upon, was still and cold; and the slim white hands, crossed peacefully above the breast, were made to hold a rosary of blood-red beads.

"Juanita!" Had he shrieked it aloud in his agony? He never knew, but the old woman drew him down beside her, and after making the sign of the cross above his head, bent weeping, over her rosary, murmuring prayers which his soul echoed, though he neither understood the words nor knew the formula.

"Juanita—" he could think nothing but the one word, which he repeated to himself softly, over and over again. Then suddenly a sharp pain clutched his heart, and he felt the perspiration starting on his forehead, and when he passed his hand across to wipe the damp away, it seemed to him they must be drops of blood, and look like the beads of the rosary in the dead girl's hands.

He never knew how long he had been there, whether hours or minutes, when he heard a soft footstep behind him and felt a hand laid gently on his shoulder.

"Come with me, my son." It was the old priest who stooped over him and helped him to rise, picking up his hat and gently leading him out of the church. Not through the door by which he had entered, but through a side door, which led to the father's habitation close by.

"Sit here, my son," he said as he pointed to a home-made settee of brightest calico stuffed with lambs' wool. He stepped into an adjoining room and brought a small glass of wine, with which he insisted his guest must at least moisten his lips. Then he sat beside him silently, with bowed head, grief in every line of his kindly, wrinkled face.

At last Captain Dunwood turned to him. "When—" he began to question, in a voice that struck him as not being his own.

"When did Juanita die?" Father Carmelo finished the question for him. "Ah! poor child—poor child; she never be very strong, and one time, American doctor, post-surgeon, he say ' the señorita have trouble with her heart'

So when Indians kill her father, I say to Maria: not tell her
yet; let me prepare her; she good child—oh! so good—I
tell her by and by, to-morrow, is to say, to-day. She had
say to me, when she hear how Indians attack sheep-herders,
she say: ' I send for the *commandante;* on my knees I will
beg him to go to my father and bring him home.' But last
night one foolish old woman she run in to see her, and she
cry 'oh! you poor child—Indians kill your father dead;
shoot him with guns, shoot him with arrows, till he die.'
Maria, she hear one loud scream, she run in to room, she
see Juanita go so—'' The old man clasped both hands over
his heart, and swayed his body to and fro. " Maria throw
her arms around her, and Juanita lay her head against her
shoulder, so—'' dropping his head to one side, " and when
Maria look in her face, she is dead.''

After a moment's silence the priest, with tears in his eyes
went on, " Good child, good daughter; when her father go
away, about a month ago, to hold *rodeo*, on the river-bank,
on his rancho, she cry and cry, 'perhaps I never see my
father again,' and I say: ' be a good girl, pray to the saints,
and ask Holy Virgin to protect him, and he come soon
again!' Next day she say '*Padre mio*, I will sing every
day, when the sun go down, one Ave Maria, till my father
come home again, and I know Holy Virgin will protect
him.' But the good God has taken her father;—was better
so, perhaps; we must not complain—''

Captain Dunwood sat rigid, and looked into the father's
face with wild, burning eyes.

" What,'' he asked roughly, in a hoarse, broken voice,

"What did she sing every evening, when the sun went down?"

"An Ave Maria; oh! it is beautiful, this Ave," the old priest continued. "It is here, in this prayer-book of Juanita's," and he took the little worn book from his writing-table; "I will find it directly." But his eyes were not so ready to find things as they had been twenty years ago, and while turning over the leaves, he spoke again: "The good sisters in Santa Fé they teach her to sing; they all love her so—" his voice broke. "Juanita's mother," he went on, "the Donna Inez, she die when Juanita was small little child, and old Maria she take care of her, always; and her heart is broken now. Here, my son, you read the Latin? Here it is, she sing it every day. You never hear her sing? Oh! she sing beautiful."

"Father—" the captain spoke without looking at the open page of the book, "Father, do you know the air, the song of 'Juanita'?"

"Song? Of Juanita?" the Padre asked, incredulously. "No, no one make song of Juanita. Why make song of our Juanita? Must be another Juanita."

His visitor arose. "Father," he pleaded, "give me the book," and without a word the litte volume was laid in the young man's outstretched palm; then, as he bowed low his head, the priest raised his hand in benediction, and Captain Dunwood left the roof that had sheltered him in his hour of bitterest pain.

Outside he staggered like one who had received a mortal blow; his face was ashen and his eyes sunken, as though years of suffering had passed over him. His way to the quarters lay past the church door; should he enter to see once more the face of the dead girl whom he would not love in life? No; no need of going in; what he should see there was mirrored on his heart so faithfully that a lifetime would not suffice to efface the picture. But his punishment was a just one, for, was not he, after all, like one of the fools and coxcombs whom he had always so despised—who believed every girl's glance to be directed to them, every woman's song addressed to their susceptible heart. A just punishment, he kept repeating, and none too great; yet how should he bear it every day of his life till he died.

Little he thought of his disheveled hair and his reeling gait, as he came in sight of the quarters; the only dread he felt was that he might encounter some one to whom he would have to speak. But that prince of cynics, Lieutenant Crane, had never left his post of observation, and, thanks to his forethought, Captain Dunwood, all unconscious of his friend's management, safely reached the room he had left that morning with his heart a-flutter. Only that morning? It seemed ages since; and would time always drag like this, till it merged into eternity? Then a heavy stupor took possession of him, he heard -no duty-call, no bugle-sound, till late in the evening when Lieutenant Crane knocked at his door to inquire whether he would receive Lieutenant Howard's report at roll-call.

When the young lieutenant stood before his commanding

officer a little later, making the official report of his expedition, he seemed utterly oblivious of the haggard face and
blood-shot eyes which it pained his tender heart to note.
During the hours that followed, Captain Dunwood moved
among his men as duty demanded, both his lieutenants,
with an adroitness born of the affection they felt for their
commander, standing between him and the things that they
felt must jar upon his feelings this day. But late in the
night, long after tattoo had rounded off the duties of the
day, and taps had warned the soldiers in their quarters that
lights must be put out, Captain Dunwood sat in his room
again, alone and desolate of heart, as he felt he should
always be.

Only the steps of the sentinel, as he paced to and fro
with measured tread, fell upon his ear; but the monotonous
refrain of "All is well"—heard a thousand times before—
made discord in his soul to-night. Then at last he took, from
where it had pressed close against his heart, the little worn
prayer-book of the dead girl, and reverently laid it on the
table before him. Hot tears shot into his eyes as he read
on, and again he heard her singing, in tones that were
pleading, beseeching, entreating, the grand old hymn to the
mother of God—

"Ave Maria—Ave Maria!
Gracia plena, Dominus tecum.
Benedicts tu, in mulieribus,
Benedictus fructus, ventris tue Jesu.
Ave Maria—Gracia plena,
Ave Maria—Ave Maria!"

" Santa Maria—Santa Maria!
  Mater Dei, ora pronobis.
  Ora pronobis, peccatoribus,
  Nunc et in hora mortris nostra, amen.
  Santa Maria—Mater Dei,
  Santa Maria, ora pronobis!"

Camp-Life in Arizona.

CAMP-LIFE IN ARIZONA.

WE reached Tucson just in time to attend Major Smith's wedding. Looking on the scene that night, I quite forgot that I was in Arizona. The bride was faultless in white *moire antique*, blonde veil, and satin slippers. Wives of the military officers and civil dignitaries of the Territory were not behind in elegance of dress and appointments, and the gay uniforms and regulation epaulettes of the officers made up, altogether, what Jenks would have called a "brilliant and *recherché* assemblage." The General, on whose arm I had been leaning during the performance of the ceremony, was the first to salute the bride, and then the band (six or eight "musically organized" soldiers on furlough from Camp Grant) struck up one of those soft, thrilling waltzes that only the dark-eyed Mexicans could have taught these susceptible individuals. I am afraid that I was less interested in the dancing than in the supper, which was a source of unlimited wonder to me, but accounted for, perhaps, in part, by the knowledge that the groom was quartermaster of the United States Army, and the father of the bride, one of the oldest and wealthiest citizens of Tucson.

I was to spend the summer in camp, some sixty miles below Tucson, and the colonel, his wife and I, started out on the following afternoon, with a dozen cavalrymen as escort, and reached camp just at guard-mount the next morning.   The officers who had not been fortunate enough to obtain the post commander's permission to attend the grand wedding, soon called at the colonel's quarters to hear the good news in general, and accounts of the festivities in particular.   The colonel's junior lieutenant had been particularly anxious to attend, and had been pining away, he said, since the colonel had left camp without him. The commanding officer himself called while he was still complaining, and, to make amends for his cruelty to the youth, the captain requested that I should choose him, the lieutenant, to act as escort and cavalier on my first ride. The lieutenant declared himself amply satisfied with the reparation made, and started joyously to prepare himself, when we were a little surprised to see him turn very abruptly, and re-enter the room somewhat quicker than he had left it.   Behind him appeared Braun, the cook, beating the ground furiously with a heavy piece of wood, and screaming, at the top of his voice, "Look out! look out! he's half dead, but he can crawl yet," and, crowding to the door, we saw a most beautiful specimen of an Arizona rattle-snake, some six feet long, trying to escape from Braun's vigorous blows.   But the blows had been well aimed, and the snake soon lay motionless at the corner of the *adobe* kitchen, inside which Braun had first discovered it, curled up on the flour-sack.

Some time after, when I left my tent, equipped and ready to mount my horse, I noticed that he stood just where the snake had breathed its last, but, since I no longer saw it there, I concluded it had been taken away from under the horse's feet, and thrown out among the weeds. What my screams were like when, on retiring to my tent for the night, I stooped to look under the bed (pursuant to a time-honored custom) before getting into it, and there found the snake curled up for a comfortable night's sleep, I will leave my lady readers to imagine; they brought half the garrison to the spot. The snake was killed over again and buried in the ground, six feet deep.

People are accustomed to think and speak of Arizona, as though the whole Territory were one waste of sand and dust; yet, could but that fearful scourge, the Apache, be removed, there are portions of this country that would soon vie, in life and beauty, with the most populous sections in California—only small portions of it, I must acknowledge— and here, at the foot of the grand old mountain overlooking our camp, was such a spot. The grass and wild flowers are always fresh and green, from the showers of rain that fall almost every week during the summer months here, and the sun, as it sinks slowly behind the mountain, tints the sky with brilliant, yet delicate hues, such as I have never seen elsewhere. Riding forth on such evenings, nothing could exceed the sense of unbounded joy and freedom I felt, not- withstanding my fear of the Indians, whom I always expected to find behind the first little hillock, or the next clump of trees, which the colonel had forbidden us to pass. Sometimes we would play '' Central Park,'' on these rides— the colonel and his wife, my companion and myself, and all the officers who did not happen to be on duty. Keeping within the lines the post commander had designated as "safe," we would pass and repass each other—some on horseback, some in ambulances, and others on foot—assuming all the style and air of New York *élite*, as we bowed and saluted afresh, every time we met.

The colonel was the only married officer in camp, so it was a matter of course that the general, who was expected on a friendly visit at the post, should be entertained at our quarters. Not that we had room enough to invite him to share our abode; his bachelor friends might give him quarters, but we would give him a state dinner, on the day of his arrival. The colonel's quarters consisted of one *adobe* room, which served as parlor, sitting-room, bed-room, and dining-room, in wet weather and on festal occasions. Beside it was the tent devoted to my use, and opposite both stood what had once been another *adobe* house, but was now a roofless ruin, with crumbling walls, containing gaps, here and there, marking the places where doors had once been projected. This was our kitchen, as a large, open fire-place in one corner, a big pile of ashes in the other, and a large home-made table in the middle of the mud floor, plainly told.

Did I say this structure was roofless? I beg pardon; there was a piece of canvas or tent cloth spread over that part of it where the cooking operations went on, only it was not long enough nor strong enough, and, when it rained, the rain water, that gathered in a pool directly over the fire-place, was always sure to break through and come down, extinguishing the fire and all hopes of dinner, just as Braun would get ready to serve that meal. It was comical to watch Braun after such mishaps. With his india-rubber blanket thrown over his shoulders, he would pick his way, through the deep puddles of water on the floor, to the ash-pile, opposite the fire-place, and there seat himself, and, with his shaggy head supported by his smutty hands, would grimly stare at the pots and pans, filled and bespattered with ashes from the recent cloud-burst of canvas.

Our supply of canned fruit and vegetables had almost given out when the time was set, definitely, for the general's visit, and we devoutly hoped that the commissary train might come in from California before the general's arrival; but when it came, we found that the usual amount of toll had been taken at Fort Yuma, so that there was very little left for the military posts in Arizona. Among the dishes served for dinner were baked beans and a meat-pie. The latter the general gallantly took to be chicken, when told that I had had a finger in the pie; but the desert was excellent, for we had still some fruits and jellies left, with plenty of sugar, spice and wine.

I have forgotten the exact words of the old saying, that "no mortal must prize himself happy before his days are ended," but I know that the colonel's wife and myself were just exchanging congratulations on the success of our dinner, in an undertone, while placing dessert on the table, when an orderly stopped at the door, and, dismounting, announced the arrival of the major from the neighboring post, together with his wife, his lieutenant and his lieutenant's wife. The ambulance was already at the door; the colonel's wife held up her hands aside in horror; Braun was rattling among the dishes at a fearful rate; where *should* we get dinner for the new-comers, if he had made away with the remnants of the feast? But, thanks to Braun, very soon a warm dinner graced the table, and the gentlemen, who had left their meal and dessert untouched on the ladies' arrival, unwittingly assisted us in serving quite a handsome repast to the late arrivals.

The next day was devoted to visiting some curious springs, not far from camp. The captain sent a large escort with us, as the place was not considered safe from Indians, but we forgot all danger while viewing the scenery along the banks of the creek, or river, into which the springs emptied. It was grand, although desolate in its utter loneliness and silence. The petrifactions made by the water of the springs were, possibly, still more remarkable. No sculptor could chisel more delicately, from marble or stone, than the leaves, the flowers, and the vines that were here preserved in undying beauty. Running over bright, green ferns, in some places, it was singular to mark how the water was gradually *freezing* the tender leaves into stone. They still looked green, but felt brittle and crisp to the touch, as though a sharp frost had overtaken them, and brushing these leaves aside, underneath were found those already brown, and in a state of perfect petrifaction.

After admiring all there was to be seen on this side of the stream, we felt a natural desire to cross over and see the other side. The gentlemen brought huge stones to pile up in the water, and the ladies were assisted over. The general acted as my cavalier, and it so happened that we were the last to cross. The rocks were wet and slippery, and stepping from one to the other, just in the middle of the creek, where the water was deepest, I glided out, or the rock turned, and I went into the water, drawing the general, who held me by the hand, in after me. Fortunately, the water was not very deep, and the sun hot, so that there was little danger to be apprehended, either from drowning or taking cold. But, for the rest of the day, it was a matter of speculation with the whole party whether the general had meant to commit suicide, or I had contemplated self-destruction; whether I had tried to drown the general, or the general had wanted to consign me to a watery grave; till it was finally determined that the double drowning-match must have been a preconcerted thing between us, as we had "plumped in" at the same time, and, but for their timely interference, would probably have reached the river Styx arm-in-arm, as we had jumped off the rocks together.

The camp seemed very quiet after our guests had departed; though dull or tedious, as many complain, a camp can never be, as long as the War Department does not take fife and drum from infantry and the bugle from cavalry—as it has already taken regimental bands from both. Reveille awakens the sleeper from his dreams in the morning, and throughout the day, the ever-changing and ever-returning calls shorten the hours till "tattoo" and "taps" send us to bed again at night. Waking up in the night, the long-drawn, monotonous "twelve o'clock, and all is well" of the sentinels on guard gives one a delicious feeling of safety and security, although, at the same time, what may seem to be the *coyotes* yelping and barking close to your tent, may be Apache Indians. During the day, every duty, military or household, is regulated and performed by the different calls of the bugle. The colonel's wife would ask of the cook, "Braun, is it not time to put the beef on the fire for dinner?" And Braun would answer, "It is only a little after fatigue-call." Or, if I asked the orderly, "When will you have time to take my saddle to the company saddler's?" he would answer, "After stable-call." "And how late is it now?" "Water-call has just gone."

There is one plague in Arizona, more to be dreaded, I think, than scorpion or tarantula, centipede or rattlesnake; it is the fever. I will leave it to the army surgeon I met in Tucson to describe the different phases and stages of this dreaded disease, and will only say that more than one-half the men of the garrison, and the greater number of officers, had succumbed to its insidious attacks before the summer was half spent. The colonel, too, was falling a victim to it, and the post commander giving the colonel permission to leave the camp in quest of health, we concluded to return the visit of the ladies at the next post. My plan to make the trip on horseback, was violently opposed at first; the colonel was too sick to ride on horseback; the captain, as commanding officer, could not leave the post (for there was no officer well enough to take his place;) the colonel's senior lieutenant was already in the camp whither we were going, on business, and the junior, with all his songs, and laughter, and gayety, was brought very near to death's door by the fever.

When the time came I mounted Black Prince, and found the captain on his iron-gray, by my side. The colonel and his wife occupied the ambulance, and the captain rode with us some five or six miles. My side-saddle contained a pocket large enough to hold a pistol, and the captain had sent me a derringer, on the previous day, to carry in it, as he did not consider my undertaking quite safe, though we had ten cavalrymen as escort. On the point of taking leave from us, the captain ordered three of the men to ride close behind me, and then turned to ask:

"Are you sure that you have that pistol with you now?"

"Why, certainly, captain," said I. "It is in my traveling-bag, in the bottom of the ambulance."

The captain looked blank.

"Just like a woman," he was impolite enough to say. "If the Indians come, of course they'll give you time to go to the ambulance, to hunt up your valise, and find your pistol."

An indignant reply rose to my lips, but the next moment pity took the place of indignation; the poor man was a bachelor. And I then and there formed the Christian resolution to introduce him to all the pretty girls of my acquaintance, in San José, Alameda and San Francisco, the very next time he came to California, on furlough.

I believe, to this day, that the captain threw an evil eye after us when we parted, or used some other spell to bring the Apaches on us, to punish me for acting "just like a woman," for when we approached the point of a range of low hills, rising out of the valley we were traversing, the corporal in command of the escort suddenly halted the train, and rode up to the ambulance. I, too, rode up, just in time to hear the corporal report to the colonel, that he had seen the head of an Indian, peering over the edge of the hill, a moment ago.

"The more fool you are, then, for halting, and giving them a chance to cut us down," said the colonel, angrily. "Tell the men to look to their arms. Ride close behind the ambulance," he said to me, hastily: "there is no time to dismount now. See—there they come!"

Around the sharp corner dashed the wild, horribly painted figures of some fifteen or twenty Apaches, mounted on little, fleet, shaggy ponies, yelling like so many devils, and leaning far over their horse's sides, they aimed their arrows at us, while following the curve of the road, that brought them directly on us. They had evidently not expected the ready fire that received them, for their horses swerved from the road. Passing to the right of us, they galloped on, shrieking and yelling, till they were far in the rear of us, and then, without a moment's hesitation or con- sultation, they abruptly turned, and charged on us once more. But the colonel had already given his orders.

"Whip up your mules," he called to the driver, "and let your horse have his head," He continued to me. "Keep close by the ambulance, and the men will cover our retreat."

We soon left the men behind, for we were on open ground, and had no ambush to fear. Once in a while a stray arrow would reach us, whizzing through the air, and frightening the animals into greater speed; but the soldiers, following us at just sufficient distance to prevent the Indians separating the ambulance from the escort, received the "brunt of the battle" on their devoted heads. I had no need to guide Black Prince; he understood the situation as well as we did. So I could turn, from time to time, to cast a hasty look on the confused scene behind me.

The colonel was by no means idle, and once, when some of the bravest "braves" had almost succeeded in cutting us off from the escort, and surrounding us, it was his revolver that sent the balls which made some of the savages yell even more horribly, before dropping bow and arrow from their stiffening fingers. I had often heard it said that the Indian warriors, when going forth to fight, were fastened to their horses in such a manner, that, even though they received their death-wound, the enemy never saw them fall. It must have been so in this case; for, though the men had counted five of them reeling, and ghastly through all their paint, not one had fallen to the ground. But they did not again attempt to cut us off from the escort. The soldiers drew closer to the ambulance, and though some of the Indians followed us for miles, probably in the hope that the one mule which had been badly wounded would give out, and leave us to their mercy, we wore out their patience at last, and reached the camp just in time to save the mule from dying on the road.

Of course, neither the men nor the horses had come off unscathed; but as no scalps had been taken by the Indians, the men regarded the attack as rather a pleasant little episode, particularly as it made heroes of them during their stay in the camp.

Quarters were not more plentiful here than they were at our post, so it was decided that we four ladies should take possession of the major's quarters, while the gentlemen—the colonel, his senior lieutenant, and the major—were to occupy the quarters of the major's lieutenant, who was also the quartermaster of the post. The colonel's senior lieutenant was quartermaster at our post, and his stay here was connected with some quartermaster transactions. When tea was over, the gentlemen adjourned to the lieutenant's quarters, opposite the parade ground, and some distance off. A long while we waited for their return, as they had promised to come back to say good-night, and when tattoo was gone, and "taps" were sounded, we retired for the night, half expecting to hear the gentlemen's knock on the only door the house contained, sometime before we fell asleep; but we slept without being disturbed. In the morning, the colonel's wife expressed her surprise that the colonel had gone to bed without bidding her good-night; the major's wife betrayed her indignation, and the lieutenant's wife—but recently married—said such a thing had never happened to her before. Nine o'clock came, and with it the colonel.

"What had kept him away last evening?" his wife asked.

"Oh, the post quartermaster had had some very difficult papers to make out, had his quarterly accounts to send in, so they had helped him till eleven o'clock, and then went to bed."

Ten o'clock brought the major.

"Why had he not returned last night?"

"Oh, the post quartermaster had had some very difficult papers to make out; it was no more than their duty to help him, so they had all sat up till twelve o'clock making out accounts, and then went to bed."

Eleven o'clock came, and with it the colonel's senior lieutenant.

"Was it right to neglect the ladies, as he had done last night?"

"Well, no; but the post quartermaster had had some very difficult papers to make out; it was no more than fair that they should help him, so they had all sat up with him till two o'clock, and then it was certainly too late to bid the ladies good-night."

The post quartermaster himself failed to put in an appearance altogether, and when his wife visited their quarters, late in the afternoon, she found him in bed, with an excruciating headache. So we all came to the conclusion that those quartermaster papers must have been *very* difficult indeed to make out.

A dark rumor reached our ears some weeks later, which, however, we utterly refused to believe. The soldier on duty as orderly, while we were at the camp, was reported to have said, that on the morning following the day of our arrival there, the floor of the "little black-room" at the sutler's had been thickly strewn with playing-cards, cigar-stumps, and empty champagne bottles. We never could quite account for this singular phenomenon; the soldiers, of course, are neither admitted to the sutler's "little back-room," nor do they, as a general thing, take champagne and cigars with their surreptitious games of cards; there had been no officers at the post except those mentioned. So the most natural conclusion we could come to, was, that the sutler, a young man of twenty-four, (who, I always thought, had quicksilver in his veins, from his utter inability to remain in one position longer than five minutes) had passed the night in that "little back-room," playing *solitaire*, and had drank champagne, and smoked cigars, to keep from falling asleep over this most harmless and interesting game.

San Xavier Del Bac.

SAN XAVIER DEL BAC.

THE major's wife had the brightest and most roguish black eyes, and the reddest lips I ever saw. The general called her his "youngest child," as the major had only recently been married, and she had just been installed presiding genius over the handsome *adobe* building on the corner opposite the general's headquarters in Camp Lowell (Tucson). The flag waved proudly above this house, since the general had rooms here, and messed with us; this circumstance being greatly in our favor just now, as we had an object to accomplish.

Captain W. had come to Tucson on a ten day's furlough, and since neither Mrs. S. nor I had ever seen the two old missions which have acquired so much distinction in the course of years, he was anxious that we should all visit them together. The mission nearest us, that of San Xavier del Bac, was only nine miles from Tucson; the other, Tomacarcori, near Tubac, was over fifty miles from there. However, it was impossible to visit even San Xavier without a strong and reliable escort of soldiers, for the Papagoes themselves, living in considerable numbers in the immediate vicinity of the old church, were not always safe from the attacks of their savage brethren, the Apaches, and to "gobble up" a party consisting of two military officers and two white·women, would have been of the greatest imaginable relish to the ferocious Johns.

So we had two points to make; in the first place, the general must be brought to give the major an eight days' furlough; in the next place, he must give us at least ten or twelve men as escort. The major's wife was careful to instruct the cook not by any means to get the roast overdone; the pudding received my special attention, and Mrs. S. also prepared the coffee with her own hand, and saw that the rice was put into the soup early enough. Of course the captain was in the secret of the attack meditated on the general, and smiled like a cynic when he heard his superior officer unwarily praise the soup and unsuspectingly ask for the second cup of coffee.

And now the fire was opened. The general resisted for awhile; he could not spare the major, his quartermaster, and how was he to spare twelve men to follow two venturesome women around the country? Besides, there was no ambulance at the post, except that assigned to his own use, and were we all four to crowd into the captain's buggy? And how was he ever to get his breakfast, if James was left to his own devices? He never got his coffee now till ten o'clock in the morning—and then it was generally cold. No, neither the major nor his wife could go—that was his fiat. Silence followed, and then fearful threats of chilly coffee, cold bread and frigid beefsteak, to the end of all time—to say nothing of pouting looks and refusals to play ''dummy'' at whist—were brought into the field. The general quailed, wavered, and finally capitulated and surrendered. Terms of capitulation were: six day's furlough granted to the major, the general's own ambulance, and ten men to protect it.

Soon after guard-mount next morning, the train was at the door; the ambulance with four mules, the buggy with two, and the ten men mounted on horses. I don't know exactly how long it took to pile and stow away all the baskets, guns, blankets, demijohns, revolvers, books, shot-pouches, champagne-baskets, powder-horns, boxes, carbines, coffee-pots and general drinking appliances, into the two vehicles; but the sun was pretty hot when we left the general in front of the house, looking after us through a cloud of dust. We all anticipated a very pleasant time;— we were to inspect the mission of San Xavier that day, and drive from there to Somebody's Ranch, where we expected to spend the night, and starting out again the next morning early, we would reach Tubac in the evening. Here we could rest for a day if we so chose, before going on to the Tomacarcori mission, from whence we were to proceed on a visit to a neighboring post.

The road, too, was pleasant enough, particularly where the Santa Cruz River wound its narrow band of silver along through the plain. The *mesquite* grows into large trees here, and though the dust was intolerable, away from the river, we should still have thought the landscape charming, considering it was in Arizona, had it not been for the numerous rude wooden crosses which decorated a great many of the trees, marking a grave at the foot of each. Americans, foreigners and Mexicans alike, have this mark of respect paid them, when the Indians have made away with them and their scalps. A wooden cross is hung up in the tree, if there is one in the neighborhood; if not, every one who passes the grave lays a stone, or, where this can not be obtained, a clod of dirt, or the bone of some defunct animal, on it.

A dozen or two of low buildings, half underground, part *adobe*, part brush, occupied by Papagoes, surrounded the mission. Of the extensively-cultivated fields they are said to have once possessed, I could see no trace, save a few acres in the immediate neighborhood; though the rank vegetation of this low-lying portion of the country proved abundantly that flourishing gardens might be established, did but the Apaches give more peacefully disposed people permission to live here. It is said that the Papagoes were the most devoted and industrious subjects of the Jesuit Fathers who established the mission, and the great regard which their descendants still have for the mission building plainly speaks for this.

The reader must not smile to find me growing enthusiastic over Arizona at times; it is a country inexhaustible in its curiosities, natural and artificial. I stood mute with astonishment when I first saw the mission of San Xavier. How was it possible that the stolid-looking, brute-like creatures, burrowing in their filthy huts, could have had any share in erecting this truly magnificent building? They— their ancestors rather—must have been not only willing but pliable tools in the hands of the padres who devised and planned the structure. It is built of hard-baked, solid *adobe*, and covered with light-colored plastering on the outside. The high wall, likewise of *adobe*, enclosing the *corral* and other buildings, had been stained with flakes and dots of brighter colors, but was crumbling to ruin faster than the church itself. This was decorated with massive cornices in appropriate places, and though the dust and sand lay thick in all the crevices and cavities of these embellishments, there was no gainsaying the fact that they had been designed by the hand of an artist. The domes and bell-towers were particularly solid, and though none of them aspired to a very great height, still we enjoyed a view " far over the land " when we ascended one of them by means of winding stairs built entirely of *adobe*.

The interior of the building is in a state of excellent preservation; the bright colors of the frescoed *plafond* and tessallated floor are as fresh and glowing as on the day the Jesuit Fathers were driven from this country by the edict abolishing the order and expelling its members from the mother-country, sometime in seventeen hundred and seventy. It is surprising that this building has not in the course of all these long years been made even with the ground by the bands of hostile Indians continually prowling through the country. But a small number of people, comparatively speaking, live in the neighborhood; still these few Papagoes seem to have beaten off successfully every attempt the Apaches have made to get possession of the treasures held within the heavy walls of the mission building. I say treasures, for though the wooden images, executed, however, with life-like fidelity, and dressed out in all the colors of the rainbow, might not be considered as such by the Apaches, still the heavy altar service, made of pure silver, would have as much attraction for them as for the white man, and the beads and flowers decorating the shrines of the wooden saints would be highly prized by the gay Indian belles.

In my eyes there was great interest attached to this altar service. I had been told by one of the American gentlemen in Tucson, who had lived there for twenty-five years, that it had been made of silver taken from a ledge owned by the padres, worked by their Indians, and covered, so as to hide it effectually from all profane eyes, when driven from the country, as above stated. It cannot be estimated how many lives have been lost in vain attempts to discover this hidden mine. That it exists there is no doubt, for documents found in the old archives of Tucson state clearly that the locality is a certain number of miles in a given direction from the old plaza of Tucson. The difficulty is, that there are not American citizens enough in Tucson to form a company to hold the territory around the supposed location of the mine for a sufficient length of time to hunt it up, and when military officers are sent out to assume command of this district, they are generally disinclined to furnish escort a second time, when they discover that the stolen-cattle-hunt or the citizen-Indian-scout for which the protection of the United States soldiers was claimed, was in reality a gold or silver hunting expedition. And so the Lost Ledge remains—a *Fata Morgana* luring thousands to disappointment and death.

From the bell tower we could look down into a narrow

churchyard, filled with unadorned but remarkably well-kept graves, the last earthly home of many of the self-sacrificing men who came here with weary feet and aching shoulders, bearing the cross they have so successfully planted in every part of the world. There were seven ponderous bells in the tower, the eighth having fallen from the decaying beam on which it swung. Great was the desire of the captain to hear the tone of these bells; but the Mexican, who had acted as cicerone, implored him earnestly not to touch the ropes attached to them. The Papagoes, he said, were extremely jealous of people visiting the mission, and would allow no one to stir or move anything on the premises. Nevertheless the captain could not resist the temptation of striking one of the bells with his pocket-knife, and the next moment a glance at the row of huts in front of us disclosed to our view a number of dark faces so ferocious in expression that Mrs. S. and I declared we would have the rights and possessions of these people no longer infringed on, if they *were* "friendly Indians," and forthwith we returned to the protecting cover of the ambulance. The gentlemen could do nothing but follow, and the ladies intimated to Francis, the driver, their pressing desire to travel at an accelerated speed.

We had soon left the Mission behind, and saw nothing but sand, a few straggling *mesquite* trees and an occasional *verde* bush, till we reached the ranch. Traveling in Arizona is not like traveling in a respectable Christian country, where houses, farms, cattle, stables, cabins, are to be seen now and then. Anyone may take up the line of march here and

continue in any direction he chooses for weeks and not see a
solitary human being in all this time, if he is not inclined to
turn out of his way to hunt up the few settlers and cast-a-
ways to be found here, providing, always, that a chance
Apache does not break up his ramble.

I have forgotten the name of the man who "kept the
ranch" at which we were entertained that night.   Nor do I
know why the place was called a "ranch;" the supposition
being that a ranch is a farm—Mexicanized, of course, but
still a place where vegetables and cereals are raised, and
cows are kept, and butter is made, and eggs laid by chick-
ens popularly believed to unalterably exist in and on such
places.   To give people who have not visited Arizona an
idea of a ranch in this delightful country, I would simply
and briefly state that we found, on an open flat, a *corral*,
in which were incarcerated five or six lean Spanish cows
(that always have one failing—they give no milk), three
lame mules, and one shadowy goat.   Furthermore there
was a house, built of the same material as the *corral—adobe;*
and in front of this house there was a stake driven into the
ground to which was securely chained—a pig! Sharing,
however, in the general aspect of things and creatures here,
he was so thin as to be almost transparent—resembling
much more the skeleton of a departed grunter than a live
pig.

The man, an American, was truly glad to see us, and his
wife, a Mexican, had probably never seen American
women before.   She was sick and looked as thin as her four-
footed *protegé*, the pig; but she jabbered most delightedly

and delightfully whenever we came within her reach. Her husband cooked a very plalatable supper for us, which consisted mainly of *chili colorado, tortillas* and *frijoles*, and after we had despatched it, in the cool of the evening, we became dimly conscious of the fact that the house before us consisted of just one room, and *it* not very large. The woman was sick, so we could not hear of her sleeeping out of doors—though the original plan had been that Mrs. S. and I should sleep in the house, and the major, the captain and everybody else, out of doors. The man felt duly grateful to us for not wanting to turn his sick wife out of the house, and kindly offered to turn his stock out of the *corral* and let us two ladies sleep there; but this offer we declined on our side—and we all slept out of doors.

The preparations and procedures in this case, I give for the benefit of those who may find themselves placed in the same situation under like conditions. Four piles of fresh hay were spread on the ground in front of the house (the pig having been previously removed out of harm's way) a distance of about ten paces between the piles; on each hay-pile was spread one blanket to lie on, another to cover with, and here, reader, we all four slept the sleep of the just. The night was pleasant, and for a wonder I was not afraid, because half the number of our escort were on guard, patroling the space in front of the house where we lay hedged in by the ambulance on one side and the buggy on the other. No matter what the earth might be where we lay, the heavens above were beautiful,— clearer, bluer than they could be anywhere else.

We started for Tubac betimes next morning, and here we found no lack of quarters. I don't mean " quarters " in a military sense, for the troops stationed here in the spring of the year had been removed to a new camp, actually leaving behind them the roofless walls of the old church in which their horses had been stabled. The house we took possession of was a comfortable *adobe* building with a stone floor and two small windows containing several panes of glass. The proprietor, an American, had taken his invalid wife "out of town" for change of air, leaving behind him, in his anxiety for the health of the enfeebled woman, everything that could not be gotten into his traveling carriage. The table, and chairs constructed of wood and cowhide, were of some value in this country, not to speak of the straw-mats and bedstead we found in one room and the *ollo* filled with sweet, fresh water, and the gourd dipper. We felt that our lines had fallen in pleasant places, and concluded to remain here the next day.

What a decayed, dead place Tubac is! So silent, so graveyard-like, that the few American gentlemen who still lived here, and came to call on us in the course of the evening, impressed me as being so many ghosts who had left their graves and were digging their way out from among wasted gardens and crumbling walls, to look upon their own kind in the flesh once more after they themselves had been " dead—long dead."

The next day was hot and cloudless, the sun burning down fiercely on the silent streets and ruined houses. It looked hopeless enough, this "deserted village," once teeming with life and industry, now lifeless and devastated from the effects of the plague that had depopulated the cities, laid waste the rural districts, and closed the mines of the territory—the Apache Indian. All along the road we traversed that day, we passed by groves of cottonwood and willows, and along neglected gardens where the vine was still clustering and the melon trailing over the untilled ground. The land looked fair to the eye where the Santa Cruz river gratefully refreshed the fields that bordered it with trees and flowers, and had it not been for the oppressive silence, in which there seemed to lurk danger and death, could we have seen man and beast laboring together in these rich fields, could we have heard the song of the ploughman at his plough, and the shout of sturdy children at play among the waving corn and the willows by the stream, nothing could have been more lovely than this scene. But instead of that, there were only silent graves among the tangled masses of vegetation which had sprung up from the seed planted there by the hands of the men who now slept in these graves; the men who had been scalped and tomahawked and racked and tortured by the red fiends, before the land they had tilled in the sweat of their brow had had time to bring forth its crops.

Why do not the philanthropists of our eastern cities, who cry out on the military authorities and the brave men who spend their lives battling against the common foe, why do not they, with their doctrine of eternal kindness, and forbearance toward the "noble red man," come out among the Apaches and try the effect of their preaching in person?

Let them but make the short trip from Tubac to Calabazas, let them count the graves by the wayside, and let them hear how this man was surprised in his little brush cabin and killed while fighting his way out of its smoking walls; how that one's scalp had been taken and his body mutilated before life had left it; how the family of five, in the graves near that pile of ruins there, had held out against the enemy year after year, till at last, after suffering tortures more appalling than the demons in hell could invent, their remains were laid to rest here by a party of white men who chanced this way after long, long days!

We were approaching a neighborhood now that had a sad interest for me, and I had obtained a solemn though reluctant promise from the captain to point out to me the exact spot where the tragedy I am about to speak of had been enacted. While on a visit at a military post some distance from here, the circumstance took place, and left an impression I can never shake off. It was nothing unusual at this place for one or two men to be "picked off" by the Indians in the course of the week. The colonel, whose wife I was visiting, spared neither himself nor his subordinate officers in regard to scouting and general watchfulness; still the Indians continued to surprise the men tending herd, or at work in the company garden, mail-carrying, or on escort duty.

One day three men came in, reporting two men killed and the third (the colonel's bugler during the war) taken prisoner. The colonel himself went in command of the scouting party sent out in pursuit of the Indians. It was horrible to think of the poor bugler having fallen into the hands of the Apaches alive,—better dead, a thousand times! But search and pursuit were fruitless, and the party returned bringing the bodies of the two murdered men. While waiting for further orders from District Headquarters, the colonel was told by a wagon-master, who had just brought in a team from Tubac, over the very ground on which this last murder had been committed, that the colonel's cousin, and another gentleman belonging to the quartermaster department, would be likely to get into camp in the evening. They were both mounted, he said, and had traveled under cover of the wagon-train till reaching a ranch belonging to an American, Mr. M., where they had stopped to take dinner and to water their horses at a neighboring spring. Night came on, but we saw no travelers coming up the dusty road, and we watched for them again in the morning, thinking they had stopped at the ranch over night. We walked quite a distance, the colonel's wife and I, to meet this cousin of the colonel's, who had grown into our affections during the long and tedious voyage we had all made together. But the man we espied at last, in the cloud of dust rolling toward us, was not the man we had come out to meet; it was Mr. M., pale and haggard from over exertion and hard riding.

There was a dead man lying by the spring, he said, and a wounded man in his house, and he himself had made his way through the Apaches as best he might to obtain help.

The colonel's cousin was dead, and his companion told us, later, of the attack by the spring. The colonel's cousin had his right hand disabled from some accident, so that he could not use his revolver, and when they stopped to let the horses drink, he had said suddenly: "I don't like this, let's go," and turning his horse, he received the first arrow in his side. Urging his horse up a little hill back of the spring, he dismounted, probably hoping to escape into the bushes; but the blood was streaming from his side, and, sinking down, the Apaches sprang on him, threw him to the ground, and pierced him through with their lances till he died.

Strangely enough, the detachment of soldiers sent to bring his body to the camp found that of the bugler in the bushes near, partly decomposed, torn by *coyotes*, and recognized only by some rags of clothing and his teeth. They were buried together, the boxes containing the bodies being taken to the burying-ground outside the camp on an army-wagon.

When we had reached almost the summit of a high hill, over, or rather along, the edge of which wound a narrow road, our train halted; for from here could be seen the spring and the little hill back of it, which we were not to pass on our way. We left the ambulance, the better to see, and to get still a better view of the surrounding country. Mrs. S. and I proposed to climb up the steep bank just above us, which was covered with brushwood and loose rocks. But the gentlemen would not hear of it; indeed, the captain proposed to place sentinels if we chose to remain long enough to dispose of our lunch in this place. Seeing that we had left the ambulance, the corporal in charge of the escort gave the men permission to dismount and they were standing and lying on the ground as best suited them to rest from riding. The ambulance-driver, too, had left his seat, and was holding conversation with his mules, while looking over the different straps and buckles of the harness, stepping very carefully on the side nearest the fall of the hill, as it would be quite a little distance to roll down, should he slip or stumble on the loose pebbles.

Though declining to take our lunch on this eminence, Mrs. S. and I nevertheless clambered into the buggy to see what the gentlemen had provided, and we were just descanting on the merits of some *tomales*, prepared and baked between maize leaves by a Mexican woman of Tubac, when a shot startled the mules, which, jumping aside, threw me from my perch to the ground. Another and another shot followed, and cries and yells mingled with them, while arrows rent the air with their own peculiar "whiz." My first thought was retreat to the ambulance; but the mules, frightened and bewildered, plunged and kicked, till an unfortunate spring brought the ambulance too near the edge of the hill, and down it went, vanishing from sight as it overturned heavily, as though trying hard to maintain its equilibrium. Mrs. S., in her terror, was trying to extricate herself from the buggy, where she had comfortably seated herself between baskets and hampers just before the attack; and the captain, unarmed, defenceless, and exposed to the musket-balls and arrows of the Indians lying in ambush among the rocks and bushes overhead, was holding the terrified mules attached to the buggy, calling on Mrs. S. to remain where she was and on the major and me to get into the buggy as quickly as we could. All was confusion and bewilderment, the worst of the enemy's fire, of course, being directed to the buggy and the women; but a number of savages breaking from cover to rush down the hill after the ambulance and secure the mules, considerably hastened my movements in entering the buggy, and the last I saw was a confused mass of major, soldiers, Apaches and horses.

I regret to say that the captain was not polite enough to wait till I was comfortably seated, but allowed the mules to rush off at break-neck speed the very moment he himself had placed his foot in the vehicle, scattering in this manner all the *tomales*, which the Apaches had not given us time to secure, and a number of hard-boiled eggs, over the road. Altogether, it was a fast drive, but I can think of others, which, if not quite so rapid, were better enjoyed by me, and besides, the captain stepped on my toe getting into the buggy, and Mrs. S. lost her new hat. But we did not mention these things to the captain till we were safe in port at the next camp, for which we made in a straight line, without turning off to visit the mission Tomacarcori, as we had intended on starting. No doubt we lost a great deal by not seeing Tomacarcori mission; but it was better to lose that, we concluded, than to lose our scalps.

CROSSING THE RIO GRANDE.

CROSSING THE RIO GRANDE.

WE were to cross the Rio Grande at Los Pinos, somewhere below Albuquerque. This was our first crossing; many and dire were our subsequent crossings of this crooked stream, which repeatedly threw itself across our path, as it pursued its course in fitful windings through the land. Orders had been issued by the general commanding the district that neither the officers nor men of the —th cavalry should enter Santa Fé or Albuquerque, and as the general's headquarters were in Santa Fé (Fort Marcy) the officers reluctantly refrained from making their appearance in a place they had an almost irresistable desire to see. Of the four ladies with our command, only one, the major's wife, had been in the Territory before; but as she spoke with no great enthusiasm of the beauties and attractions of Santa Fé, we, for our part, were tolerably content to pass by within twenty-five miles of it. There had been heavy rains throughout the Territory, and the low land along the river was mostly under water; but in the spot which the colonel had selected for fording, the water was shallow, and we expected to cross in safety.

Our train was quite respectable in size,—three companies of cavalry, some twenty-five army wagons, two or three pieces of ordnance, and the carriages and ambulances which we were occupying. The mounted men were to cross the river first.   It was singular to see how many of the horses rebelled against going into the water, and distressing to witness the terror they displayed when the treacherous quicksand gave way under their feet, and the wicked flood seemed to engulf them deeper and deeper. The colonel, in his light carriage, guiding the horses with his own hands, next went in, followed by the carriages of his subordinate officers, ranged strictly according to the rank of their respective owners.   I gave a convulsive gasp when the water, coming into the bottom of our travelling-carriage, first touched my feet; the running of the current made me dizzy and faint, so I covered my eyes with my hands, and opened them only when I felt the water rise higher and higher over my feet.   When we had gained the other side, the officers rode from carriage to carriage, offering the ladies congratulations on the first safe passage of the Rio Grande, and—a draught of commissary-whisky from their field flasks.   I, for one, accepted both with thanks; for the little keg stowed away under the seat was empty; in fact, we were out of supplies of every kind, as we had counted on drawing from the Santa Fé commissary.

The captain had been stationed in the Territory before the war, and, as it happened, our present colonel had been his commanding officer then.   We were to pass almost within sight of Albuquerque on the following day, and the command was to camp some eighteen miles above, at Peralta, for the night, and upon these facts the captain based his plans for mutiny on a small scale.   When we had reached the top of a low chain of hills, he ordered Melville, the driver, to stop, and said to me:

"There is a road leading down from here across the flat into Albuquerque. If I can but remember the road, we can drive into Albuquerque, get supplies from the quartermaster, and reach Peralta before nine o'clock to-night."

I was delighted with the prospect, for the brown sugar with which we had of late been compelled to sweeten our coffee, was not at all to my liking; I knew there was white sugar in the commissary at Albuquerque, so I did not in the least object to going there, although contrary to orders. Our orderly, with the saddle-horses, was to continue on with the command, while we were to turn down the mountain road, here, where we were out of the colonel's sight. But the mules drawing our carriage were warmly attached to my white horse, and they set up such an atrocious screaming on seeing him led off, that we were forced to recall Mohrman and let him take the lead with Toby.

Reaching the flat, we found the *acequias*, the deep ditches dug by the Mexicans for the purpose of irrigating their fields with water from the Rio Grande, all overflowed, and covering the fields with water; but we managed to pick our way over the precarious road, and soon discovered a low round sand-hill in the distance. Pointing toward it, the captain said: "There is Albuquerque;" but, open my eyes as I might, *I* could see nothing but the sand-hill and a strip of water beyond. The windings of the river had left us far in the interior of the country on the previous day; now as we approached the Rio Grande again, I saw at the foot of the hill a number of low *adobe* buildings.   It was one of the largest cities in the Territory, this clump of mud-houses growing up out of the cheerless, monotonous plain, where neither a blade of grass nor a single wild-flower sprang up to gladden the heart.   Over toward the mountains, the country was more pleasing, and a number of Pueblo Indian women, bearing baskets filled with the most delicious of grapes, peaches and melons, testified to the fact that all of New Mexico was not a sterile plain, and that all of its Indians were not savages. Mexican women, with the inevitable *revoso* covering head and shoulders, flitted through the streets, or haunted the shops kept by a few enterprising Jews.

Making our way to the Quartermaster's Department, we were somewhat startled to see the colonel's light carriage drawn up in front of it.   We were on the point of beating a hasty retreat, when the colonel's querulous voice accosted the captain:

"Don't you know, sir, that the commanding general's orders are that neither officers nor men of the —th cavalry are to enter Santa Fé or Albuquerque?"

"I was not aware that any exception had been made in favor of the colonel commanding the —th cavalry," answered the captain, recovering himself, and for the rest of the day the captain was invisible to the colonel's *official* eye, though they met at every corner they happened to turn.

The captain knew that his salvation depended on reaching camp in advance of the colonel. Should the colonel make the camp before we did, he would immediately inquire for the captain, and place him under arrest, if not court-martial him, for "absence without leave." So we hastily concluded our purchases, entered the carriage, and were just about to leave the quartermaster's corral, when we discovered that Mohrman was missing. Great was our distress, and many and deep, I fear, the captain's curses. The men's quarters were hunted through, and all the saloons of which the city could boast were searched, but our Dutchman was not to be found. At last the bugler was ordered out, and the first note of the well-known signal brought Mohrman to the spot, flushed and excited, but totally ignorant of the unpleasant consequences which his delay might cause the captain.

. I must stop here to state that the servant-girl whom I had engaged at Leavenworth City had basely deserted me and gone over to the enemy;—that is, she had married an infantry sergeant at Fort Union, leaving me without cook or laundress. So Mohrman, still panting and breathless, and turning his hat around in his hands very fast, came out with:

"Madame, I know you don't like Charlie for a cook, and you have no laundress; now, I found such a nice Mexican girl here this afternoon,—her name is Joaquina. I think she would learn to cook very easily; and if you would only get me the Captain's consent, I'd marry the girl right away, so that she could wait on you all the time."

The Captain answered in my place; I could not tell exactly what, but I know ˋthe guard-house was mentioned.

Night was on us before we had left the neighborhood of the ranches surrounding Albuquerque; but the *acequias* were growing less frequent, so that I flattered myself we should have little difficulty in reaching camp. It grew darker and darker, until at last it was almost impossible to distinguish Toby's white form as he was led just in advance of the carriage. The captain thought he could not have forgotten the "lay of the land" in seven short years, and assured me that it was perfectly safe travelling along the sand-hills that border the Rio Grand, where there is not an inch of ground between the carriage-wheel and the precipice high over the river. The stars were reflected in the waters far below me, and I knew that one false step of our mules would send us all down to those bright orbs in the water. On the other side, the hill rose high above us; and had the driver turned but the length of a finger to that side, the rebound would have capsized the carriage and hurled it over the bank.

Thus the minutes crept on; and when I rejoiced at last to find that the road descended and I could no longer see the stars below me, I was rudely torn from my fancied security by the most savage yells that ever greeted humnan ears. They proceeded from a spot not very far distant, where a crowd of half-naked and demon-like forms were dancing around a flickering fire.

"Oh, heaven!" I exclaimed, "we have fallen into the

hands of hostile Indians,—and you always told me there were only friendly ones here!"

The Captain tried to explain to me that they were only celebrating some feast, and proposed to take one of the Indians with us to act as guide to Peralta; but I refused to consent, and Melville gave them a wide berth, landing us after a little while in the midst of *acequias* and numberless pools of water forming one endless ocean.

My terror was considerably increased when I heard the heavy plunging of a horse, laboring through the morass behind us. "Those are robbers," I whispered, "and they will challenge us directly." But, to my horror, the Captain addressed the rider, whose figure I could now discern close to the carriage. He was a Mexican, who had seen where the "Cabelleros" were camped near Peralta, and would guide us there. So he rode before the orderly, and we followed Toby as well as we could, though it seemed to me we were getting into deeper water at every step. I could distinguish trees, too, such as I knew grew only along the Rio Grande; and I felt convinced that the treacherous Mexican was leading us straight into the river. The water had long since saturated the bag of white sugar which I had put under the seat with my own hands, and the package of tea beside it would not be improved in flavor by the muddy water; but all this did not trouble me so much under these circumstances, my chief aim being at present to keep myself out of water and my eye on Toby—the latter rather difficut, I must own, in the Egyptian darkness. Suddenly I heard the Mexican call out something in Spanish, and Toby vanished into an abyss of some kind before my eyes, while the carriage at the same time struck against something hard, and was lifted out of the water. Then the truth of the happy escape we had made, dawned on us. The water from the neighboring river had flooded the whole flat, and had hidden from our sight the deep *acequia* cutting through the country here; the Mexican had given warning, but Mohrman, not understanding the language, had missed the bridge which we were fortunate enough to strike. The camp-fire flashed on us a few moments later. Charlie had made the tent look so comfortable, and prepared so excellent a supper, that I was glad to think "Joaquina" had not superseded him. The colonel's orderly had not yet inquired for the captain; so I presumed, with a great deal of complacency, that our revered commander was still floundering in the slush and water of the Rio Grande.

There were long and dreary day's marches to be made between here and Fort Craig, where the headquarters of the —th Regiment were to be established; and there, too, I should lose the company of the other ladies—the adjutant, the major, and the lieutenant all belonging to the colonel's staff. We had but one more stream to cross together—the Tecolate "creek" at the village of the same name. I did not know why the officers should show so much more aversion to crossing this "creek" than they had evinced at the passage of the Rio Grande. Thinking, perhaps, that "ignorance is bliss," they had not enlightened me, but left me to enjoy my ramble among the ruins of an old church, or mission, which I had discovered in the neighborhood of the little town. The other ladies not becoming so deeply interested in the scraps of glass and pottery strewing the ground here, had returned to the carriages; and when the colonel sent word that the large hospital ambulance in which we were to cross were ready, I could not be found. When I made my way to the "creek" later, the ambulance had already returned and was waiting to carry me over. The creek was a wild, turbulent stream, rushing along with a fury that had already carried the strong bridge before it, and had lodged it against a sharp bend in the river, where the skeletons of the first three army-wagons that had been launched in the flood were keeping it company.

"Is there no other way of crossing beside getting into that ambulance?" I asked in a very subdued manner.

"None," was the colonel's answer; "but the mules are led by ropes, and an escort follows the ambulance."

It was not an easy task to hold conversation in the immediate neighborhood of the stream. The colonel screamed at the top of his voice, to make himself heard above the loud roar of the water, and I was compelled to repeat every word I said three times over;—so I entered the ambulance without another syllable. The ropes attached to the heads of the mules were taken in charge by four mounted men; the officers, including the captain, had been ordered to remain with their respective companies, but they came to the river a moment to speak some encouraging words to me, after which the signal was given and we started. It seemed impossible for the mules to drag the heavy vehicle behind them when they had once lost their footing, and they were themselves almost dragged along by the ropes which the soldiers held. One of the soldiers allowed his rope to slacken when the mules first began to swim, and in an instans it was twined around the animal's legs; the mule struggled and kicked, frightening the others, and soon I could see nothing but one wild mass, battling and plunging in the water. From the shore came confused cries of, "Let the mules go—" "Cut the ropes—" "The ambulance is going over—" "Hold on to the ropes—" and a hundred other things that seemed still to ring in my ears after the ambulance had toppled over, and I was clinging to the covering with all the energy of desperation. I must have lost my hold after a while, for I was thrown against the ruins of the bridge with such violence that my consciousness returned all in a moment, and I clung to the beams and planks until rescued. I was taken to a Mexican house, where I was wrapped in the blankets which the soldiers, who had already crossed, carried rolled on their saddles. It was not very cold, still I should not have voluntarily gone swimming with my clothes on, just that day, for one of the three wrecked wagons had contained my trunks, and none of the other ladies could have furnished me with any of their clothing, even had they known of my predicament; for their trunks were still on the other side.

Mohrman had been left to keep watch at my door, to be ready in case I should want for anything, and I asked him presently:

"Did the other ladies get over the river safely?"

"Yes, madam," was the grave answer; "only the escort

riding so close behind the ambulance splashing so, the ladies were wet through, and the colonel, who was over here when they came, put them out on the little flat, just behind the bank there, to dry, and he has placed a sentinel so that nobody can come that way till the sun has dried them.''

I could not help smiling to think what two interesting groups we formed, the three ladies ''drying in the sun,'' and I enjoying all the luxury of a regular ''water-cure pack,'' rolled up in a dozen gray soldier blankets.

From Fort Craig, Company M proceeded alone, crossing the Rio Grande once more before entering on the *Jornada del Muerto*, the '' Desert of Death.''   It was a long and tedious march through the desert, really almost a ''Journey of Death,'' for the sun was fearfully hot and water scarce. To be sure the Rio Grande could be reached by turning a distance of ten or twelve miles out of the straight line of march; but what the penalty of such a rash act might be, I learned as we neared the Point of Rocks, a favorite ambush of the Indians, for we were in the Indian country now, since we had left Fort Craig behind us.

I saw a number of moving objects as we approached, and was greatly alarmed; but with the aid of the captain's field-glass, soon made them out to be a party of soldiers. They drew up in line when they saw the captain approaching; perhaps they had not discovered my presence in time, for before the sergeant could throw a blanket over the cold, stark form lying on a pile of rocks by the roadside, I had already seen the ghastly face and mutilated limbs of the wretched man who had found a cruel death here only the day before. It was the usual story; two men (civilians), mounted, were crossing the desert together, when, driven almost crazy with thirst, they had attempted to turn down to the river to fill their canteens, but were attacked and chased for miles by the Indians; one man escaped to Fort Selden, but the other fell into the devils' hands, to be tortured to death. The soldiers dug his grave, wrapped him in a gray blanket, and laid him to rest on the silent and lonely desert. Many such scenes have I witnessed since; but there, by this stranger's grave, I knelt to say a short prayer, while the soldiers, with uncovered heads, threw the last earth on the low mound.

We reached Fort Selden in the evening; after a night's rest we crossed the Rio Grande there, for the third and last time, leaving it behind us, on the way to our still far distant post.

An Episode of "Fort Desolation."

AN EPISODE OF "FORT DESOLATION."

"How much you resemble Mrs. Arnold!" exclaimed the Doctor's wife, after an hour's acquaintance, the day we reached Fort Craig. It was not the first time that I had heard my resemblance to this, to me, unknown lady remarked on. A portion of the regiment of Colored troops to which Doctor Kline belonged, and which we met on their way into the States, as we were coming out, had been camped near us one night; and a colored laundress, who had good-naturedly come over to our tent to take the place of my girl, who was sick, had broken into the same exclamation on first beholding me. Captain Arnold belonged to the same regiment, and was expecting, like all the Volunteers then in the territory, to be ordered home and mustered out of service, as soon as the body of Regular troops to which my husband belonged, could be assigned their respective posts. Their expectations were not to be realized for some time yet; and when I left the territory, a year later, a part of these troops were still on the frontier.

Fort Craig was not our destination; to reach it, we should be obliged to pass through, and stop for a day or two, at the very post of which Captain Arnold had command—which would afford me excellent and ample opportunity for judging of the asserted likeness between this lady and myself. I must explain why we were, in a measure, compelled to stop at Fort Desolation (we will call it so).   It was located in the midst of a desert—the most desolate and inhospitable that can be imagined—in the heart of an Indian country, and just so far removed from the direct route across the desert as to make it impracticable to turn in there with a command, or a large number of soldiers; for which reason, troops crossing here always carried water-barrels filled, with them.   A small party, however, such as ours was then, could not with any safety camp out the one night they must, despite the best ambulance-mules, pass on the desert.

With most pardonable curiosity, I endeavored to learn something more of the woman who was so much like me in appearance; and I began straightway to question Mrs. Kline about her.   The impression of a frank, open character, which this lady had made on me at first, vanished at once when she found that Mrs. Arnold was to be made the subject of conversation between us.

" Is she pretty? "

" Yes—quite so."   Ahem! and looked like me.   But my mother's saying, that there might be a striking resemblance between a very handsome and a very plain person, presented itself to my memory like an uninvited guest, and I concluded not to fall to imagining vain things on so slight a support.

" What kind of a man is Captain Arnold? "

" The most good-natured man in the world."

" Oh!"   Something in the manner of her saying this in praise of Captain Arnold made me think she wanted to say nothing further; so I stopped questioning.

We left the doctor and his wife early the next morning,

and reached Fort Desolation at night-fall. The orderly had preceded us a short distance, and, when the ambulance stopped at the captain's quarters, Mrs. Arnold appeared on the threshold, holding a lantern in her hand. She raised it to let the light fall into the ambulance; and as the rays fell on her own face, I could see that she looked like—a sister I had. The captain was absent, inspecting the picket-posts he had established along the river, and would return by by morning, Mrs. Arnold said; and she busied herself with me in a pleasant, pretty manner. She could not resemble me in height and figure, I said to myself, for she was smaller and more delicately made; nor had anyone in our family such deep-blue eyes, save mother—we children had to content ourselves with gray ones.

The night outside was dark and chilly; but in the captain's house there were light and warmth, and it was bright with the fires that burned in the fireplaces of the different rooms—all opening one into the other. I was forcibly struck with the difference between the quarters at Fort Craig and Mrs. Arnold's home at Fort Desolation. Comforts (luxuries in this country) of all kinds made it attractive: bright carpets were on the floors here; while at the Doctor's quarters at Fort Craig, one was always reminded of cold feet and centipedes, when looking at the naked *adobe* floors. Embroidered covers were spread on the tables, and white coverlets on the beds; while at the doctor's all these things were made hideous by hospital-linen and gray blankets. Easy-chairs and lounges, manufactured from flour-barrels, saw-bucks and candle-boxes were made gorgeous and comfortable with red calico and sheep's-wool; but the crowning glory of parlor, bed-room and sitting-room was a dazzling toilet set of china—gilt-edged, and sprinkled with delicate bouquets of moss roses and foliage.

"Where did you get it?" I asked in astonishment—*not* envy.

"Isn't it pretty?" she asked, triumphantly. "The captain's quartermaster, Lieutenant Rockdale, brought it from Santa Fé for me, and paid a mint of money for it, no doubt."

At the supper-table I saw Lieutenant Rockdale, who commanded the post in the captain's absence, being the only officer there beside the captain; and, as he messed with them altogether, I need not say that the table was well supplied with all the delicacies that New York and Baltimore send out to less highly favored portions of the universe, in tin cans. Lieutenant Rockdale was a handsome man—a trifle effeminate, perhaps, with languishing, brown eyes and soft voice. He seemed delighted with our visit, and took my husband off to his own quarters, while Mrs. Arnold and I looked over pictures of her friends, over albums and at all the hundred little curiosities which she had accumulated while in the territory. The cares of the household seemed to sit very lightly on her; a negro woman Constantia, and a mulatto boy of twelve or thirteen, sharing the labor between them. The boy seemed to be a favorite with Mrs. Arnold, though she tantalized and tormented him, as I afterward found she tormented and tantalized every living creature over which she had the power.

I had noticed, while Constantia and Fred were clearing off the table, that she had cut him a slice from a very choice cake, toward which the child had cast longing looks. Placing it carefully on a plate, when he had to leave it for a moment to do something his mistress had bidden him, in the twinkling of an eye she had hidden it, and when the boy missed it, she expressed her regret at his carelessness, and artfully led his suspicions toward Constantia. Hearing him whimpering and sniffling as he went back and forth between dining-room and kitchen, his childish distress at losing the cake seemed to afford her the same amusement that a stage-play would, and she laughed till the tears rolled down her cheeks. Later, he was summoned to replenish the fire, and, knowing the little darky's aversion for going out of the house bare-headed (he had an idea that his cap could prevent the Indian arrows from penetrating his skull), she hid the cap he had left in the adjoining room, and then laughed immoderately at his terror on leaving the house without it. The next morning, she led me out to the stables to show me her horse, a magnificent, black animal, wild-eyed, with a restless, fretful air. Crossing the space in front of the house, she called to a soldier with sergeant-chevrons on his arms, a man with just enough of Negro blood in his veins to stamp him with the curse of his race.

"Harry!" she called to him, "Harry, come hold Black for me; I want to give him a piece of sugar." She opened her hand to let him see the pieces, and he touched his cap and followed us. He loosened the halter and led the horse up to us, but the animal started back when he saw Mrs. Arnold and would not let her approach him. Harry patted his neck and soothed him, and Mrs. Arnold holding the sugar up to his view, the horse came to take it from her hand; but she quickly clutched his lip with her fingers, and blew into his face till the horse reared and plunged so that Harry could hold him no longer. Laughing like an imp, she called to Harry:

"Get on him and hold him, if you can not manage him in that way: get on him anyhow, and let Mrs. —— see him dance."

The mulatto's flashing black eyes were bent on her with a singularly reproachful look; but the next moment he was on the horse's back, the horse snorting and jumping in a perfectly frantic manner.

When Mrs. Arnold had sufficiently recovered from her merriment, she explained that the horse had not been ridden for a month; the last time she had ridden him he had thrown her—she had pricked him with a pin to urge him on faster.

About noon the captain arrived, and I found him, as Mrs. Kline had described, "the most good-natured man in the world," and, to all appearances, loving his wife with the whole of his big heart. He was big in stature, too, with broad shoulders, pleasant face and cheerful, ringing voice. The shaggy dog, who had slunk away from Mrs. Arnold, came leaping up on his master when he saw him; the horse he had ridden rubbed his nose against his master's shoulder before turning to go into his stable, and Constantia and

Fred beamed on him with their white teeth and laughing eyes from the kitchen door.   Later in the afternoon, he asked what I thought of his quarters, and told me how hard his colored soldiers had worked to build the really pretty *adobe* house in strict accordance with his wishes and directions.   But I could not quite decide whether he was more proud of the house or of the affection his men all had for him.   Then he told me the story of almost every piece of furniture in the house, and, moving from room to room, we came to where their bed stood.   Resting beside it was his carbine, which the orderly had brought in.   Taking it in his hand to examine it, he pointed it at his wife's head with the air of a brigand, and uttered, in unearthly tones:

"Your money or your life."

With a quick, cat-like spring, she was by the bed, had thrust her hands under the pillow and the next instant was holding two Derringers close to his breast.   Throwing back her head, like a heroine in velvet trousers on the stage, she returned, in the same strain:

"I can play a hand at that game, too, and go you one better!"

She laughed as she said it, the laugh that she laughed with her white teeth clenched, but there was a "glint" in her eye that I had never seen in a blue eye before.

When once more on the way, my husband asked me how I liked Mrs. Arnold.   "Very well," said I; "but—" and I did not hesitate to tell him of the peculiarities I had noticed about her.   He himself was charmed with her sprightliness, so he only responded with, "Pshaw! women!"

after which I maintained an offended (he said, offensive) silence on the subject.

Not quite four months later, my husband was recalled to Santa Fé, and we again crossed the desert, with only three men as escort. I had heard nothing from either Mrs. Arnold or the captain in all this time, for our post was farther out than theirs; indeed, so far out that nothing belonging to the same military department passed by that way. It was midsummer and the dreary hills shutting in Fort Desolation and running down toward the river some distance back of the place, were baked hard and black in the sun; the little stream that had meandered along throug the low inclosure of the fort in winter time, was now a mere bed of slime, and the plateaux, which had been leveled for the purpose of erecting the captain's house and the commissary buildings on them, could not boast of a single spear of grass or any other sign of vegetation. The captain's house lay on the highest of these plateaux; lower down, across the creek, were the quartermaster and commissary buildings (here, too, were Lieutenant Rockdale's quarters), and to the left, on the other side of the men's quarters, was the guard-house, part *jacal*, part tent-cloth.

How *could* any one live here and be happy? Black and bald the earth, as far as the eye could reach; black and dingy the tents and the huts that strewed the flat; murky and dark the ridge of fog that rose on the unseen river; murky and silent the clefts in the rocks where the sun left darkness forever.

It might have been the fading light of the waning day

that cast the peculiarly sombre shadow on the captain's house as we drew up to it; but I thought the same shadow must have fallen on the captain's face, when he appeared in the door to greet us.   Presently Mrs. Arnold fluttered up in white muslin and blue ribbons; and both did their best to make us comfortable.   How my husband felt, I don't know; but they did not succeed in making me feel comfortable. Perhaps the absence of the light fire made the rooms look so dark, even after the lights had been brought in, there was certainly a change.   Supper was placed on the table, but I missed Constantia's round face in the dining-room. In answer to my question regarding her, I was told she had expressed so strong a desire to return to the states that she had been sent to Fort Craig, there to await an opportunity to go in.   Lieutenant Rockdale's absence I noticed also. He did not mess with them any more, I was informed.

My attention was attracted to a conversation between Captain Arnold and my husband.   The guard-house, he told him, was at present occupied by two individuals who had made their appearance at Fort Desolation several days ago, and tried to prevail on the captain to sell them some of the government horses, and arms and ammunition, offering liberal payment, and promising secrecy.   They were Americans; but as the number of American settlers, or white settlers, in this country is so small, it was easy for the captain to determine that these were not of them, and their dress and general appearance led him to suspect that they belonged to that despicable class of white men who make common cause with the Indian, in order to rob and plunder, and, if need be, murder, those of their own race.   Of course they had not made these proposals directly and openly to the captain—at first representing themselves as members of a party of miners going to Pinos Altos; but they soon betrayed a familiarity with the country which only years of roaming through it could have given them.   He had felt it his duty to arrest them at once, but had handcuffed them only to-day, and meant to send them, under strong escort, to Fort Craig, where the regimental commander was stationed, as soon as some of the men from the picket-posts could be called in.

It was late when we arose from the supper-table, and the captain and my husband left us, to go down to the guard-house, while Mrs. Arnold led me into the room where their bed stood.   This room had but one window, of which window the captain was very proud; it was a *French* window, opening down to the ground.   Throwing it open Mrs. Arnold said:

"What a beautiful moon we have to-night; let us put out the candle and enjoy the moonshine," with which she laughingly extinguished the light, and drew my chair to the window.

From where I sat I could just see the men's quarters and the guard-house, though it might have been difficult from there to see the window.   We had not been seated long when I fancied I heard a noise, as though of some one stealthily approaching from somewhere in the direction to which my back was turned; then some one seemed to brush or scrape against the outside wall of the house, behind me.

"What's that?" I asked, in quick alarm. It had not remained a secret to Mrs. Arnold that I was an unmitigated coward; so she arose, and saying, " How timid you are!— it is the dog; but I will go and look," she stepped from the low window to the ground outside, and vanished around the corner of the house. Some time passed before she returned, and with a little shudder, sprang to light the candle.

" How chilly it is getting," she exclaimed; and then continued, " It was the dog we heard out there. Poor fellow; perhaps the cook had forgotton him, so I gave him his supper."

Rising from my seat to close the window on her remark about the cold, I stepped to the opposite side from where I had been sitting; and there, crossing the planks that lay over the slimy creek, and going toward the comissary buildings, was a man whose figure seemed familiar; I could not be mistaken, it was Lieutenant Rockdale. No doubt the man had a right to walk in any place he might choose; but, somehow, I could not help bringing him in connection with "the dog, poor fellow," for whom Mrs. Arnold had all at once felt such concern.

Soon the gentlemen returned, and we repaired to the parlor, where a game of chess quickly made them inaccessible to our conversation. The game was interrupted by a rap at the front door, and Harry, the sergeant whom Mrs. Arnold had compelled to mount her black horse that day, appeared on the threshold. In his face there was a change, too; his eyes flashed with an unsteady light; as he opened

the door, and ever and again, while addressing the captain
—whose thoughts were still half with the game—his looks
wandered over to where Mrs. Arnold sat. We were so
seated that the captain's back was partly toward her when
he turned to the sergeant; and he could not see the quick
gesture of impatience, or interrogation, that Mrs. Arnold
made as she caught the mullato's eye. Involuntarily, I
glanced toward him, and saw the nod of assent, or intelli-
gence, he gave in return.

The seargeant had come to report that the prisoners in
the guard-house had suddenly asked to see the captain:
they had disclosures to make to him. When Captain
Arnold returned, his face was flushed.

"The villains!" he burst out. "They had managed to
hide about $5,000 in United States bank-notes about them,
when they were searched for concealed weapons, and they
just now offered it to me, if I would let them escape. Not
only that, but from something one of them said, I have
gained the certainty that they are implicated in the massa-
cre of the party of civilians that passed through here about
two months ago: you remember, the general ordered out a
part of K Company, to rescue the one man who was supposed to have been taken prisoner. The wretches! But
I'll go myself, in the morning, to relieve the men from
picket-duty; and select the best from among them to take
the scoundrels to Santa Fé!"

When about to begin my toilet the next morning, I gave
a start of surprise. Was *that* what had made the house
look so dark and changed? Before me stood a large, tin

wash-basin—of the kind that all common mortals used out here—and the beautiful toilet-set of China, with its splendors of gilt edge and moss roses, had all disappeared, all save the soap dish and hot water pitcher, which were both defective, and looked as though they had gone through a hard struggle for existence.

When our ambulance made the ascent of the little steep hill that hides Fort Desolation from view, I saw three horses led from the stable to the captain's house—the captain's horse and two others. He was as good as his word; and before another day had passed, the two men penned up in that tent there would be well on their way to meet justice and retribution. A solitary guard, with ebony face and bayonet flashing in the morning sun, was pacing back and forth by the tent; and walking briskly from the commissary buildings toward the men's quarters, was Harry, the mulatto sergeant.

From the first glance I had at Mrs. Kline's face, when we reached Fort Craig, I knew that the mystery of the change at Fort Desolation would be solved here. Constantia was there, and acting as cook in Dr. Kline's family. She was an excellent cook, and we did ample justice to her skill, at supper time. The gentlemen leaving the table to smoke their cigars, Mrs. Kline and I settled down to another cup of tea and *médisance*. From what Constantia had stated on coming to Fort Craig, it would seem that in some way Captain Arnold's suspicions had been aroused in regard to the friendship of Lieutenant Rockdale for his wife. About two months ago, he one day pretended to start off on a tour of inspection to the picket posts, but returned, late the same night, by a different road. Stealing into the house through the kitchen, he had, rather uncermoniously, entered the bed-room, where he found Lieutenant Rockdale, toasting his feet before the fire. Raising his carbine to shoot the man, Mrs. Arnold had sprung forward, seized his arm and torn the gun from it. In the confusion that followed, the toilet-set referred to, and other articles of furniture, were demolished; but Constantia, who had crept in after the captain, to prevent mischief, if possible, gave it as her opinion that Mrs. Arnold "had grit enough for ten such men as him an' de leftenant."

"If you did but know the ingratitude of the creature," continued Mrs. Kline, "and the devotion of her husband has always shown her!" And she gave me a brief sketch of her career: Married to Arnold just at the breaking out of the war, and of poor parents, she had driven him almost to distraction by her treatment when thrown out of employment some time after. At last he went into the Union forces as substitute—giving every cent of the few hundred dollars he received to his wife, who spent it on herself for finery. Later, when for bravery and good conduct he was made lieutenant in a negro regiment, she joined her husband and finally came to the territory with him. In their regiment it was well known that he always blindly worshiped his wife, and that she had always ruled him, his purse and his company with absolute power.

Before retiring for the night we debated the question: Should we remain the next day at Fort Craig or proceed on

ur journey? The mules needed rest, as well as the horses,
or the quartermaster could not furnish fresh mules which
e had rather expected; still, my husband was anxious to
each Santa Fé as soon as possible—and we left the question
f our departure where it was to settle it next morning at
reakfast. The news that came to Fort Craig before the
ext morning, made us forget our journey—for that day, at
ast. Captain Arnold had been murdered! The big, true-
earted man was lying at Fort Desolation—dead—with his
roken eyes staring up to the heaven that had not had pity
n him—his broad breast pierced with the bullet that a
oman's treachery had sped!

Before daybreak a detachment of six men had come in
om Fort Desolution to Fort Craig, to report to the com-
ander of their regiment that Captain Arnold had been
ssassinated, and Sergeant Henry Tulliver had deserted,
aking with him one horse, two revolvers and a carbine.
aptain Arnold had started out the morning before, with
nly two men, to call in the picket posts. An hour later
he two men had come dashing back to the fort, stating that
hey had been attackted and Captian Arnold killed by the
wo white men who had been confined in the guard-house.
t was ascertained then, for the first time, that the prisoners
ad made their escape. A detachment of men was sent
ut with a wagon and the captain's body brought in—the
en with their black faces and simple hearts gathering
round it with tears and lamentations—heaping curses on the
illians who had slain their kind commander.

Suddenly a rumor had been spread among them that

Harry, the sergeant, had set the prisoners free, and instantly a hundred hoarse voices where shouting the mulatto's name—a hundred hands ready to take the traitor's life. Vainly Lieutenant Rockdale—who, after the captain's departure, had at once repaired to his house—tried to check the confusion that was quickly ripening into mutiny: the excitement only increased, and soon a crowd of black soldiers moved toward the men's quarters, with anything but peaceful intentions. Perhaps Harry's conscience had had warned him of what would come, for while the mob were searching the quarters, a little figure sprang over the planks across the creek, ran to the stables below the captain's house, and the next moment dashed over the road mounted on a wild-looking black horse.

Could they but have reached him—the infuriated men, who sent yells and carbine balls after the fugitive—he would have been sacrificed by them to the *manes* of the murdered man, and perhaps this effect had been calculated on when the fact of his having loosed the prisoners had been brought to their ears.

"How did it come to their ears?" I asked the doctor, under whose care one of the six men, overcome with fatigue and excitement had been placed. It seems that Mrs. Arnold had expressed her conviction of the Sergeant's having liberated the prisoners, to Lieutenant Rockdale, in little Fred's hearing; and the boy had innocently repeated the tale to the men. In the afternoon of the same day the detail had been made of the men who brought the news to Fort Craig, but when the detachment had been only an hour or two on the way, they found the trail of the escaped prisoners. The men could not withstand the temptation to make an effort, at least, to recapture them. They knew them to be mounted, for two horses which Sergeant Tulliver had that morning separated from the herd were missing; but the trail they followed showed the tracks of three horses, which led them to suppose that Harry had found the men and joined them.

But the trail led farther and farther from the road, and fearing to be ambushed, they turned back, leaving the man who had been driven from the companionship of his brethern by a woman's treachery, to become one of the vultures that prey on their own kind.

TOBY.

TOBY.

She was the most nervous woman I ever met. Not nervous in the common acceptation of the term; she did not scold, or fret, or worry and lay it to the state of her nerves; nor was she fidgety, or cross, or irritable. But she would grow pale at an unexpected knock at the door, or flush painfully red if she heard a quick footstep behind her. I have seen her grasp the banister for support, if, looking down the stairs into the hall-way, she discovered a form not instantly familiar to her eye, and at night, when she first came to our house, she used to beg piteously that I should leave the door between her room and mine open, so that I could rouse her quickly when her cries for help told that she was dreaming the one dream over and over again.

We were as good friends as two women get to be after a six month's acquaintance; she told me many things of her past life, but I felt that she did not tell me all there was to be told. She said she abhorred a "woman with a history," yet I knew *she* had a history if ever woman had. Long after we had parted I was surprised, one day, to find that she still thought of me, nay, she even missed me. I give you the letter as I received it from her,

You have often asked me, dear Delia, what became of Toby, the horse I so loved in my "cavalry days." As often have I answered that I could not tell you this without telling you at the same time a somewhat lengthy story. Since you have gone abroad I have so missed you that I think I can best find time now to write what you always wanted to know.

Though I have an idea that you are not a devoted reader of ''Reports and Statistics,'' you may still have seen or heard something of the ''Personal Narrative'' of J. R. Bartlett, of the Boundary Commission of the United States and Mexican Boundary Survey. The Santa Rita del Cobre, the ancient New Mexico copper mine was selected for the headquarters of the Boundary Commission in 1850–51, and fifteen years later, in 1866, after the close of the war, the United States troops (regulars) to which my husband belonged, were sent by General Carleton to build a fort where, during the war, a camp had been established by the California Volunteers, within eight miles of these famous old mines.

It is one of the loveliest spots the sun ever shone upon. Grand as well as lovely; a pleasant valley, the low green hills surrounding it overshadowed by the Mimbres mountain range, in which the copper mines are lying; while the Sierra Diavolo, holding the treasures of the Pinos Altos, was blue in the distance, and far off, like a misty dream, the outlines of the Three Brothers, mountains in Mexican territory, rose phantom-like against the horizon.

We had the clear blue sky of California there, but as I had not then been in this blessed land of ours, I hailed it as a boon and compensation to those who were cut off from civilization and home comforts at a lonely frontier post. Every morning seemed to me a fresh spring day breaking over the camp. Our tents were comfortable, the commissary well supplied; game could be easily found; fresh meat was always abundant, as we carried a large herd of cattle with us, and last, but not least, the cook and waiter, whom we drew from the company, were both faithful and diligent. The consideration of commissary supplies may seem " of the earth, earthy," to an ethereal being like yourself; but a few month's residence in a country where Apache Indians, a few scattered sheep-herds, and fat tarantulas are the chief agricultural productions, would effectually cure you of turning up your delicate little nose at the contents of the commissary department.

The company laundress was an Irishwoman, and the only white woman except myself within a distance of over a hundred miles. Though my husband was not commanding officer, I enjoyed all the privileges, benefits and amenities that generally fall to the commanding officer's wife; for this gentleman was not married, and I was the only lady in camp. So, whatever there was of comfort, convenience or pleasure to be found in or about this isolated post, was lavishly bestowed upon me, and all that could make life pleasant or enjoyable was literally at my tent door. For, as I looked out, the fair land lay bathed in sunshine before me; the laughing waters of the tiny brook that flowed through the camp flashed into my dazzled eyes; the soft winds stirred the live oak by my tent, and Toby, saddled and bridled, came up with a whinnied greeting to bear me off up into the mountains.

Dilapidated mining-shafts, covered by the growth of half a century of gnarled trees and mountain shrubs were explored; in the ravines and gulches we came upon old arastras, and remnants of habitations of a later date, but moldering and in ruins, too, with the skull of an Indian unearthed here and there, and a half-hidden grave to show that the victims of treachery or savage ambuscade had been decently buried by those who had escaped the Indian's scalping knife. They were dreary enough, some of these places, down by the waters of the little camp-brook, which here had turned into a brawling, rapid-running stream, hemmed in by steep banks, from which hung blackberry vines and the wild growth of the country. Then up again a steep ascent, that taxed all Toby's strength and agility, though it was not a heavy burden under which he labored, and having by this rough pilgrimage gained several miles in a "cut-off," the clear stream that runs through the *cañon* leading to the copper mines winds bright and sparkling before us.

How Toby loved this stream! "Whitewater" we called it, for "Coppermine Creek" did not seem pretty enough. Its bed was paved with pebbles glistening in a thousand different hues,—Pescadero and its pebble-beach could not have vied with it in wealth of color. The old Presidio at the copper mines was then invaded. Half fort, half smelting works, as it had been off and on since the beginning of the present century, there could be found in and about it the traces of murderous Apache arrows, and the rank growth of the vine and the peach tree, planted and cultivated once by the Spaniards, later by Mexicans, and destined to be replanted and nurtured by " us Americans." For the iron horse now goes snorting and shrieking by a strip of fair country which in those days lay so entirely outside the reach of civilization that in my wildest dreams I should never have forseen its connection with the rest of the world.

Here lunch was spread, the extensive works were inspected, the enormous piles of copper gazed at, and regret at the thought that the grand old place had been abandoned and was falling into ruins was uppermost in every mind.

Before the shadows grew long we remounted, for these mountain *cañons* were not pleasant in the gloaming, and more than once have I been startled by the trunk of a tree, which, with its turning leaves, looked like the blanketed form of a lurking Apache. On these occasions Toby was my sole reliance. He seemed to have the same kind of shuddering horror of an Indian that I had, and I think he would have saved me by his swift feet without my ever drawing rein on him, and wherever we dismounted he was always beside me. Anywhere near the water I could take off his bridle and let him go. He would splash in the water, drink his fill, and come back. The saddle always remained on him; but, though he had no respect for the gay saddle-cloth and would come back with it dripping, he never once attempted to roll with the saddle on him.

There was something human in his affection for me.

Many a time did he stand beside me while I poured all my trouble and my fears into his ear, which he seemed to bend nearer to me, stamping the ground sometimes as if to say, "Too bad! too bad! Come, let's up and away."

When we got tired exploring the copper mine region and the abandoned shafts lying about it, we would wend our way in the direction almost opposite, to Pinos Altos, as well known for its wealth of gold as was the Santa Rita del Cobre for its inexhaustible treasures of copper. In former years, before the war, there were only the rich placer diggings worked here, but now, since the returning troops had once more given at least nominal protection to the place, there had been a saw-mill established, and many of the magnificent tall pines from which the Mexicans had named the place were being felled and fed to the horrid buzzing monster with the sharp, insatiable teeth that seemed always crying for more—more!

The mountains we climbed to reach the spot were called the Diavolo Range, though I failed to see anything about them that was diabolical. The miners, perhaps, who battled with the Indians here after the troops had been withdrawn from the Territory at the beginning of the war, may have had a different opinion. To me the country seemed very grand and beautiful—different in character from the copper-mine region, a little sterner in feature, I thought, but the same cloudless sky smiling above it, and the same deep, unbroken, eternal silence brooding over it. I cannot realize that the hum and traffic of a growing settlement are now awakening echoes that have slept for centuries. Yet they tell me that Silver City has been established within ten miles of the very spot that once looked so hopelessly death-like and so deserted to me in my despair.   For I *was* in despair. Beautiful as was the country, pleasant as seemed my surroundings, in spite of the devotion shown me by the soldiers who composed the garrison, the repect and attention of the officers, and last, but not least, the undivided affection of my white horse, Toby, I was not only in despair—that is too mild a term—I was living, day and night, in sunlight or darkness, in a state of terror, fear, and suspence, such as cannot be described.   In the midst of apparent safety and protection, death stared me constantly in the face—not the swift, sudden death that the Indian's arrow or the ball of an assassin grants, but the slow tortures with which the cunning of the maniac puts its victim to the rack; for my husband was a madman and a murderer, and I was given, helpless and without defence, into his hands.

I tnink the discovery must have paralyzed me, for I cannot now explain to myself the dazed, unresisting state in which I remained for months after I knew the whole truth. Partly, perhaps, the consciousness that I was thousands of miles away from where help could reach me from my own people, the natural reluctance of a wife to disclose her misery and wretchedness to strangers, and the knowledge of the power which to a certain degree my husband possessed, at least, over his immediate subordinates—all these considerations, a mixture of fear and pride, held me in thrall for long, long days,   Another thing, rediculous as it may seem, prevented me from seeking protection at the hands of my husband's superior officers. Months afterwards, when I had at last made my escape, one of the ladies at Fort Union asked me:

"Why did you not call on the captain for protection?"

"How could I?" I asked in return. "You see, whenever Mrs. Mack (that was our laundress) had had a hand-to-hand misuuderstanding with her husband, Dennis, overnight, she always went to the captain to complain ol him in the morning. Dennis got three days in the gaurd-house, and straightway on coming out got drunker than he had been before. Now, I could not go and complain to the captain of *my* husband as Mrs. Mack did of hers—could I?"

No! But I would tie a strip of flannel around my throat and complain of a bad cold, in order to hide the marks that his fingers had left where he had strangled me just one degree short of suffocation. With what feeling of gratitude I used to step to the tent-door in the morning—when my liege lord gave permission—to take one more look at the sky above me, after a night passed waking, in momentary expectation of a blow from a hatchet he had concealed about the tent during the day, or with the silent horror of the situation growing on me till I was ready to shriek out, "Be merciful! Kill me at one blow, or pull the trigger the next time you hold the death-cold muzzle of your pistol to my head"—for you must know it was a favorite way he had of amusing himself. He would hold the revolver pressed close against my temple and let that horrid "click-click" sound in my ears till I was fairly numb with terror. Then he would explain to me in a low voice how utterly impossible it would be for any help to reach me in time if I screamed for help; would dilate upon the numerous strings and loops he himself had added to the fastenings of the tent, and would describe how he could cut me into small bits, and roast the bits in the fire, before being discovered, if I ever so much as dared to breathe what passed in those quiet, peaceful-looking quarters of ours. For out tent had really a cheerful home-look about it. Strictly speaking, there were two tents set up close together in one, and the soldiers, in their solicitude for my comfort, had built a wall some four feet high about it, and the canvas had been partly removed at either end to make room for a fire-place they had built of mud and stones, the chimney reaching high above the tent. So that in reality we had two rooms, a fire-place in each; and altogether our quarters were looked upon as exceedingly fine and comfortable, exciting surprise and envy in the minds of the few stray visitors that passed through camp.

That these visitors were few and far between was a great blessing, as I soon found; for after my husband had once admitted to me that he had been a murderer and had fled from justice, he was seized with an insane idea, whenever an arrival was announced in camp, that the officers of the law had tracked him here from Texas, where the crime had been commited years ago, and that *I* had communicated to them where he could be found. He had cut a round opening in the top of the tent and through the fly—as if the space had been intended for the passage of a stove-pipe—and from this point of observation he could see the dust flying up in the road when any one approached the camp. Then he

would make a spring at me—as a tiger springs upon his prey
—grasp my throat with both his murderous hands, and urge
me to confess for whom I had sent, and by whom I had sent
the message, swearing direst vengeance on all concerned did
he did but discover them.   If, however, the orderly came
to the door the next moment to announce that Mr. So-and-
so, or Such-a-one, had arrived and desired to see the lieutenant, this gentleman was all good nature and condescension,
sending an immediate invitation to the visitor to come to our
tent, or going in person to meet him.   I had to smooth my
ruffled feathers then as best I might, for I knew that the least
failure to appear happy and cheerful in. the presence of the
guest would be rigorously punished as soon as the stranger's
back was turned.

Oh, the abject, trembling misery of that time!   Often
when the captain saw us as we left camp without escort—as
the lieutenant was inclined to do—he remonstrated with us,
telling my husband how wrong it was to risk my life, even
if he chose to expose his own, to an Indian ambuscade.
Little did the kind man think that I was actually praying—
God forgive me!—that an arrow or a bullet should come,
quick and painless, and put an end to my wretched existence.

Little, too, did he know that these lonely excursions were
undertaken because his lieutenant deemed it necessary, or at
least expedient, to find a place of shelter where he could hide
—when that dreaded sheriff's *posse* came from Texas—till
he could be supplied by me with means and ways for his
escape.   How is it possible that a crazy man can have the
sense, or at least the cunning, to plan and prepare every

detail and particular for his own flight, and for the baffling of his pursuers? And yet he *was* crazy; for in the muster of arguments that could be used for his defence should he be tried for murder, he placed his main reliance on the fact of his having been for two years the inmate of a Philadelphia lunatic asylum.

Not over three miles from the camp, on the left of the road that comes up trom the Mimbres River crossing, there was a dreary, flat, table-like rock, without a trace of verdure or a sign of life about it. Underneath this, amid broken stones and drifted sand, was a small opening into which a man could crawl, where there was a small cave or burrow. This spot he selected; and here I, who was afraid of the very darkness itself, was to come every night and bring him food, water, and everything he needed, until he should find a chance to quit the country. You must remember there was nothing in this country then save military posts at long intervals and a very few poverty stricken Mexican towns and settlements, separated by hundreds of miles of waterless sand-deserts and barren rocks, with Indians of different tribes, but all alike hostile, sprinkled over the whole *ad lib-itum*. And yet I was often on the point of braving all those horrors to escape the terrors of my captivity and torture. Often when Toby came whinnying around our quarters, I was sorely temped to cut the fastenings of the tent and make a bold dash for liberty or death: for you must understand that during the lieutenant's absence from the tent I was never permitted to go to the entrance under any excuse. I might have taken an opportunity of that kind to appeal for help, or send word of my wretched condition to the commanding officer by a passing soldier—don't you see? And this he was determined to prevent. Poor Toby, never coralled or hobbled as the other horses were, would clatter around the tent for hours, pawing the ground, tugging at the ropes and scratching at the entrance; but never till the lieutenant made his appearance was I permitted to give him the lump of sugar or other tidbit I had ready for him.

Day by day my life grew more intolerable, and I don't know how soon it might have been ended, either by that man's hand or my own, had he not finally bethought him of a way in which I could perhaps benefit him. He had been placed under arrest for some trifling neglect of duty soon after we reached camp, and, though this might have been all the more pleasant under ordinary circumstances as giving him more time to pursue his own pleasure, he began to chafe under this inactivity, and at last concluded that it was a deep, underhanded plot of his superior officers to injure and annoy him. If the conception of this idea strongly suggested one of the common fancies of the insane, the remedy he concluded to adopt certainly afforded proof conclusive that his brain was turned. As, however, I saw in it a possible means of escape, I grasped at it as a drowning man grasps at a straw.

His plan was this: I was to apply to the commanding officer for an ambulance and escort as far as Santa Fé, and there I was to lay his grievances personally before General Carleton, and ask at his hand redress and protection for my husband. Redress and protection for *him!* The bitter irony and humor of the thing was not lost upon me even in the abject state of mind I was then in; but I took good care to allow no trace of my real feelings to appear upon my face.

The purpose was quickly carried out. Next day the orderly bore a note from me to the captain, written, I need hardly say, under the eyes of my tormentor; and in a little while after, a polite note from him assured me that my train would be ready at the hour mentioned, the following morning. Very gladly had this kind-hearted man consented to my request; for, as I learned later, something of the true condition of affairs at our quarters had become known to him through our orderly and the cook, and the captain felt but too happy to grant me safe escort on my way back to my friends, which he thought I was now taking.

Women, however, are the most foolish, unaccountable, soft-hearted idiots in creation. The night preceding my departure was spent in great part by the lieutenant on his knees, imploring my forgiveness, vowing reform, and explaining how it was only his great love for me that had made him at times a little tyrannical. Then, the outrageous treatment under which he had been suffering at the hands of his superior officers had well nigh driven him mad, he said. To be sure, I had seen nothing of this "outrageous treatment," except that Uncle Sam paid his salary as regularly as that of the other officers; that the commissary supplied him with the best there was; that his brother officers showed him all the courtesy he allowed them to, and that his time was entirely at his own disposal. Only in one

direction had any restraint been used. The commissary
clerk had been restricted to a certain quantity of commissary whisky to be issued to him. To this restriction I
think I owe my life. A madman pure and simple is bad
enough, in all conscience; but let this same madman intoxi-
cate himself with liquor, and a demon would blush to own
him for a brother. I know whereof I speak.

At last the morning dawned. The ambulance stood at
the door; our orderly was seated beside the driver; six
mounted men and a sergeant had been detailed as escort.
Much as I had begged, the lieutenant had not allowed Toby
to accompany me; the Indians would see me if I rode
Toby, whereas they would never know that a woman was
inside the ambulance. The captain, who came to take
leave of me, said my husband was right, that the escort was
not large and that it would be like tempting Providence—
and the Indians—for me to ride through the country on
horseback.

Toby, poor fellow, had been confined in the corral, and
his whinnies grew first rebellious and then heart-breaking,
as, dragging at his chain and wildly pawing the ground, he
saw the train moving out and leaving him behind. My
heart smote me at the horse's cries, for they were cries, if
it was only a horse; but the lieutenant had got into the
ambulance with me, to go as far as the limits of the post,
and was giving me his parting instructions and making his
parting promises of repentance and reform, and I did not
even dare to express my grief at leaving my dear, devoted
friend. Pinkow, the orderly, for whom the lieutenant had

obtained the captain's permission to accompany me all the way to Santa Fé and back, sat beside the driver of the ambulance, as I said, while the lieutenant and I sat in the seat behind. My mounted escort was to return when we reached a post where a fresh escort could be conveniently furnished, either at Fort Cummings, Fort Selden or Fort Craig. Fort McRea, but lately established at a distance of a mile or two from the Rio Grande, and to be reached only by turning aside some eight or nine miles from the straight road across the much dreaded *Jornada del Muerto*, had no soldiers to spare. There had been a line of picket posts established near the river, to protect from the ever-lurking Apache those coming here for water, on their weary journey or prospecting tour, and it required all the men they had to keep the Indians in check and afford the necessary pro-tection. But the captain felt confident that at either of the other posts I could exchange my escort and draw fresh mules for the ambulance.

Hardly had the lieutenant left the ambulance and vanished from sight when Pinkow turned in his seat and faced me with an eager, questioning look in his eyes. I was startled by the man's sudden movement, and asked in some alarm:

"What is it, Pinkow?"

"Thank God!" he cried, with a great sigh of relief. "You are free, madam. I have counted the moments since the lieutenant came into the ambulance with you, dreading that he would change his mind at the last minute and drag you back to that horrid tent, to murder you at his leisure."

"Why—Pinkow—" I protested, "the lieutenant—"

"—is my commanding officer and has detailed me to wait on you, with secret instructions to bring you back from Santa Fé dead or alive. Alive, if possible; dead, should you refuse to return of your own free will to the prison he has prepared for you. Do you think, madam, that because your silent, uncomplaining endurance of the lieutenant's tyranny was honored by the captain and the other officers, it is not known at headquarters? And in the company there is not a man who has forgotten your courage and kindness on the long march out here. All these men here will go into Santa Fé with you if you but say the word, and once under the general's protection the lieutenant can never more approach nor harm you. The captain, though not advised of your intention, feels convinced that you will never return to our camp or the lieutenant again. I have his orders to see that everything you may need on your journey in, whether undertaken with a military escort or on the overland stage, be furnished you; though indeed the general himself will see to that, and the captain also thinks that some of the other officer's wives are at Fort Marcy (Santa Fé) at present."

"But, Pinkow," I remonstrated, tremblingly, "I promised to come back; he will come after me if I break my promise; I know he will, and kill me wherever he finds me."

"Do you suppose the captain will give him permission to leave camp to follow you? Not while he thinks that you will seize upon this opportunity to make your escape. He is under the firm impression that you are anxious to get out of that madman's clutches, and would be surprised if he heard that you had conscientious scruples about breaking your word with him. Do you know," he continued, in a lowered voice, "that he is a condemmed criminal, that he escaped the gallows only by flight, and lives in hourly dread of being recognized and handed over to the civil authorities by his brother officers? And to such a man's power you would return?"

"It will break his heart if I go and leave him in his trouble," I cried, thinking of his parting appeals and promises. "He is not bad, Pinkow; he was young and hot-headed when that man in Texas enraged him, and he shot him in a fit of passion, It has been kept secret so long; why raise up that dread ghost now? And think of Toby, I should never see Toby again, and you heard how he cried. I must go back, Pinkow, oh, I must go back!" and I burst into tears.

It was not so much the recollection of the horse that made me cry—my nerves were suddenly unstrung; the prospect of life and liberty before me was overpowering; I feared to give room to the flattering hope that tried to take possession of me. It looked so utterly impossible that I could really become free once more; that I could ever again breathe without fear and dread, as other people did.

"That is just what the lieutenant counted on," pursued Pinkow; "he knows how you love the horse, and told me to insinuate to you, in case you should refuse to come back, that I thought he would beat and starve the poor brute to death.   I do not doubt that he would if he got the chance, but I have posted both the captain and the men, and they would look after Toby for your sake, if not for his own.''

The farther away I got from the post, the higher my spirits rose.   I dried my tears at last and asked the faithful fellow if he really and truly thought I could get away and reach my friends in safety.   He made it appear so plain that it depended on my own wish alone, that I began to breathe more freely, and at last said:

'' Be it so; I will at least try for my life.''

Then I made him promise to say nothing of my intention till I had reached Santa Fé, partly because my pride rebelled against being looked upon as a runaway wife, and partly because I so dreaded my husband's pursuit that I felt as if a word spoken aloud might be carried back to him on the passing breeze.

Once determined on gaining my freedom, I could not travel fast enough.   I urged the driver to hurry his mules to the utmost, telling him I was anxious to reach Fort Cummings before nightfall.   Though I gave no hint of my real intentions, I felt that he, as well as the soldiers of the escort, knew why I hurried them; and all through the day we traveled briskly over that silent and desolate portion of the country where the Southern Pacific now runs its daily trains.   Not a human soul did we meet; a herd of antelope came scudding down the broad valley of the Mimbres River while we were passing through; and in the mountains, toward where the copper mines lay, one of the soldiers suddenly spied a thin, blue column of smoke arising.   The sergeant grew alarmed for my safety, and asked whether I preferred turning back to the post, as there was no doubt that the Indians had discovered us and were communicating our presence on the road to some distant portion of their tribe. But the sun was still riding high in the heavens, and I felt that I would rather brave death out here, under the blue sky, than encounter it in the gloomy darkness of that dreadful tent. So I told the sergeant to keep on, asking if there were an extra revolver I could have. Pinkow had prepared for everything, and a neat deringer proved to me that the captain had been consulted on this point, too. Then we hastened on, stopping only long enough at the crossing of the Mimbres River to refresh the horses and mules, and at nightfall we entered the rocky *canon* which takes its name from the spring that has gladdened the heart of many a weary traveler on this road. Cook's Cañon has an unpleasant sound in connection with Apache reminiscences, and even the spring, a large, square sheet of water, surrounded by a low, hand-built wall of rock, looked black and inhospitable in the darkening night.

The commanding officer of Fort Cummings received and entertained me with all possible kindness, saying it was not surprise to him that a lady should grow weary of the solitude and hardships of camp life. But I hastened to explain that indeed, *indeed*, I was not tired of living in camp; that I was only going to Santa Fé to urge General Carlton to grant my husband an early trial by court-martial, as he wished to be restored to duty, and that I intended returning without delay as soon as my object was accomplished.

Whether he believed me or not, I don't know; but he offered me fresh mules for my ambulance and an exchange of escort when I refused to remain the next day and rest before continuing my hard journey. I declined both offers, from an insane fear that the very mules in the ambnlance might have caught a whisper of the word "Flight."

The first day's journey had really not been a severe one, and I felt that it was neither cruel nor selfish to order an early start the next morning. We had nearly sixty miles before us, and no water to be had till we struck the Rio Grande; but I did not want to carry water-kegs till it was absolutely necessary; we would have to come to that soon enough.

I had no eyes for scenery or surroundings. Magdalena Pass was to me only something to be hurried through in order to reach a place of safety, as I felt Fort Selden would be to a certain degree, for I knew that I should find a lady there—an old friend she seemed to me, for we had met at Carlisle Barracks, and her husband, like mine, belonged to the Third. He was commanding officer at the time, Captain Tilford having not yet arrived in the territory. And this lady I had determined to take into my confidence. Good, warm-hearted woman! How she wept over me and deplored the vanishing of all my hopes and illusions! We had been so happy together at Carlisle—I had looked so hopefully and fearlessly into the future!

A plucky little woman she was, too; and she declared that if my tormentor should really evade the vigilance of the officers at our camp, she would never allow him to pass through theirs. He was under arrest and had no right to leave camp, and a transport of soldiers should carry him back to Fort Bayard if necessary by force, she vowed. We deemed it best to send back the escort from here, and the sergeant of my new escort was instructed as far as necessary by the post commander. This escort was to remain with me till I reached Santa Fé; there were no married officers at any other post between here and Santa Fé, except at Fort McRea, and I shrank from making the necessary explanation to any but a woman, while I knew they could spare no soldiers from the last-named post. Having fresh mules I could start early in the morning, and, kindly as I had been treated, tenderly as I had been cared for, I was eager to shake the dust of Fort Selden from my feet.

It was a terrible day's journey we had before us. No soldier who has ever crossed the dreary, hopeless stretch of ninety-five miles, where neither water nor shade can be found, called the *Jornauda del Muerto*, speaks of it without a shudder. A scorching sun above, a barren waste beneath; a chain of dull brown mountains on the right, a ridge of low hills far to the left. Thus the road winds, drearily, silently, changelessly along. Hour after hour you gaze upon this blank, vast monotone, never daring to hope that one bright spot may greet the eye, but dreading ever that the brooding stillness of the heavy air be rent in sudden horror by the Indian's savage cry. Oh, the long, slow hours that dragged their leaden wings across this waste! To me, there were twin demons lurking in every isolated clump of lance-weed that we passed. Where the men looked

for only one enemy, I feared two—the Indian's painted vis-
age was not more dreaded by me than the diabolical smile
I had seen on that madman's face. And I could not shake
off the feeling that he was pursuing me—that he was even
now on the road I had just passed over.

Though it was still daylight when we turned off from the
direct line across the desert into the road that leads to Fort
McRea, it was nearly dark when we reached this desolate
post; and the uninviting features of the spot looked still
more repulsive in the heavy gloom of the coming night.
The captain's wife was extremely kind to me. Captain
Horn —of the volunteers—himself was absent at one of the
picket-posts on the river I spoke of before. There was a
band of white marauders making the country unsafe at that
time, which was as much to be dreaded as the red Indians;
and therefore these pickets by the river were constantly
inspected personally by the captain.

The next day's journey was a short one, and we reached
Fort Craig while it was yet day-light. I am unable to
explain why it was that a volunteer officer, Colonel Gerhart,
was in command of this post at that time, though to be sure
it was months before the volunteer forces in the territory
were everywhere replaced by regular troops. Doctor Day
also belonged to the volunteers, and his wife had the coziest
quarters in all this large fort. The colonel, young and full
of life, called at the doctor's quarters and grew enthusiastic
over the prospect of the pleasant day we should all pass together to-morrow, Sunday. The tire had come off the
ambulance wheel, and he was rejoiced to say that there was

not another ambulance at the post that could be got ready in less than forty-eight hours' time.

I felt the color leaving my face at this disclosure, but hoped it might only be a pleasant little *ruse* of the colonel's, when suddenly Pinkow's woe-begone countenance appeared at the door to report that the blacksmith had pronounced the wheel in urgent need of a soaking, or a scraping, or some other like attention—I have forgotten what, but I knew we could not proceed in that ambulance. I sat dumb with dismay, and I fear the colonel thought me very dull and stupid. I spent a restless night, was up by six o'clock, and summoned Pinkow.

"Pinkow," I said "we *must* go on. All last night I dreamed of the lieutenant; he had overtaken us, and everywhere around me was blood—blood. I am going on; if here is no ambulance to be had they can give me a horse, or I will ride one of the ambulance mules. Somehow, I feel that the lieutenant knows by this time that I mean to escape, and if he catches up with us now he will kill me sure."

Pinkow could have replied that even if one of the "L" Company soldiers had known of my design he could not have yet imparted it to the lieutenant had he been so inclined, as the escort was to rest for two days at Fort Selden; and the probabilities were all against any of the soldiers playing traitor toward me. But the poor fellow was himself so thoroughly impressed with the unhesitating wickedness of the gentleman in question, that he believed him capable of all sorts of unheard-of deeds.

"You are right, madam," he said; "and I was only afraid they would pursuade you to stay. I have discovered that the post sutler has a very handsome ambulance, more like a carriage, but very strong. If we could get that."

The sutler was known to me by reputation as a well-bred man, one of the prominent men of the territory. a personal friend of the general; and when I had at last prevailed upon the colonel to ask for his carriage, of course it was gladly given. Nevertheless, it was eleven o'clock before we could set out on our journey, and we had agreed in the council held that I should stop at San Antonio, where a discharged soldier kept the government station. Doctor Day said I looked as if I needed rest, and Mrs. Day, dear soul! packed me a splendid lunch—which my soldiers relished exceedingly.

For my part the anxiety I had undergone since the previous night, the fear of being delayed one whole day, had completely prostrated me with nervous headache, and all through that blowing, blustering autumn day I lay back half unconscious in the cushioned seat of the ambulance. I had tenaciously clung to my Fort Selden escort, though the colonel had wanted to replace them with men from his own command. I knew that Sergeant McBeth had been made acquainted to a certain extent with the real object of my hasty journey, and he seemed to be such a manly, kind-hearted young follow that I felt great reliance on him. They were all good men. Indeed, who ever heard of an unworthy act on the part of a soldier, whether he wear bullion epaulettes or the coarse cloth of the rank and file?

When we reached the station at San Antonio, Pinkow and Sergeant Brown, who kept the station, an elderly bronze-faced man, lifted me out of the ambulance and helped me into the house. It was an *adobe* built in the regular frontier New Mexican style—the house the base of a hollow square, high *adobe* walls forming the other three sides, with a heavy gate opposite the house, and never a door or a window to be seen on the outside of the entire structure. The court-yard was bare of foliage, flower, or fountain, such as are sometimes found in the habitations of the wealthier residents along the Rio Grande. But the interior of the house was kept faultlessly neat, as might be expected of an old soldier like the sergeant. A number of very comfortable beds were kept for the officers and their families who passed by this place at long intervals; and on the most comfortable of these beds I threw myself, without removing any article of my clothing for fear of being unable to replace it in the morning—I was so completely exhausted, so thoroughly convinced that I was pursued, and so firmly determined to continue my journey at daylight.

I remember well that good Sergeant Brown brought broiled chicken to my bedside—an unheard-of luxury—and tea, and the sweetest kind of Mexican bread. In one corner of the room was a queer, triangular little fire-place, and in the grate was burning a bright fire of coal brought up from the bowels of the Soledad Mountain, in whose somber shadow we had but yesterday been traveling.

Day had hardly dawned, when Pinkow knocked at my door to know if I was able to resume the journey. I convinced him of my determination by ordering a cup of coffee and the ambulance, which, to satisfy me, was at once dragged out of the court-yard and left in front of the open gate where I could see it.   The mules had not yet been fed, and I actually scolded Pinkow for being so tardy.   I said he wanted to see me murdered right there; I knew the Lieutenant was close on our heels.   The good-natured fellow protested—not against my injustice, but against my wearing myself out with unnecessary fears.

"They will not allow him to pass any of the posts," he said, "for they all know he is under arrest; and where else could he find anything for himself, his escort, or his animals to subsist on?"

But who ever succeeded in reasoning a woman out of her determination to be afraid?   So I clambered into the ambulance, bade Pinkow fasten back the curtains, and looked out upon the dreary scene.   Truth to tell, I was more dead than alive, and nothing save the most absolute terror could have given me strength to venture out in the bleak, raw blustering morning.

San Antonio was more name than habitation at that time. The two or three wretched *adobe* houses that made up the place were a fitting relief to the dry, barren country.   Sluggish, gray, and sullen, the Rio Grande passed at a little distance from the spot; and while I lay back in the cushions, peering anxiously in all directions that my eye could reach, a strange *cortége* came slowly gliding down the stream. Was it the funeral barge of Lily Maid Elaine drifting across the River Usk of Mexico?   Ah, no! Something sadder far than this. The Indians in making another raid on a large herd of sheep had killed the herder and driven off the sheep, and this was the funeral procession. His mother, a widow, had crossed the stream the night before, and was now bringing back with her the body of the murdered man—her only son.

The sight struck a chill to my heart, and I turned to Pinkow, who was hovering near.

"A terrible omen that," I cried. "Oh, Pinkow, if we were only safe in Santa Fé, I should tell the general all I have suffered, and I know he will protect me. Why don't we start?" I asked in conclusion, trying to raise myself to look back into the court.

Sergeant Brown was just crossing it with a lunch for me, and the mules were led up to the ambulance at the same time, while the escort prepared to mount.

A cold wind swept over the hard ground, whirling up small clouds of sand and red *adobe* dust, and a dull gray sky made everything around look inexpressibly dreary. There was something heavy and oppressive in the atmosphere in spite of the keen air, and the falling in line of the escort reminded me of the military funerals I had seen. Sergeant Brown lent a hand while the driver was putting in the mules, and when they were ready he wished me a last "good-bye." His hand was still raised to his cap, when, as the ambulance felt the first impetus of the straining mules, one of the springs snapped, and the whole cavalcade was thrown into momentary confusion. Pinkow was on the ground in an instant, and the driver had just reined in his frightened mules, when a commotion among the escort, a low exclamation from Pinkow, caused me to turn my eyes in the direction to which they all pointed.

A horseman, indeed a stranger of any kind, was an unusual sight here in those days; but the sight of *this* horseman turned my heart to stone, and paralyzed every nerve in my body.

"The lieutenant!" said Pinkow, faintly; and involuntarily Sergeant McBeth urged his horse closer up to my ambulance.

I did not not faint, but there was a blank of several minutes in my memory, and then I heard a hissing whisper close to my ear.

"So you tried to get away from me, did you? But you see I have overtaken you, and alive you will never get away from me again. Don't scream or call on those men for help—I have two revolvers with me. I would kill them all, and then tie you to Toby's tail and let him drag you to death. Do you hear me?"

There must have been something death-like in my wide-open eyes, for he bent over me with sudden apprehension; but I had heard him. Every word of his had burned itself into my brain as with a searing-iron. The words are there to this day—the Lord help me!—and I answered, hardly above a breath:

"I hear you."

Not that I wanted to whisper or speak in a low tone. I could not have spoken a loud word if my life had depended on it, as perhaps it might.

"Come back into the house with me," he said in a louder

tone; "I am hungry and tired; neither Toby nor I have had rest or food since leaving camp, except what we could get at a Mexican ranch back there. I knew that they would keep me back at the posts, in order to give you a good start." He lowered his voice again, and his strong yellow teeth gleamed viciously behind his drawn lips. His hollow eyes were burning with the fire of madness, and strands of long, uncut hair were hanging wildly about his face. He laid his talon-like hand on my arm.

"Come," he continued aloud; "we shall not be able to go from here to-day; the ambulance will need an overhauling. Come into the house with me."

"Never!" I said, speaking low, and trying to speak firmly. "Kill me right here, if you want to—I shall not go into the house with you."

"Then you insist upon bloodshed and open disgrace." He spoke close to my ear again. "Remember that I promised to reform, and that you promised to be patient with me and aid me. Is this what your promise is worth? You want to deliver me into the hands of my enemies—to see me wronged and murdered. Come with me and I will forgive you."

He to forgive *me!*

"But refuse and I will kill you and the rest here on this spot."

And he raised me from my reclining posture and lifted me from the ambulance to the ground.

Pinkow stood by, pale and motionless with suspense, but Sergeant McBeth had dismounted and stepped up to me.

"Madam," he said, touching his cap, "the damage to the ambulance can be repaired in half an hour's time; you need not even alight, for we shall not take the mules out at all."

"Have the mules taken out, sergeant," the lieutenant interposed sharply, "and let your men dismount. My wife will not continue her journey to-day."

But the sergeant approached still nearer, and with an inclination of the head replied as sharply:

"My instructions are to obey madam's orders and I see none of my superior officers here who could countermand the order. As soon as madam signifies her wishes, I shall hold my men in readiness to carry out her commands."

Every man of the escort had dismounted, and they stood clustered about me as if ready and eager to carry out any order I might give. I saw an appealing look in Pinkow's eye, and noted the gleam of hate and fury that flashed on him from the lieutenant's blood-shot orbs, while with a quick movement he threw back the old soldier overcoat he had on and displayed the shoulder-straps on the cavalry jacket he wore under it. But even now the gallant sergeant would not submit.

"Your orders, madam?" he asked with eager eyes and glowing cheeks.

"I have none to give, sergeant," I replied sadly, "except that you take the best care of the outfit in your command. I thank you and the men for their attention and obedience, and I want them all to have a rest after their long journey."

"Stand aside, sergeant," the lieutenant said harshly; "I

will now take charge of the command, and herewith relieve you of all further responsibility. You will consider yourself under orders to me.''

He gave me his arm and led me back into the court-yard, where, somehow, all the escort had collected, and again I was reminded of a military funeral as I passed through the file of sober-faced, heavily armed men.

Entering the low door which I had left but an hour ago forever, as I thought, I turned my head wistfully back, and there, at the foot of the court-yard, near the gate, stood sergeant McBeth, the wind blowing about the folds of his short soldier's cape, his hand resting on the hilt of his cavalry saber, and his eyes following me with a questioning, pitying look. Sergeant Brown stood gravely holding the door open for us, offering the lieutenant a military salute; but I vainly sought Pinkow with a last, despairing look.

Suddenly his voice came, rough and broken, from the open gate of the court-yard.

'' Madam,'' he cried in evident distress, ''madam—oh! it is too late. Toby is here, but—''

Toby! True, had I not seen him totter under the lieutenant's cruel spurring when he was urging him up to the ambulance a while ago? Swiftly and with sudden strength I snatched my hand ·out of the lieutenant's encircling fingers and was flying back across the yard and outside, where I saw Pinkow leaning, sobbing against Toby's neck. The animal was trembling in every limb, but when he spied me a low whinny struck my ear, and he moved forward a step to reach my side. I rushed toward him, but before I could reach him he had tottered and fallen at my very feet, with a deep, almost human groan.

I cried out with grief and knelt by his side, stroking his white, silky mane and trying to bed his shapely head in my lap. But his eyes broke even while I was caressing him, and I bent over the faithful, long-suffering animal, and my tears fell hot and fast—tears as honest and sincere as any I ever shed for a human being.

FLIGHT.

FLIGHT.

A SEQUEL TO "TOBY."

LET me confess, dear Delia, that, next to a woman with a history, I abhor a woman who faints; though my own experience has been that we cannot in all cases escape either the one affliction or the other, no matter how hard we try.

I know, at least, that when Toby had drawn his last breath, I tried my best not to succumb to the numbness I felt creeping over all my senses after the first storm of grief had passed. But I can not remember, for the life of me, how I got back to Sergeant Brown's adobe house. The first thing I remember was the lieutenant's haggard face bending over me, and most unexpectedly his protestations of affection, repentance, and reform were as profuse as they had been on the night preceding my departure from Fort Bayard. He needed my sympathy he said, and my aid; for we *must* now proceed to Santa Fé; it was almost a matter of life and death with him, an officer under arrest, to escape from camp and venture directly into the lion's den—the Commanding General's headquarters.

I was to assist him in denouncing to the general the constant and systematic annoyance and persecution to which he had been subjected by the other officers at the fort, and which had driven him to this step at last. To retort that I

had seen and known nothing of these annoyances and per-
secutions would have been of no benefit to me or the gentlemen in question; whereas, the prospect of going to Santa
Fé instead of returning to Fort Bayard held out at least a
faint hope for me.   So on toward Santa Fé we proceeded
the next day; and no devoted lover, no model husband,
could have been more attentive and affectionate.   The
trouble was that he was too attentive; so completely en-
veloping me, as it were, that not even to Pinkow could I
speak a word, either in public or in private.

From Albuquerque the lieutenant was wise enough to
send back the escort; it would hardly have been advisable
to enter the presence of the district commander with flying
colors.   As it was, the ambulance alone attracted immediate attention as it rolled through the narrow, crooked streets
of Santa Fé; and we had barely entered the old *fonda* near
the plaza, when an orderly of the general's came to inquire
what officer had arrived, and on what business?   The lieutenant's trepidation was plain to me, though he forced himself to an air of bravado.   Of course, he could keep me
locked up in the close, low room with him, but he could
keep neither Pinkow or the ambulance-driver there.   I
trembled lest a word of my trouble or attempted flight
should escape them, for I knew they could do nothing to
help me under existing circumstances, and knew that I
should feel the effects of the lieutenant's wrath sooner or
later, no matter how honeyed was every word he spoke to
me now.

Not an hour had passed till the general sent back his

orderly to request the lieutenant to report, at once, to the general in person.   He hastened to obey, locking the room-door on the outside, and taking the key with him—a proceeding at which I was not even surprised. But in a moment he returned, his eyes aflame, his face purple with suppressed rage.

"Put on your bonnet, and come with me," he said.

"To the general's?" I asked, in astonishment.   "But that is impossible; he has ordered you to report to him—he will think me crazy to come with you."

"Do as I say," he insisted, and to hear was to obey.

In five minutes I was ready; and in passing out through the principal entrance of the *fonda*, which was reading-room, lounging-place, and hall in one, I suddenly comprehended the reason of the lieutenant's dragging me with him. Colonel Lane, one of the most highly-esteemed officers of the Third, came up to shake hands with me, regretting that Mrs. Lane had not come with him to Santa Fé (they were stationed at Fort Union) but consoling me with the information that Mrs. Suttorins, the wife of the adjutant, was here, and one or two other ladies of the Third.

General Carleton was too well-bred a man to let me feel the awkwardness of my position. I thought I could read in his eyes that Pinkow had been talking (indeed, I felt that that also was the way to account for the colonel's presence at the *fonda*); and in his kindliest tones he inquired whether I was on my way into the States: adding that the overland stage left the *fonda* every morning at seven; but by stopping a week or two with the ladies, at Fort Union, he thought he could promise to send me in with a military outfit.   I trembled when I looked up at the lieutenant's face; but he controlled himself so far as merely to answer in my place:

"No, general, madam is *not* going in; she is going to remain with me."

As we rose to go, the general detained the lieutenant a moment, saying to him, half aloud:

"Lieutenant, you will return to your station at once and report to the commanding officer, under arrest.   The captain will receive further instructions from me."

The shades of night were already falling, as we left the general's quarters.   The colonel was still standing at the door of the *fonda*, but after an ineffectual attempt to detain the lieutenant in conversation, I saw him wend his way toward headquarters, as I half turned my head on entering the house.   The lieutenant ordered supper in the room, bidding me hasten to retire after supper, as we should have to be up and away before daylight in the morning.   I clenched my hands in dumb despair as I listened, but did not dare to answer a word.   Just then a hubbub arose at the door.   I raised my head, and the lieutenant silently laid his revolver on the table beside him.   But they were only light knocks resounding at the door, and women's voices and laughter reassured the lieutenant so far that he opened the door to admit the adjutant and his wife, Mrs. Lieutenant Ennis, Colonel Lane and one or two other officers.   The gentlemen at once surrounded the lieutenant; and Mrs. Suttorins, approaching to greet me, whispered in my ear:

"Come home with me—I must see you alone."

I grasped her hand, but already the lieutenant's eyes were fastened on me, in spite of the friendly demonstrations of the visitors to absorb his attention. Conversation became general for a little while, and Mrs. Ennis, with perfect *sang froid*, exclaimed suddenly, to me:

·"Oh! Before I forget, I want you to deliver a confidential message from me to Mrs. Captain Horne. But the gentlemen must not hear it," she continued, laughing— "they talk too much. Come out into the corridor with me."

But the lieutenant stood beside her in a moment, laying a detaining hand on her arm.

·"You will have to excuse my wife from going into the cold with you; she is not well, and much fatigued. And besides, we shall hardly see Mrs. Horne, as we do not intend to stop at McRea, but shall camp out on the *jornada.*"

There was an uneasy movement among the gentlemen; I noticed that one of them put his hand into his breast-pocket, and Colonel Lane—bless his kind heart—sent a long inquiring look over to me. But I felt the lieutenant's basilisk eye fixed on me, and I did not dare to raise mine. Neither of the ladies were allowed to approach me, on taking leave, and I saw my friends and would-be preservers depart from that low, gloomy room with the feeling of the condemned prisoner, who takes leave of his last earthly ties.

Months later, when I met them all again at Fort Union, they blamed me for the passive submission to a man who was a coward at heart, though a bully in behavior.   Ah, yes; that was easy enough said, but they had never stood in my shoes.   The gentlemen had all been armed that night at the *fonda*, knowing so much of the circumstances as Pinkow could relate, and fully appreciating what manner of man they might have to deal with.   But not a word or a sign from me told them that I wanted their help, and how could they interfere without or against my wish and desire?

We did not start as early the next morning as the lieutenant had said we should.   Indeed, we staid long enough for me to hear the call of the postilion-horn, as the overland stage stood ready to start at the door of the *fonda*, and oh, how the notes tore my heart!   Then the ambulance came and I climbed in, leaving all hope behind.

And I was right to leave all hope behind.   I had never believed that the lieutenant's repentance and conversion were sincere, in spite of his demonstrations and protestations and I soon had proof of it.   During the few hours of our stay at Santa Fé, Pinkow, who perhaps thought it policy, on my account, to regain the lieutenant's favor, had, somehow or somewhere, managed to capture a dog, a splendid, long-haired hunting-dog.   He *said* a soldier had given the dog to him, and I really don't think Pinkow would have "pressed" the dog if he had not fancied the animal might serve as a lightning-rod to divert the storm from my poor head occasionally.   If such was his intention, he succeeded at once.

When we started, the dog stood apparently in high favor; he was taken into the ambulance, where he crouched down at my feet, and would lick my hand whenever I stroked his hair or patted his head. I stopped caressing him when I saw the lieutenant's face commence to darken, fearing that perhaps it offended him. It was of no avail, however; the dog was thrust out of the ambulance at the first opportunity, but the lieutenant's humor did not improve. Pinkow cast uneasy glances, now at the lieutenant, now at the poor dog, who seemed bewildered and more than half inclined to turn back to Santa Fé. Pinkow whistled to him, but the lieutenant bade the driver stop the ambulance, sprang quickly out, called the dog to him, held him down with one hand while he drew his revolver with the other, and reversing the weapon had beaten the struggling animal's brains out before I fairly knew what he was about.

"I'll teach you to try and get away from me," he shouted in mad fury, and pointing to the quivering body of the brute, he called out to me: "That is the way I serve all runaways," and then quietly proceeded to rub his hands clean in the dust of the road, before re-entering the ambulance.

I sat in speechless horror, for I knew now what I had to expect. Oh! why had I not cast all fear and false shame aside, and seized the helping hands held out to me in Santa Fé? But regret was unavailing, and afraid almost to breathe, for fear of exciting my tyrant's displeasure, I rode on through the long, dreary day, hardly daring to lift my eyes to the gray sky, but unconsciously trying to count the rain-drops that came slowly drizzling down from there. This day was but a precursor of many similar ones.

Wherever he could, the lieutenant avoided stopping at the military posts, making night-journeys whenever it was possible, and camping out, passing through the forts during the day, remaining only long enough to draw forage and rations, and hurrying on under the excuse of the General's orders to report to his post-commander as soon as possible.

Perhaps it was well for me that he so hurried by the posts, for the surprise that was more implied than expressed on seeing me return, gave me anything but a comfortable feeling in my tyrant's presence. Not till we reached Fort Craig did he ask for escort: two men were furnished him—or rather me; for I really do not think that any one would have cried much whether the Indians got the lieutenant or not.

My friend at Fort Seldon fairly trembled when she came to the ambulance to greet me; it was not fear that shook her, it was rage that flashed from her eyes, and in very ungracious tones she addressed the lieutenant:

"I think you are trying to kill your wife, hurrying her through the post like this. Come out and rest with me a day or two—" she turned to me—"my husband will see you safe to Fort Bayard, whenever you want to go there."

"My wife goes there with me," the lieutenant replied in my stead, "and I must ask you to permit us to proceed; we wish to get through Magdalena Pass before night."

"But you will have to wait till my husband's return," she persisted; "he has gone to Doña Ana, and may be back in an hour or two."

"I have no orders to that effect," the lieutenant retorted;

"my instructions are to report to the post-commander, at Fort Bayard, as soon as possible."

Perhaps the most puzzled of all was this same post-commander, when he discovered that I had returned, together with my tormentor. All circumstances considered, it was only proper that he should not call to greet me on our arrival, but he immediately sent his servant to me with supper and compliments. My husband had reported to him at once, had been ordered not to leave his quarters without special permission, and late at night the captain sent an orderly to demand his side-arms. The lieutenant was furious, but I knew what it meant, though the future proved that all the captain's efforts to insure safety to me were futile.

For a day or two he seemed cowed; but, unfortunately, one of his men, mistaking his quiet bearing for reform, allowed himself to be persuaded into having the lieutenant's two-gallon keg filled with whisky at Pinos Altos. The poor fellow went to the guard-house, where he had time to repent of his mistaken kindness; but the lieutenant enacted such scenes that a guard was placed at our quarters, ostensibly for the purpose of preventing the lieutenant from leaving tent, in reality to protect me from his murderous attacks. So day and night I heard the passing of the sentinel, up and down, up and down, by the side of the tent. A bright fire blazed all night in front of it, and when the relief came I could hear them exchange a few low words with each other, as they stood for a moment warming their hands at the flames. But even this proved no protection; and though his side-arms had been removed, the Lieutenant found no difficulty in obtaining access to the tool-chest of the company carpenter, and a hatchet is as formidable a weapon, in the hands of a crazy man, as a pistol or revolver.

One day a great excitement took possession of the Lieutenant. He had learned that General Alexander, (brothe-in-law of the late General Upton) formerly of the Third, but just then transferred to the Eighth, was coming as Military Inspector to the camp. After a few preliminary admonitions, that he would kill me in the most frightful manner, should he discover that I had sent to him to come with the sheriff from Texas, he settled down to a persistent watching of the General's every step in camp. The little round opening in the roof of the tent was hardly ever unoccupied now, and woe to me did ever the General and the Captain, as it sometimes happened, approach the vicinity of our tent. It was *I* who had called them there; they were spying out the best way to cut into the canvas of the tent, to let the sheriff in on him; but I should be made to die a thousand deaths, he said, before they should take him away.

I sat by, silent, trembling, and hopeless. I had given up all thought of escape, and was fast sinking into a state of utter helplessness. Pinkow was allowed to come into the tent to assist me in cooking, though he had originally been our orderly, and Richard our cook. But the Lieutenant grew so morose that the men all feared him, and Richard, who with Pinkow had built their little tent close beside ours, much to the lieutenant's disgust, was allowed to attend to the lieutenant's horse, while Pinkow attended to our commissary supplies, and brought the mail to our quarters when the mail-rider came in. The letters I wrote to my friends were short and unsatisfactory, to me, at least; for I could write only under my prison-keeper's eye. He read every word of what I wrote, and then sometimes tore the letters up before my face, saying he had detected a hidden meaning in the lines; and sometimes following Pinkow to the door of the tent and destroying them, without my knowledge. Nor did I receive all the letters intended for me; but I knew that my friends were now all in California with the exception of one brother.

Before the inspector had left, the lieutenant had been notified of the convening of the court-martial at Fort Bayard, during the early part of the following week; and with it another fruitful source of excitement for the lieutenant, of threats and violence for myself, was established. His time was now spent between watching the arrival of the conveyances bringing in the officers from the different posts, and heaping choice and various curses on their heads. I knew that the sitting of the court-martial would be as much, and more, of a trial for me than for the lieutenant; for at the very worst his judges could not and would not take his life, while the preservation of mine would be highly problematical.

The very first session proved that my theory was correct. The fact alone of his being led to the tent where the officers held their sittings, under guard, was sufficient to arouse his ire; but there was another circumstance which enraged him far more than this. With his characteristic cunning he had

closely watched the proceedings, in order to find the least
loop-hole by which he could escape his sentence, and he
was just exulting because an oversight in the initial steps
gave him the hope that he could overthrow the whole proceedings of the court, when Quinton Campbell, junior lieutenant of the Fifth Infantry, called the attention of the
others to the error they were about to commit, or the form
they were about to omit.   I think Lieutenant Campbell
must have seen in the crafty face of the man they were about
to try, the quick gleam of malice and satisfaction which announced that he had fastened on something of which he
could take advantage.   The oaths he heaped on the devoted
head of the junior lieutenant when he returned to the tent
were fearful, and the threats of vengeance he uttered against
one and all of the officers assembled, showed him to be
either a fiend or a' coward.   I think he was both.   That I
did not sleep on roses that night, I need hardly say; for with
all his rage there was mingled that fear that now, since he
could not constantly guard me in the tent, I might pluck up
courage enough some day to make another attempt at escape: and I did—but not until I had been frightened and
tortured almost into madness.

The session of the court generally lasted from ten or eleven
till three or four o'clock in the afternoon.   Pinkow, as I
said, was my aid and assistant in house-keeping; and after
the lieutenant and I had taken dinner, Pinkow always had
his dinner in the tent, and then proceeded to clear off the
table, wash dishes, and restore order in the kitchen department generally.   One day the lieutenant returned home

earlier than usual, and more frantically mad than ever. Since he could not watch me while he was at the trial, I sometimes ventured to the door of the tent—but never outside; I did not dare to disobey orders so far. This day I had stood at the door full two minutes, looking up at the clear sky, and drinking in the beauty of God's creation. After dinner was over the lieutenant ordered Pinkow to "pack all the stuff over to his own tent, or throw it away; he wanted it no more." Pinkow's eyes flew over to me involuntarily; he knew the signs of a coming storm as well as I. Then the tent was closed at once, and to my horror the lieutenant drew a hatchet out from under the mattress of the bed, where he must have concealed it while Pinkow was "packing out the stuff."

"Kneel down," he commanded, "and fold your hands. I am going to cut your head open."

I knelt down, but in that short moment my whole life passed before me, and mother's face and the picture of the blue sky and the bright land I had seen only that morning rose up before me with strange vividness. Why had I not escaped that very morning? Why had I not fled from the camp alone and unobserved, and run till I had reached a hiding-place or dropped dead in my tracks? I would, if I ever again should see the light of day, I vowed in my heart; no fear, no pride should ever deter me again. All this time I was kneeling before him, my own hands folded, while one of his spanned my throat and the other held the hatchet above me. I knew there was no use resisting, so I fell at last into a stony indifference. I think this saved my life, for

he thought I was not feeling keenly enough the horrors of
my position.   Never speaking above a whisper, and moving
with the utmost caution, for fear of arousing the suspicion
of Pinkow or the guard, he approached the bed, on which
lay a piece of sewing upon which I had been engaged in the
morning.   Lifting it with the helve of the hatchet he flung
it into the fire-place, where the coals were still bright.

"There!" he said, chuckling—"let that go first.   You'll
not need it any more—you're going the same way."

Then he snatched the cover off the table, a note-book
lying on it, a little shawl I wore, and an apron—all went the
same way.   Next he reached out for a heavy blanket under
which I had hidden the little two-gallon keg, which I knew
still contained above a quart of whisky.   I had been afraid
to empty it out, but had hoped he might forget it in his excitement over other affairs.   Now it suddenly rolled out, and
the hollow noise it made seemed like a death-knell to me.
He sprang upon it with ferocious exultation, snatched a
tumbler from the chimney-board and filled it with the liquid
fire.   It was but a short respite for me; the shades of night
were falling around the tent, and long, dark hours lay black
and death-boding before me.   Contrary to all expectation,
however, the whisky seemed to lull him to sleep; and, after
emptying one glass after the other, he stretched himself on
the bed, bidding me lie where he could touch me with his
hand, lest I should open the tent during his sleep and let the
soldiers in to murder him.

I, too, slept at last, after I had seen the guard-fire blazing
up brightly outside, and heard the sentinel relieved at nine

o'clock at night. What woke me up I never knew, but as I opened my eyes they fell directly on the sharp edge of the hatchet, and the maniac face of my husband grinning fiendishly behind it. In a moment it flashed on me that he was taking deliberate aim so as to kill me at the first blow, fearing, doubtless, that in my death-agony I should scream for help, if the blow were not planted full in my brain. Before I could move my head, his other hand was grasping my throat and pressing my head back on the pillow; but the struggle, faint as it had been, had changed the position of the weapon in his hand. Then I saw that not only was he trying to get in the most telling blow, but he was also calculating the exact position in which the shadow was thrown on the roof and wall of the tent. He had evidently replenished the fire, as the night was cool, to convince Pinkow and the guard that serenity and harmony prevailed in our tent, and the glitter in the drunken fiend's eye was hardly less cruel than the glint of the cold steel of the hatchet. I raised my hand imploringly, and tried to speak.

"Not a word out of you," he hissed into my ear with an oath. "I can cut you into little pieces before the guard can get into the tent, and I'm going to do it. So much you get for asking for a guard to protect you. Then I am going to roast you alive, for telling the Judge-Advocate all about me."

And he pressed my head back, and again took aim. Presently he laughed, shifted his position and declared he didn't want my brains spattered all over his hands, like the dog's, and putting his heavy hand on my forehead he brought the hatchet within an inch of my throat, making the motion of drawing it across and across.

"Steady," I heard him mutter, "steady."

Wheather he meant the admonition for himself or for me, I never knew; but after a moment's balancing he rolled over, the hatchet fell from his nerveless hand on my breast, and in a moment more he slept the heavy, sottish sleep of the drunkard. Hardly daring to breathe, I lay with my eyes wide open, praying for daylight to come, and for some helpful hand to lead me from this dark, dreadful tent, and out of the dreary, desolate graveyard of a country.

At last the day dawned; Pinkow called to the lieutenant what hour it was, and when he saw from the lieutenant's looks that this gentleman had slept all night with his clothes on, he knew that the remnant of whisky had been found. Coming in to light the fire, he started back when his eyes fell upon me; and well he might, for when I approached the little mirror over the chimney-board, I saw that there were white hairs among the brown on my head. Without a word Pinkow placed breakfast on the table, carried the two chairs from the back part of the tent to the front, where the table was laid, and started to go, taking up a tin dish with a great deal of racket, I thought.

"Fresh beef at the commissary this morning," he explained, "and I mean to cook a real nice broth for the lieutenant to-day."

I thought the remark a little ambiguous, but the lieutenant seemed to take it in good faith.

Pinkow had not returned when the guard came to lead

the lieutenant to the court session.   Glad of an excuse to get, if only a few feet distant, away from my tormentor, I busied myself with the preparations for dinner, leaving the table laid for Pinkow's breakfast.   When the guard tapped at the tent-door I turned to call the lieutenant's attention to the summons, and he had just time enough to shake his clenched fist in my face and vow to "have my heart's blood to-night," before leaving the tent.   Pinkow must have lain in wait somewhere behind the tent, for he stood before me as soon as the lieutenant's back was turned.

"I have summoned Mrs. Mack to come to you," he said. "To be sure, she is only the laundress, but she can tell you how you look this morning, and what you are coming to."

"I can see it myself, Pinkow," I replied, "and I made a vow to myself last night that I will go from here, on foot, if necessary, into the mountains where the Indians can catch me—anything rather than stay here another night."

And I told him of what had taken place in that tent since our late dinner of yesterday.

Mrs. Mack came into the tent while I was talking; she cried out at my changed appearance—it was weeks since I had last seen the good woman—and heaped curses, loud and deep from her Irish heart, on the lieutenant's head.

"Let me go to the Captain," she urged—"he'll come the minute you send for him."

"No, no!" I cried, "not yet.   Let us consider first what we had better do.   And Pinkow," I added, the fear of the household tyrant still uppermost in my mind, "put the beef-soup on the fire; it is after eleven o'clock: he will scold if everything is not ready when he comes." I must add that our cooking facilities were not ample, and one dish had to be cooked after the other.

"Curse the lieutenant," Pinkow blurted out. "I beg your pardon, Madam, for my rudeness. But where is the large knife, then, to take out this bone with?"

He searched the table for the knife without avail. He went to his tent to hunt, without success. We looked in the ashes of the cook-fire, but it was not there. Then a sudden thought flashed through my brain. I raised the mattress of the bed; there lay the knife, in all its hideous sharpness of edge and breadth of blade.

Mrs. Mack screamed in fright, and Pinkow set his teeth.

"And now, madam?"

" I am going, Pinkow."

But *how?* was the next question. I had no doubt the captain would help me, and I was determined to leave the camp before night; but I did not want the captain to call on me at our quarters, nor would I go to the laundress' quarters to meet him. I did not want even the sun above us to see that any preparations were making for flight—I had such a dread of exciting the lieutenant's suspicion. But I was fully roused at last, and would kill him before he should get me into his power again. In the meantime, the precious moments were slipping by. Mrs. Mack combed out my long, tangled hair, and bathed my face as she would have done a child's, while Pinkow had gone to have the captain summoned from the court-room, and hold council with him. When he returned, the final steps were decided on, and, with many parting adjurations not to abandon my resolve, Mrs. Mack left the tent shortly before the lieutenant was expected to return.

I saw his face darken as he approached.

"Seems to me you are keeping open house to-day; looks very inviting," he snarled, pointing to the flaps of the tent, which Pinkow had fastened away back, leaving the front of the tent as open as possible.

"Madam had a headache this morning, and the sun is so pleasant that I fastened the canvas back like that," and already Pinkow was bustling around, placing dinner on the table, and setting the chairs.

"I've cooked you a nice broth, lieutenant, as I promised," he continued, ladling out the soup, and then leaving the tent as if he had forgotten something outside.

My heart beat with great heavy throbs as I sat opposite to the lieutenant at the table, and as I scanned the haggard face and drawn features before me, I almost felt the old pity creep into my heart again. But he raised his eyes at that moment, and all the pity went out of my heart, as he asked, fiercely:

"Why do you look at me? They haven't got me yet, but I'll get you first."

The gleam in his eye was as cruel as the flash of the knife I had discovered that morning, and my purpose became more firm than ever. Just as we were about to leave the table, Mrs. Mack tapped at the tent-pole—punctual to the second—and innocently asked if she could speak a few words to the lieutenant.

"Come in, Mrs. Mack," I said; and really my voice did not tremble, nor did I change color, though I knew that now the time had come.

I had invited her to a seat on the bed, and while she was addressing the lieutenant in regard to some little favor she pretended to want shown her when he should be returned to duty, I placed his chair facing her, and with his back to the entrance or front of the tent. While she was still speaking, Pinkow entered the tent, and rising from the chair I had been occupying near the lieutenant's, I said, half aloud:

"Why, poor Pinkow has no chair to sit at the table," picking up my own chair as if to place it at the table for him.

And I did. I set the chair down quite noisily, whispering to Pinkow:

"I am going now," and the next moment I had gathered my skirts close around me, glided softly from the open tent, and was flying swiftly down the lane which the tents of the "L" company soldiers formed to the left of our quarters.

At the very first tent stood Corporal Cook, who pointed silently in the direction of Mrs. Mack's bell-shaped tent, for I had been so confined and guarded that I knew only the general direction of her tent. I had never yet seen it. In an instant there were footsteps resounding on all sides of me. At a signal from the corporal there were suddenly soldiers in front of me to lead the way, soldiers beside me to guard my steps, soldiers behind me to avert any possible pursuit. In two minutes I had reached my harbor of refuge; a shout went up on the outside of the tent as I sank down on a pile of fresh-laundried clothes, and an answering shout came from the direction from which I had just fled. Dennis Mack sprang forward from the depths of the tent, and Mulhall, the blacksmith, stood in the door.

"What is it, Mulhall?" I asked, wildly; "why do the men shout so?"

"It's because you are safe out of that tent," he replied, and he threw back the flap of the tent. "See—the men have drawn a complete cordon around this tent, and twenty of them are guarding the lieutenant from breaking through his lines."

"For God's sake let them guard him well!" I panted; and just then Mrs. Mack came speeding along almost as swift of foot as I had come.

She, too, flung herself on a pile of clothes, gasping for breath, and fanning herself vigorously with her apron. Dennis stood helpless between us.

"Bridget," he asked in great concern, "Bridget dear, sure you're not kilt?"

"It's kilt I am inthirely, Dinny," she replied. "Och! the murtherin, black-hearted divil!"—shaking her fist toward the tent I had just deserted; "but it was me he wanted to kill, too, whin he found his wife had got away."

And she proceeded to relate how the shout of the soldiers had first called the lieutenant's attention away from her.

"Where's my wife?" he had asked, turning with quick apprehension to the front of the tent. Then with a fearful oath he had sprung upon her, accusing her of conspiring against him, and helping me off; and only the timely interference of the guard outside had saved her from his clutches. Once outside, she took time to relieve her feelings by informing him that she *had* helped his wife to get away from him, and then made for her tent, while the lieutenant was checked by the guard, and reminded that he must not leave his quarters.

"But I want my wife," he had insisted; to which the guard replied that he thought he had seen me walking toward the sutler-store.

"Then I'm going to follow her!"—and he made the attempt, but the clicking of the carbine in the sentinel's hands, and his decided "Halt! or I fire!" had brought him to his senses, while the threatening faces he saw all around him proved that one more step would be fatal to him. Then he turned at bay; and calling Pinkow, he ordered him to bid me return at once, or suffer the consequences. Giving the men a sign to take him inside, so that he should not see the direction he took, Pinkow came straightway to the tent of the laundress, and reported the proceedings. He threw his cap high in air as he cried:

"I promised to cook the lieutenant a fine broth to-day, and, please the Lord, I've done it."

"Shall we hang the lieutenant?" Mulhall asked earnestly, "we'll do it in a minute. Or shoot him?—though shooting is too good for him, and we'd prefer to hang him, and we'll do it, whether or no, if he ever tries to approach you again."

I strove to quiet their ardor: but for the captain's approach just then I don't know what might have been done. Those in the tent fell back respectfully, and after a short interview the captain left to consult with the other officers in regard to the best course to pursue, as I had expressed my determination not to remain in the same place with that madman overnight. I wanted, if possible, to set out with as many men as could be spared toward Fort Bowie, (Apache Pass) and so by way of Arizona into California, where most of my friends were now living. After half an hour's deliberation, the officers decided that I could not go that way. Fort Bowie was something over a hundred miles from there, the way lying through the worst part of the Indian-infested country, and the highest number of men they could give me would be only twenty-five—partly infantry at that. So it was decided that I should retrace the road I had once before traveled toward Santa Fé. At Fort Union it was thought that I might still find General Alexander and wife, who were going in with a military train of which the General had command.

The captain brought me kind messages from all his brother-officers. I had their sympathy and their respect, and had I been revengeful I might have triumphed over my persecutor in advance, for I knew that he would be ultimately expelled from their ranks. But there was no revengeful feeling in my breast then, for when it was decided that I should again have six men and a sergeant for escort, with Pinkow to wait on me, I nearly broke the poor fellow's heart by imploring him to stay behind and wait on the lieutenant. I knew that he would fare badly among all these hostile men, and I knew that Pinkow would keep his promise, if I got it, to treat him well.

A number of the commanding-officers of the posts through which I should have to pass were assembled at the court-martial, and therefore the letter which the captain gave me was addressed to those whom they had left in command. Whatever request or instructions the letter contained I never knew. It had been placed in my hand open, but I had not been bidden to read it. It was returned to me by each commanding officer on my road, and retained by the last. It secured me new escort, fresh ambulance-mules, and every possible kindness and attention I could wish for; but I never read the magic words.

The sun was sinking when the ambulance drove up to Mrs. Mack's tent. The captain had insisted on having at least my trunk and side-saddle brought from the lieutenant's tent, though I wanted to leave everything behind, and not let him know I had left camp at all.

"He will follow me this very night, captain, I know he will," I protested—"you know how he did the last time."

The captain smiled his quiet smile.

" The lieutenant taught me a lesson then. He will not follow you again; at least, not to-night. I will promise you that."

And when Pinkow came with the men bearing the trunk, he said that the lieutenant was lying on the bed, a guard with drawn revolver sitting at the foot, a sentinel pacing up and down in front of the tent, another at the back, and " L " Company men all around the tent waiting and hoping for him to attempt an escape.

The trunk was lifted into the ambulance; the men kept

piling in stores of blankets, bread, tea, sugar, coffee—though the captain had had a mess-chest placed inside, and a lunch-basket well filled besides, with a pair of his own blankets spread on the seat. Richard instead of Pinkow sat beside the driver; the captain came to bid me a last farewell and "good-speed," and just as the first shadows of the coming night fell on the earth, I passed slowly and for ever from out the tents and soldiers' quarters of Fort Bayard.

At the captain's quarters stood assembled the officers who formed the court-martial, with uncovered heads, ready to bid me farewell. But I knew that the rumbling of the ambulance fell like the wheels of the juggernaut-car on the heart of the wretched man in the tent close by, and bidding the driver in half-stifled tones not to stop, I passed slowly along the line of officers. The last I saw through my tears was a cloud of waving handkerchiefs and hats raised aloft; then the ambulance made a sharp turn, and I pressed my hands to my face and cried bitterly. But I was not left long to my grief; a rush of footsteps behind the ambulance caused the driver to look back. It was Pinkow and Mulhall with more blankets, more bread, more canned fruit and renewed injunctions to Richard to take good care of me.

"And, Madam," urged Mulhall, "suppose you let Sergeant Horine repeat his instructions to you, just to impress it well on the minds of the men, you know."

"Very well," I said, willing to humor them all, for I knew they wanted me to feel safe. The ambulance halted; the sergeant rode up.

"Sergeant," I said, "I should like to know what your instructions are."

"My orders are to escort the ambulance to Fort Selden, and shoot the first man who approaches madam against her wish."

Mulhall was satisfied; Pinkow wiped the tears from his face, and they both said good-by for the last time.

The grey dawn was breaking when we entered Fort Cummings. The commanding officer was instantly aroused, and he promised at my request to put on double guard while I remained at the post. It was only to sleep for a few hours, and the men, who declared that their horses were still quite fresh, were ready to go on. They were to go only to Fort Selden; for, since it was open flight this time, I could ask without hesitation everywhere for the means to carry it out successfully, and I was confident that Sergeant Horine's orders would be reissued to the men at every post.

When we had emerged from Magdalena Pass, Richard insisted on calling a halt. He wanted to cook a cup of coffee for his madam for the last time, and the least I could do for him was to gratify this very reasonable wish. I left the ambulance, and the escort dismounted. A fire soon blazed up, with the water hissing above it. I was seated on a little knoll, watching the road we had come, almost involuntarily, when Richard came up; in his hand a large white cup from the captain's mess-chest. The wind blew back his bushy hair, revealing a long, badly-healed gash on his forehead—a souvenir from the swamps of Richmond; and a deep scar on his cheek, a memento of the Vicksburg trenches, lost itself in the waves of his heavy beard.   But there were tears in the big man's eyes, and as they trickled slowly into his mustache, he said in a broken voice:

"It's the last cup of coffee I shall ever cook for my madam.   And—and—I'm so glad you're going away."

He laid the cup down and turned away; and while I drank it, more than one tear fell into the coffee.

If her husband had suddenly been promoted brigadier-general, my friend at Fort Selden could not have been more delighted than when she discovered me in my ambulance. That my new escort was fully instructed as to its duty by her husband, I need hardly say.

I hurried through from post to post as fast as I could; for though the guards were doubled wherever I stopped, and I was assured everywhere that the lieutenant could not possibly escape from Fort Bayard, I thought my own thoughts, knowing the man better than any one else.   My fears grew when we left the chain of military posts behind, and, nearing Albuquerque, we were sometimes compelled to stop overnight at some Mexican village, or lonely adobe house, along the Rio Grande.   At such times my escort did guard duty, patrolling in front of the door of the *casa* the whole night through.   Fortunately these *casa* possess only one door, as a general thing; the window, if there is any, being high up in the wall on the same side of the house with the door.   Only in one house there was a small window opposite the door, and on this occasion both sides of the house were guarded.   Still I did not feel safe, and looked around the room in search of something I could hurl at the lieutenant's head should it suddenly appear through the little narrow window.

Now, if the window itself was rather an American feature of this *casa*, the deposit of bottles I discovered in one corner, under an old mat, added considerably to the coloring. They seemed a perfect godsend to me, however, and on the bench in front of my bed I set up a perfect battery of empty bottles. I remember them very distinctly, for a bottle which had once contained some sort of bitters, of stout glass in the shape of a primitive cabin, seemed the most powerful weapon of defence to me, and I patted it lovingly ere I stood it up in front of me. Then came black bottles that might have contained whiskey or wine in their day—common bottles enough, I dare say, and perhaps never before looked upon with such satisfaction and affection.

Then we reached the crossing of the Rio Grande, seven or eight miles before entering Albuquerque, and here we found fresh trouble in store. The river had overflowed and swept down stream the large scow that served for a ferry-boat, leaving us helpless and unable to cross the stream.

There was no possibility of fording the stream at this place and this season. To me this misfortune seemed doubly great, as I knew that the overland stage was nearly due here at the crossing, and nothing could shake my belief that that miserable man had got away from Fort Bayard, and was in the stage.

I descended from the ambulance, and mounted one of the horses, and together with the sergeant rode up and down the river-bank to see if we could discover any trace of boat, skiff, or canoe. I would have encouraged the men to "press" anything in this shape, without a moment's hesitation. Away on the other side of the river we could discern a hovel of some kind, the habitation of the ferry-man, perhaps, when there was a ferry; and my men bethought them of firing off pistols and carbines, and waving handkerchiefs and blankets in order to make any one who might be over there understand that we wanted to be helped across.

The moments flew. I feared that darkness would overtake us there, and that dreaded stage-coach might come in sight at any time. At last the sergeant consented to comply with my wish, which was nothing more or less than I should be allowed to mount one of the soldiers' horses, and, accompanied by the sergeant, should swim the stream.

"It is as much as your life is worth, Madam," he remonstrated; "of course the horse will swim, but your head will swim, too, and you can never hold yourself on the horse."

"But I can slide off," I suggested, "and hold on to his tail, and he will drag me across in that manner."

I don't remember where I had picked up this piece of wisdom, but I was determined to try this novel method rather than stay on this side the river.

The sergeant had already advanced quite a distance from the shore ahead of me, when a shout from the men called us back, and they pointed to a black speck moving toward us from the other side. It proved to be a tiny canoe, in which, on nearer approach, were discovered a Mexican and an Indian, both of whom sprang out of the craft when a few hundred yards from the shore, and hauled the vessel in after them out of the current, which was very strong. Quickly the soldiers helped them land the boat and clean it out, after which I was helped into it, and cautioned not to stir. There was barely room for the sergeant beside myself and the two dark-faced Charons. For many yards both of them waded in the water, the one guiding the boat, the other pushing.

The current was strong, the river fully a mile across, and there was water, water, everywhere around me. I closed my eyes when the two ferry-men, after many shouts and responses, at last got into the canoe. As we approached the middle of the stream I could feel the current drawing us swiftly down the river, and when I felt the sergeant moving in the boat, and heard his voice mingling loudly with that of our pilot, I dropped my hands from my face and looked fearlessly out over the water. I saw that the boat had drifted far down the stream; but I saw the ambulance still in the same place on the other shore, and the waving of handkerchiefs proved that we were closely watched by the faithful men we had left behind. With hands tightly clasped, I sat perfectly still. No need to make the burden resting on the sergeant's shoulders heavier than it was, by showing fear or lack of courage. If he had risked *his* life to carry me safely over, I would certainly show no fear for mine.

At last the other shore was reached. The low *adobe* hut was barely discernible a mile above us, and to this we had to retrace our steps, as it was the ferry-man's abode, and there we should have landed. Inside we found his wife, (a dark

Mexican) and one child.   Here I was to remain till the sergeant, mounted on an old mule belonging to the ferry-man, should return from Albuquerque with an ambulance and escort.   There was no fear but what he would return in the shortest possible time, and with everything he wanted, for he carried the magic letter with him.   What I dreaded was, that the overland stage should come while the sergeant was gone.   In vain he explained to me that the high water throughout would probably detain the stage from reaching this crossing; that the stage could not float over; that the soldiers on the other side would not let any of the passengers cross; and that he had instructed the ferry-men not to cross the river again until he, the sergeant, had returned. As the military generally ruled supreme in the territory, the ferry-men, I knew, would obey the sergeant.   I knew, also, that the soldiers would recognize the lieutenant even in disguise, and would shoot him down with a great deal of pleasure, should he try to get over before they had seen the Albuquerque ambulance depart with me in safety.

Still, I sat in fear and trembling in that low adobe room, trying to speak pleasantly to the brown-faced woman and the little child, but listening intently for splash of oars or tramp of horses, and counting the minutes that must pass before the sergeant could return.   After all, he came sooner than I expected.   The ambulance was drawn by four mules, panting and sweating from the violent run of an hour; and out of the ambulance sprang Captain Cain, of the Third. His wife was waiting for me, he said—had been waiting for me ever since the time I had passed through Albuquerque a prisoner in the hands of my own husband. In fact, he said, they had all been looking for me; and at Fort Union, from whence he had just returned after attending court-martial there, they had been expecting for weeks to hear of my death or my flight.

It is almost needless to say how kindly the captain and his young wife cared for me, and how much they wanted that I should stay and rest at least one day. The captain, occupying the *adobe* house in town, had soldiers from the barracks stationed in and about the place and sentinels paced all night long in front of the room which Mrs. Cain and I occupied. But I could not rest.

"I know he will follow me—let me go on," was my constant refrain.

And on I went—none too soon as it afterward proved.

Nearing Algadones the following day, the ambulance-driver suddenly drew up in the road, pointing to a comfortable *adobe* with broad veranda in front.

"The General," he said; and I ordered him at once to drive up to the house.

General Carlton spoke so kindly to me, that the tears sprang to my eyes, as he held my hand and looked into my worn face.

"You are almost home now," he said. "Mrs. Alexander is waiting for you at Fort Union, and you will find everything ready provided for your journey in with her and her husband."

"Mrs. Alexander!" I repeated; "waiting for me—"

"Yes," he replied; "for when the general, on his return

from his tour of inspection, told her what he had heard and seen at Fort Bayard, she insisted that the marching of the general's command should be delayed, so sure was she that you would make your escape and try to return to your friends in the East. So—go with God; I could not place you in better hands than those of General Alexander and wife; and I will see that you are not pursued or harassed any more."

Santa Fé was almost deserted when I got there. All the officers of Fort Marcy, except Captain Hawly, were still at Fort Union; and as I had the best of mules and swiftest of horses, I reached Fort Union in an incredibly short time.

I shall never, while life lasts, forget the sensation of rest and relief which I felt when my eyes fell for the first time on Mrs. Alexander's face. It had so happened that I had never met or become acquainted with the general and his wife. They had not crossed the plains with our command, coming into Fort Union long after we had left it for Fort Bayard. But neither of us remembered that we had never been introduced, when tired, worn, and sorrowful, I was lifted from the ambulance in front of the general's quarters. Mrs. Alexander came to meet me; and when she looked into my face I don't know what expression she saw there, but she laid her arm around my neck, and as I rested my head for a moment on her shoulder, she whispered:

"I want you to think you have just come home to a sister now. I will care for you and be to you as to one of my own."

And she kept her word. If ever an angel descended

from heaven to live upon earth, it was that woman.   Long years have passed since then, but the memory of that hour has never grown dim.

And now it only remains for me to tell you how, when we reached Fort Lyons with the general's command, an express rider followed him to say that the lieutenant had escaped from Fort Bayard the day after the court-martial had adjourned; had been arrested at Fort Selden, and placed under guard; had escaped to Albuquerque, been re-arrested and placed in irons; had here called upon the civil authorities, always at variance with the military powers, and had been set free; had then proceeded to Fort Union where he was now—safe.   He could follow us no farther; but later I learned that a medical commission had been called, who had pronounced him insane, and advised the authorities to send him to a lunatic asylum.   But again he called upon the civil authorities; found some lawyer, with little else to do, to " defend his case," and managed to go unharmed as usual.

Then the proceedings of the court-martial were returned from Washington, unapproved, because of some flaw this same lawyer had managed to pick in them with the lieutenant's aid, and the other officers had still to tolerate him until a second court-martial could be called.   In the meantime, in the regular routine he had advanced one step on the army register; but by the second court-martial he was sentenced to be cashiered the service.   The sentence was approved at Washington; the officers were but too glad to expel him from their brotherhood, and I have never learned in what corner of the earth he lives or lies buried.

But to you, dear Delia, I had always intended giving the satisfaction of an explanation—ever since the time when you were in danger of being looked upon as a keeper of a crazy woman. Do you remember the incident? It was shortly after I had come to board at good Mrs. B.'s, and you were kind enough to accompany me in some of my wanderings, in quest of something to do. I had just been promised a position as language teacher, at one of our public schools; and though to me the thought of having to live between the cold, white walls of a dreary school-room, day in and day out, was anything but enticing, I still had reason to thank my stars that I had found employment, and a means of independent livelihood so soon.

You remember that a troop of cavalry passed the door of the building where the rooms of the Board of Education were then situated—soldiers being rather more plentiful, all over the union, than they are now. But there was an officer mounted on a white horse at the head of this column, and, just as they passed the door, the bugle sounded the cavalry-call, and the whole troop went off on a trot.

Soldiers! Cavalry! A white horse! A flood of memories swept through my heart—bitter thoughts of the past, and what might have been—and while you stood by, distressed and uncertain what to do, I sat crouched down on the lowest step of the hall-door, my shoulders swaying back and forth, my hands pressed over my face, and, as the bugle call grew fainter in the distance, I still sobbed aloud:

"Oh, Toby! Toby! Poor Toby! Poor Toby!"

A Miner from Arizona.

A MINER FROM ARIZONA.

SHE had met him in the hall twice before that day—unmistakably a fresh arrival, dressed, from the hat to the boots, in new store clothes, bought ready-made, without much judgment or taste as to fit or material. When he walked it was with a deliberate, rather shambling, but by no means heavy step; when he stood still it was with feet wide apart, and a general air of surveying a big stretch of country around him, calmly expectant, half alert, half indifferent—too discreet to court danger, but conscious of the power to do it battle. Not an old man, and a handsome man withal, his beard blanched from exposure more than age, and the lines in his face speaking of hardships and much solitary life.

He had planted himself with his back against the balustrade surrounding the stairway, and waited for her approach, without the slightest tone of disrespect, but evidently with the intention of addressing her. Such a heart-hungry, longing look as there was in his large eyes of bluish-grey—such an expression of being lost and alone here, in the large, strange city, more than ever he had been on his wildest, most solitary prospecting trip. Uncovering his head, he said:

"Excuse me, madam" (which proved him a Southerner —a Yankee would have said Miss), "but I have seen you several times since I came here, and don't know anyone else to ask: Is this really the Worthington House, or not? I can't get any kind of satisfaction from the lady I rented my room of."

"This is the Worthington House; yes, sir."

"How comes she to say, then, that she is not my old pardner's wife? Old Worthington told me, years ago, that if I ever came to San Francisco, I must stop at his wife's fine lodging house, on Kearny Street. The house is fine enough; I haven't seen anything finer in Arizona"—a humorous smile lit up his face—"but that"—indicating the parlor with a bend of his head—"ain't old Worthington's wife, and I know it."

"You are right; the present landlady purchased the place of Mrs. Smith, who bought out Mrs. Worthington several years ago. Perhaps Mrs. Ward feared to lose you as a roomer if she disclosed the fact at once that she was an utter stranger to Mrs. Worthington, or anyone connected with her.

"Reckon I'll stay here now," he decided, after meditating, "seeing that I've got comfortably fixed, and found someone to talk to. You are the lady that paints the pictures?" pointing to a door at the end of the hall, where a sign announced that portraits were painted in oil and water-colors. He moved slowly up to the door and contemplated a number of small portraits, mostly of actresses in elegant costumes, which were displayed in one large frame. He regarded the bright, graceful figures for a while, and then turned to his amused companion.

"What's the reason," he asked, with blunt directness,

pointing with his finger to the frame, ''that these women, and most all the women I see on the street, have got such bright, pretty dresses, and things on them, and you only wear a black gown like that? I didn't hurt your feelings, did I?'' he asked, apprehensively, as he saw the laughing, hazel eyes suddenly droop, and tears gather on the long lashes. ''Indeed, I didn't mean to—and you so kind to me. Why, I'm not fit to be a white man,'' he continued in self-abasement; ''I'm worse than an Indian to go and do such a thing as that.''

''I know you did not mean to give me pain,'' she replied, softly. ''How could you know? It was my little sister who died about eight months ago, and I am wearing mourning for her. Don't you understand?''

''Where is your mother?'' he asked presently.

''Dead,'' was the reply.

''And your father?''

''He died two years ago in Napa. He failed in a quicksilver mining enterprise, and died of a broken spirit, I think, rather than a broken heart.''

The hungry look in the man's face had changed to one of intense curiosity. He was not yet satisfied; it was, perhaps, the old prospector's instinct that urged him to push investigations further. Perhaps, too, he had never struck just such a ''lead'' before.

''Brothers?'' he continued the examination.

''None,'' she answered, smiling in spite of herself. ''No relatives in the world that I know of, and no friends—at least none in this part of the world.''

She had opened the door to enter her studio, but noting the face of her new friend fall suddenly back into the old dreary expression, a quick pain touched her heart that any being should be more forlorn than she herself had been.

"Come into my studio," she said, "and I will show you my little sister's picture—painted by myself, from memory."

There were different pieces leaning against the wall in various stages of progress and completion—simpering faces of fat old dowagers, toned down into something like humanity by the touch of a genial brush; faces of lovely women, and handsome bearded men; but on an easel rested a flower-piece, the creamy yellow and velvety red of the rose mingled there with the sky-blue of the forget-me-not. A reflection of the warm, rich coloring seemed to flash across the stranger's features as he planted himself in front of the picture.

"My stars, but that's fine!" he explained, with quite unlooked for animation. A rapid, half contemptutous glance swept the line of portraits. "I shouldn't bother with those things if I could paint like that," pointing to the flowers.

A weary sigh escaped the lady's lips.

"I paint those flowers only for recreation; the portraits pay better, and are a surer source of income to me."

He cast a keen look around the room. It was plainly furnished, though tastefully decorated.

"Must cost lots of money," he said, "although it's only a back room."

"No doubt the landlady has made him sensible of the

value of a front room," she commented, inwardly. Then she said:

" Not that so much; but I still have debts to pay, contracted during the lingering illness of my poor little sister. Afterward I can indulge my own taste more than at present."

She pointed to a miniature suspended near the easel—a small body, but a head of ideal beauty.

"Was she a cripple?" he asked, hastily.

"Helplessly so. I lifted her from the bed to the lounge, and back again, to the day of her death."

"And now mourning for her like that! She must have been no end of trouble and expense to you."

She looked at him a moment, with gentle pity in her eyes.

"Have you never had any one to love—any one whom you had to care for? Don't you know that it is the purest joy we can find on earth to know that we are all in all to some one who is entirely dependent upon us—"

She hesitated and blushed. What right had she to be lecturing this man, a stranger to her? He had regarded her silently, and with a new light breaking in his eyes.

" You're a mighty good woman," he said, with his usual directness. "Seems to me you are like my mother."

" Where is she?"

" Dead, I reckon."

"And—allow me to return some of your own questions— have you no other relatives?"

" Yes, dozens. Brothers and sisters—some in Arkansaw and some in Texas, some in the 'nation,' and some back in Georgy, whar we were all bo'n." He had imperceptibly fallen into his native dialect during the recount. Recovering himself, he went on, as if in half apology, "But I never hear from them nowadays. The half of them may be dead for all I know."

"And you are on your way now to hunt up as many of them as you can still find?"

"Oh, Lord, no!"

It was said with such sincere horror that she repressed a laugh with difficulty.

"I came in from Arizona to see what I could do here with several mines I have in the Territory; some of them terribly rich, too. If I can sell, or only bond, them before I go back, I don't care if I buy half a dozen of your pictures myself. Flower-pictures, I mean," he added, hastily. "I don't want.any of the old women you've painted here."

There was no use struggling any longer; she must laugh, in spite of herself—the merriest, heartiest laugh she had indulged in for many a long day—while he stood by, calm and unmoved, neither offended nor roused to join in her merriment.

"I mean what I say. My name is Calhoun Kendal," was all he felt called upon to offer as voucher of his honesty of intention," and if I sell only one or two of my claims, I shall have money enough to buy stacks of such things."

"Which will be very fortunate for me," she replied, gayly. "And as you are to be a patron of mine, I cannot do less than invite you to visit my studio whenever you feel inclined. I shall always be glad to see you," she added, with sweet sincerity.

Then he made her a short bow, and left her to work on her portraits with what relish she might. One thing is certain—the lady with the most pugnacious nose had that aggressive feature of her face softened into comparative loveliness in the course of the afternoon; the artist seemed to paint something of her own beauty into the picture.

Margaret Benson's sitting-room adjoined her studio; and she belonged to that large class of much-to-be-pitied San Franciscans who go, day after day, to eat their solitary meals at a restaurant. Not but that San Francisco restaurants are good. Let him who dares find fault with any of our "peculiar institutions"—but it does seem a very undomestic manner of living. Flushed with triumph at having accomplished that much dreaded and dreadful nose, Miss Benson took up her hat and wrap and started in search of her unsociable dinner. On the stairs she overtook her new friend, who stood still, to give her the opportunity of passing by or addressing him, as she might choose.

"One more unfortunate, going in quest of dinner?" she asked, laughing. "Come with me, if you have not yet established yourself permanently at any one place. I know they make you pay three times as much as you ought to at the place where you have been in the habit of going."

"How do you know where I have been in the habit of going?" he asked, with a quick, suspicious look, which one would have hardly sought for in his face.

She did not notice it. "I have not the remotest idea

where your haunts may have been, Mr. Arizona," she
answered, with comical gravity. "I only hazarded that
opinion on the strength of the general appearance of things,
and as the result of my own keen observation." And
when they had finished their very comfortable dinner, he
was free to own that her "keen observation" had not mis-
led her.

Mr. Calhoun Kendal was not an idle man, by any means.
Of the different mining properties which he owned, some
alone and some in partnership with others, a number were
almost sure to find a market in San Francisco, he thought,
though it was "mighty slow work," as he often complained.
It always seemed a relief to him to find an asylum in the
studio of Miss Benson, and the lady herself, as well as those
who happened to be sitting for portraits, were equally entertained by the man who could tell of "hair-breadth 'scapes,"
and incidents in which the romantic and horrible were
strangely blended. He soon came to be a well known
figure, and the wonder among her lady patrons was that
Miss Benson should not induce him to sit for his picture.
So much character in his face, they said, and altogether so
striking a head, with the flowing beard and the high, fur-
rowed brow. But he would not listen to any proposal
tending in that direction. He didn't want to be made a
figure-head, he told her in confidence, one day. She might
paint as many flower-pictures as she wanted to for him, and
he'd buy 'em all some day, when he had sold a mine; but
face-pictures!—no, not for him.

Some days his hopes ran high in regard to these mines,

and other days he seemed discouraged and hopeless of doing anything with them.

"You see," he explained to her, "those strikes that were made by myself when out prospecting all alone I could sell or bond at low figures and make something at it, but places that three or four of us together took up have got to be held at higher figures, or neither of us make a cent. Now, these fellows, my pardners, have put this thing into my hands, and, of course, I'm not going back on them. If I can't sell or bond something for them, I'm not going to bond or sell anything for myself alone—and that's just how matters stand."

"And did you go through the country alone—all by yourself? Where did you get anything to eat? How did you keep the Indians off? You could not fight them single-handed, could you?"

He answered her questions in rote and conscientiously:

"Yes, I went through the country alone frequently, and sometimes, if I thought I had found a pretty good showing, I rigged up a tent with blankets or branches, and stayed while my provisions held out, if there was water and feed for my mule, when I had one. Sometimes I footed it, and then I carried what grub I could, and went back to some settlement for more when it gave out. I never fought a large number of Indians single-handed but once. I was living in a shanty in the mountains, and discovered about thirty Indians prowling around early one Sunday morning, when I peeped through a chink in the wall. One of them came up near enough for me to take aim at him through a small opening by the fire-place, and he jumped into the air with a yell, and fell down dead. The rest seemed to think there was a whole garrison concealed in the shanty, and they made off, leaving the dead one behind. Then I went out, dug a hole, tied a rope around the Indian's neck, and dragged him into it. After that I saddled my mule, went to Tucson to get my grub for the week and looked around to see if I could discover more of them skulking among the timber.''

She had clasped her hands in horror. The thought of the dead Indian, dragged along by the rope around his neck, made her shudder with terror.

'' But were you all alone—no other human being near?'' she persisted.

'' There was a cat—as smart a cat as ever I saw. She liked fresh meat best, but as the supply was short, I used to shoot game for her, and she knew whenever I took up my gun early in the morning, before going out to work, that the game was for her. You should have seen her watch, and bring in the rabbit, or squirrel, or birds I shot! It was just fun.''

"And the Indian—did you stay there, where you had put him into the ground?''

'' Certainly. It is much safer prospecting near a dead Indian than a live one.''

A horrible prosaic being, she called him, with a little shiver, and so utterly devoid of sentiment or romance, but with such uncompromising honesty of purpose that all his faults and peculiarities vanished, in her eyes, before his good qualities.

He seemed best satisfied when they were alone, and she worked at the flower-pictures. He followed every move of her hand, and wondered how human fingers could perform such deft and delicate work. His own hands were singularly awkward. There was nothing they touched or lifted but was set down awry or bent, and whatever could possibly be broken by contact with the ground was sure to find its way there out of his hands. In fact, he liked best to hold quiet possession of a comfortable corner of the lounge, to which she was in the habit of bringing him the paper he wanted to read, the glass he wanted to drink from, or the fruit she always had ready for him to eat. To her it seemed so much less lonesome since she had some one to provide for again, while he followed with his eyes her every step and motion when attending to his comfort, as though he meant to paint her from memory some day, as she had painted her dead sister.

They went out together sometimes, though he said that an hour's sight-seeing made him more tired than a month's prospecting, but if any show were brought to him, he said, he didn't object to looking on. It was the procession in celebration of the national holiday he was speaking of, and he was not a little proud of his front room on this occasion, as it looked out on Kearny Street, and he could solemnly invite Miss Benson to see the "show" from his windows. But if the sun of the Arizona deserts had never caused him discomfort or a headache, the sun of San Francisco, glittering on the polished steel of the unstained arms of the warlike militiamen, caused him great discomfort and a most

distressing headache.   Without the slightest regret at losing
so fine a sight, Miss Benson instantly drew the blinds, and
made the patient recline on a lounge.   Then she went to
her landlady's kitchen prepared a cup of strong tea, and,
between keeping ice-water on his head, and compelling him
to drink his tea black and without sugar, she restored him
to his usual health in an hour or two.   While he lay on the
lounge his eyes followed her, as usual, in spite of all she
could say to the effect that the eyes must be closed to drive
off a headache.

"But I can't see you, then," he protested; and as she was
about to change the wet cloth on his forehead, he suddenly
seized her hand, and pressed it to his lips.

"You are a mighty good woman," he said, simply.   Our
friend was not the man to lift his fancy to the height of "an
angel."   "I can't think why you should be so kind to me.
Nobody ever has been before."

"Just for that reason," she replied, with a pitying look
at the hard, weather-tanned hands.

"I am going to work now in earnest," he said the next
morning, stopping to look in on her before he left the house.
"I want to know whether I'm going to be a rich man for the
rest of my life, or a poor one, and—act according.   If these
capitalists here want any of my mines, they will have to say
it pretty quick, or I'll go on to New York with them."

Margaret wished him the best of luck for his day's work,
and could not prevent the rich blood from showing clear and
rosy in her delicate face.

For a week or two it seemed doubtful whether he would

retire on a hundred thousand dollars or go back to Arizona "dead broke." Then he came home one day to pack his valise (he had never owned a trunk in his life), and start back for Arizona to consult his different "pardners" in regard to their willingness to consolidate some half dozen of the mines, as he had just "struck" a number of moneyed men who would incorporate as the "Kendal Consolidate" under certain conditions, and give stock equal to $50,000 to each partner for his share and claim.

"Shall you be gone long?" Margaret asked, with a slight tremor in her voice.

"From six weeks to three months. Shall you be here when I return?"

"Yes."

"I'll buy those pictures if I come back with money," he said, taking a last look around the room, and he turned to go.

For two months she heard nothing from him; then a slow step came up the stairs one day and approached her room. She sprang to open the door to a mixture of dust, sun-burn, and flowing beard, her face flushed and her eyes sparkling.

"Welcome home!" she exclaimed, with a thrill of delight in her voice.

"Powerful hot down there," he said; and he quietly dropped into his old corner of the lounge. "Looks like home here," he continued, after a pause; "and you are certainly the best woman in the world," as she approached him with a glass of cool water and took his hat from his hands.

Mrs. Ward had already heard of his arrival, and hastened

to inform him that his old room would be vacated and ready
for him in half an hour.   And before a full hour had passed
it seemed to them all that he had been gone only since yesterday.

His trip had been successful, he told Margaret, and the
Kendal Consolidated had been incorporated during his absence.   He could have returned in a month's time, if it had .
not been that he wanted to re-locate, for himself, a very good
prospect he had come across years ago, and which would be
valuable now in view of the railroad to be built through
Arizona.

Early the next morning he visited the office of the Kendal
Consolidated, and seemed to have grown an inch or two
while there.   He had met so many people at the office who
were eager and anxious to see the Mr. Kendal who had discovered the great Kendal mine.   It chimed in well with the
interests of the directors that the name and fame of Mr.
Kendal should not be hidden under a bushel; and the secretary had not only told him that the stock already sold higher
than they had expected it to go, but had undertaken to
bring him together with parties who would take his last location off his hands without once looking at it.

"I'm a rich man now, sure; and as big a man as any in
the city."

Margaret laughed, as she had laughed at all his oddities
since she had known him.   The next day, however, when
he returned from "our office," and told her of a fine young
man to whom he had been introduced, and who was to take
him to his father's house, she did not laugh.

"Has a sister, he says—a nice young gal that he wants to introduce me to."

She looked at him in an odd, startled sort of way. Not that any eccentricity of orthography or grammar in his speech could have surprised her, however; she had grown accustomed to that. When he really left the house that evening to pay the visit, she was a thousand times more lonesome than she had been during all his stay in Arizona. Long after ten, when she heard his step on the stairs, she hastily turned off the gas, but listened at the door. Yes, his step halted there before he passed on to his own room.

In the morning she was at work on a portrait, but laid it aside for a "flower-picture" when Mr. Kendal came in to sit with her a little while.

"Fine gal, that sister of young Briscoe's," he broke out, as enthusiastically as was possible for Calhoun Kendal. "Our Secretary said he would introduce me to some high-toned people, and he kept his word. Highly respectable family. The mother wears a real point-lace cap and tucker —or whatever you call it, and the young lady was dressed the prettiest I ever saw. Very stylish, and the last *mode*, Dick says—that's the boy's name. Live in good style, too —very genteel house and elegant bricky-brack furniture, and all that."

Margaret listened in surprise to words which she knew had not belonged to her friend's vocabulary till within a day or two; but Mr. Kendal talked on, regardless of the girl's silence.

"We're all going to the theater—the old lady, Dick,

Sadie and the father, too, I reckon. I didn't see much of him, though; guess he hasn't got much to say. Wanted to go to-night, but Dick says we must go respectable, and I must get a black dress-suit first. He's going to take me to his own tailor; guess he'll fix me up pretty fine. Of course, I want to look respectable when I escort a stylish young lady. I just wish you could see her—she's a *mighty* pretty gal. But, here—I'm doing all the talking. Have you nothing to say?''

Mr. Kendal, of the Kendal Consolidated, was not very quick of perception, or he would have observed that the hand holding the brush had trembled so that that little implement of art had to be laid aside, and a pair of wax-white hands lay idly folded in the girl's lap. But suddenly he was struck with the stillness pervading the whole form, and he bent forward to look into her ashy face.

''What's the matter?'' he asked, in alarm. ''Are you sick, or in pain? You look fit to die.''

''What difference would it make to any one?'' The words were uttered below her breath; yet Mr. Kendal's somewhat dull ears had caught their import.

''Why, Margaret,'' he stammered, shocked at the sudden change in her being, ''how can you talk like that? You know I would give half the money I've got, and run a hundred miles without stopping, to see you relieved or cured if you were sick. Shall I go for a doctor, or call Mrs. Ward?''

''No, no.'' She looked full into the large, honest eyes, bent upon her with such a genuine expression of concern.

"It was only a sudden faintness, and will pass in a little while. Go to your office now, and I will rest a little."

But if Margaret had hoped for an hour to herself, she had made a miscalculation. Mrs. Ward said she had orders not to leave Miss Benson alone, as she came in. "And I'm to send for the best physician, and he is to prescribe the most costly drugs; and I'm to take Miss Benson out in a carriage, and I'm to hire a nurse, a parson, a circus-band, and a barrel-organ—all to restore the health and cheer the spirits of Miss Benson. Precious Miss Benson! She will be wrapped with gold-cloth and hung with diamonds pretty soon," Mrs. Ward added, laughing heartily at the recollection of Mr. Kendal's concern.

Margaret smiled, but with pale lips. "An excellent man is Mr. Kendal, and a true friend."

He would not even go to look after his black suit in the evening, he was so glad to find Margaret better, an l was overjoyed to find her at her easel again early the next morning. She had left the door open for him purposely, and now, while they were both commenting on the form just springing into life on the canvas, a voice outside, inquiring for Mr. Kendal, attracted their attention. The servant dusting and brushing in the hall approached the door, followed by a young man, who very unceremoniously looked into the room over the domestic's shoulder, and did not even wait for Mr. Kendal to invite him to enter.

"These your rooms, old fellow?" he asked, without seeming to notice the other inmate.

"This is Miss Benson's studee-o. Miss Benson, allow me

to introduce Mr. Briscoe. Miss Benson is my oldest San Francisco friend, and a great artist. I consider it a favor to be admitted here, and am sensible of the privilege granted me to watch so highly gifted a lady practicing her art."

If the lance was somewhat unwieldy which the knight of the sun-browned hands was breaking in the cause of chivalry, his friend understood that it was meant to rebuke the lack of courtesy and deference shown a lady, and Dick Briscoe was quick to take the cue.

"Ah! beg pardon," contracting his eyebrows, as though the light from the one window might have blinded him. "Happy to meet Miss Benson—a friend of yours and an artist. Beautiful!" he exclaimed, standing before the flower panels on the wall. "How Sadie would admire those! We must ask permission of Miss Benson to bring my sister in to see them some time," he said, alert as usual, turning to the honest Arizonian, whose face was relaxing at the praise bestowed on his friend.

The new black suit was sent home to Mr. Kendal in due time, and he presented himself to Margaret in his fine array on the night of his visit to the theater with the Briscoe family.

"Do I look respectable in my new clothes?" he asked.

"Eminently so," was the truthful reply, "but I liked you far better in the more unconventional dress you wore when I first saw you."

"These don't feel so comfortable, either," he admitted.

Mr. Kendal was charmed with his glimpse of what he considered fashionable life, and he went in pursuit of it to the church or the theater with equal gusto. As a crowning piece to his stylish outfit, he had purchased a black cylinder hat, to the amazement of Dick Briscoe himself, who came to conduct him to the church where the Briscoe family rented a pew.

"Ain't it rather a bore, though?" he asked, considerately.

"Well, yes," Mr. Kendal admitted, cheerfully; "but then, you know, a black silk hat *is* the most respectable kind of a hat to go to church in, after all."

"That's so," assented the accommodating youth, and moving his own tile a little to one side, he stepped to the window to conceal a smile. He himself had put the "respectable" wrinkle into his friend's head, but this was out-Heroding Herod. However, if his Arizona friend was pleased, why should he object?

"I've done it," exclaimed Mr. Kendal, rushing into the studio one morning, sinking into a chair, dropping his tile, and wiping his heated brow on a scented pocket-handkerchief. "I've talked to her father—she said I might last night, at the theater. I am going up to see her this afternoon, to tell her that he's willing."

Margaret wished him joy, and the happy man started on his visit at the earliest proper moment. Dick Brisco himself opened the door for him, and led him into the parlor, where Miss Sadie received her elderly lover without any attempt at coyness. He was bewildered a moment by her beauty and seductive smile, but after the first confusion he timidly approached, and laid his hand on one of the long braids of yellow hair that fell gracefully across her shoulder. "My stars," he gave word to his admiration, "I never before knew that you had such a beautiful head of hair."

"No, by Jove, nor I," chimed in Dick, who had posted himself on a sofa opposite to the lounge on which his sister was airily seated, evidently for the purpose of enjoying Sadie's first reception of an accepted lover.

"You, Dick!"

With a single cat-like spring she was beside her brother, shaking him by the arm, and threatening him with her pretty little hand.

"Let me alone," he protested, choking with laughter. "Mr. Kendal call her off. She hates me for being in the room. I'll go now," and he rushed out, leaving Sadie to her adorer.

Of course Miss Bricoe was pretty, very pretty, with bright black eyes, and a full suit of fashionable yellow hair, bewilderingly arranged, and a form as lithe and swift in its motions as that of a panther or a cat. There was something audacious about her, that had at first astonished and attracted the unsophisticated man, while the petted-child air she could assume had made him long to stretch out his hand and caress her as he would a playful little kitten. That the young lady had been christened "Sarah" in her infancy detracted nothing from her good looks, but she hated all who ventured to be familiar with her original name.

If there was any change in Margaret Benson, Mr. Kendal did not notice it; he still came into the "studee-o," but it was generally only to tell of some new excellence or beauty he had discovered in his *fiancée*, or to draw comparisons between the female portraits there and Miss Sadie Briscoe always, of course awarding the palm to that young lady.

"How old are you?" he asked of Margaret one day, after he had been confiding to her his discovery of some new merit in his betrothed.

"Twenty-five—nearly twenty six," was the composed reply.

"My stars! Why, that's what we call an old maid in my country."

"I am afraid it is called so here, too," she assented smilingly.

"Now Sadie is only seventeen—and she says she has always wanted to find in the man she loved one who would be companion, husband, and father to her at the same time." (The truth of the matter was that Miss Sadie had passed her second decade; "but," as she said to brother Dick in confidence," the old fellow wants a young wife for his money, and I think I'll fill the bill.")

One morning shortly after breakfast Mr. Kendal was seized with one of his sudden headaches, and remembering Margaret's former kindness he saw no reason why he should not again appeal to her Samaritan qualities. She darkened the room, bathed his head in ice-water, and was making all preparations she thought necessary, when Dick Briscoe, not having found the Arizonian at the Kendal Con. office, came to inquire into the cause of his absence.

"You can't think how good that woman has been to me," said the patient, when Margaret had left the room, "and she knows just what is good for me when I get sick."

"But how do you think Sadie would like it if she knew of Miss Benson's coming into your room when you are sick?"

" I should think very poorly of any woman who was too nice to take compassion on a fellow-being when sick," Mr. Kendal declared.

Mr. Dick made a note of it. "But she might be jealous," he suggested, insinuatingly.

"Sadie jealous of me?" A pleased smile broke over the Arizonian's face. "But she need not be jealous of Miss Benson, I'm sure."

Dick seemed so concerned for Mr. Kendal's health that he made him promise not to leave the house till he should call for him; and though the patient had recovered within an hour or two, he kept his word scrupulously and to the letter, and did not leave the house.

Early in the afternoon there was a faint rustle of silk along the hall by Margaret's room, and directly the door of Mr. Kendal's room flew open, and a dazzling array of wavy yellow hair, fleecy lace, and glittering jewelry rushed into the outstretched arms of the happy man.

" Oh, what a dear little puss you are," he said, after she had breathlessly related how pa and ma [it was "the old man" and "the old woman" between Sadie and her brother in private] both believed her gone to the matinée, and how shocked and grieved they would be if they knew that dear brother Dick had consented to her prayers, and had brought her to see her dear suffering darling.

"How can I ever show dear brother Dick my gratitude?" and he held out his hand to that noble young man, who had discreetly turned to the window till the first transport should have subsided.

"Ah! but you wicked, naughty man had a strange lady tending you, when you knew that I would gladly have braved everything to come to you if you were sick. Where is the wretched woman that dared to take my place? Let me see her at once."

More delighted than he wanted to own, her lover assured her that she should not only visit the "studee-o" of the lady, but that he had a surprise in store for her there; and he marshaled the brother and sister across the hall. With due pride he introduced his betrothed to the tall, self-possessed woman at the easel, who received her visitors pleasantly, inquiring of Mr. Kendal about the pain in his head.

"And now for my surprise," said Mr. Kendal, as Sadie was complimenting Miss Benson on the different flower-pieces by her hand. "Them's all mine"—waving his hand toward the pictures, and forgetting his grammar in his anxiety to give his beloved pleasure. "Miss Benson has been a long while painting them for me, and the price is no object, as they are to be a present to you, my dear."

Miss Briscoe quickly raised her eyes to Miss Benson's face. Had this handsome woman really never fascinated her husband *in spé*? And had Miss Benson never tried to secure the prize for which she herself had so eagerly striven? There was a flush on Margaret's face, and Miss Sadie eyed her keenly; but after a moment the glittering black orbs drooped involuntarily before Margaret's clear hazel eyes.

"I shall prize them so highly," Miss Sadie said, sweetly, "both as a gift of Mr. Kendal and as the work of a true artist."

But once in Mr. Kendal's room again, she stamped her pretty little foot in uncontrollable passion.

"You shan't have that old maid come into your room any more—I won't have it—do you hear? I am jealous, you know," she continued softly, when she saw the look of displeased surprise in his face. "If I didn't love you I wouldn't be jealous of you—would I?

He answered the argument with a kiss, and Miss Sadie returned to the attack. "Who is your friend, anyhow? You say she has no relatives, no friends, earns her own support, and lives here all alone? H'm—I don't think that is strictly respectable, and I don't know that pa would approve of my marrying a man who was intimately acquainted with such a person."

"I am sure," her lover cried, in alarm, "I mean to do nothing to hurt your feelings, but Miss Benson is really the best woman—"

Miss Sadie made the spring at him which she often made at her brother, and which Mr. Kendal thought so charming.

"But I tell you I'm jealous, and never want to hear the woman's name again."

She stood on tip-toe before him, and made playful attempts at choking him.

After a while they passed out through the hall together,

and Margaret, lonesome and forgotten in her room, came to her door as the party began descending the stairs to the street. Just then a gentleman met and passed them, looking around in the corridor to read the different signs. Without a glance at him, Margaret drew back into the room, but the gentleman had caught sight of her, and hastened to her door before she could close it.

"Margaret—Miss Benson!" he exclaimed, extending both hands, while Margaret, opening wide the door, looked searchingly into his face.

"Philip!"

Her surprise brought the red blood to her face, leaving it all the more pale the next moment.

"And is this your—your home?" he asked, looking around the room he had entered.

"My studio, home—what you will," she answered, with an attempt at firmness and cheerfulness.

"Oh, Margaret, poor child," he cried, pitingly, "don't try to make me believe you are happy and contented. I saw the pain and heartache in your face before you knew who I was."

She had dropped her head on her arm, which rested on the table beside her, and sobbed like a tired child. He laid his hand on her soft hair a moment.

"Could you find no way of communicating with us? Only two months ago I heard of your father's death and—and misfortune. We were losing ourselves among the pyramids of Egypt when Providence sent a fellow Californian in our way, who spoke of it. We started home at once, I by the most direct route, but my mother was compelled to return by way of Paris. The Lord only knows what extravagances she has been indulging in—spangled dresses and red shoes for aught I know.''

Margaret smiled as the image of Mrs. Dufresne, grand and calmly dignified, arose before her.

'' As well Semiramis or Zenobia in frizzled hair and a Dolly Varden.''

'' Well, whatever she brings you may depend there will be something to replace this black gown of yours.''

'' A terribly ugly dress this, is it not?'' she asked bitterly. '' It has cost me many a pang.''

''You have had great trials, but your friends should not have allowed you to remain alone here, brooding over the past and its irrecoverable losses.''

A harsh word arose to her lips.

'' I could find no friend after poor papa was dead. I doubt that I would have had the courage to write to your mother, if I had known where to address you.''

'' So hard has the world dealt with you? Ah, well, mother will be here soon now, and you shall forget all coldness and unkindness. I am to put mother's own house in order for her, and I will have to go to Oakland to-morrow, and talk my prettiest to the Elliots, to induce them to give up the next two years' lease. You know we were to have been absent for five years. Then we must re-furnish the house. I shall depend a good deal on your assistance, and altogether on your taste. And, by the way, there you have four pretty flower-pieces to decorate the walls of your *boudoir.*''

"They are not mine any more. They are sold." Her lips trembled, and he looked compassionately into her white face.

"Yes, it must be hard to part with, for money, what has grown dear to us and a part of us in its very creation."

She hid her face in her hands, and he looked on in distress a moment, till he gently tried to remove them.

"Why, Margaret, girl, is there any other sorrow in your heart than what I know of? Tell me of it. You know you may confide in me."

She brushed the tears from her lashes.

"There, I am better now, and shall never again be lonesome and forsaken. I know you will always be to me a true friend—a kind brother."

Philip Dufresne started.

"Yes," he said, after a pause, "your best friend, I hope; always."

Mr. Kendal had parted with the brother and sister Briscoe at the next street corner, and they pursued their way home.

"I say, Sal——" began the graceless brother.

"Shut up, you imp. My name is Sadie," interrupted the sister.

"Oh, bother ! I say, I had a great mind to try this afternoon how far the gratitude of my prospective brother-in-law would bear stretching. I'm in a tight place, and the old man can't be stirred a peg. What's a fellow to do?"

"At any rate, not to blackmail Mr. Kendal," returned Miss Sadie, indignantly.

"Not, at least, till you are fairly married to him, you

mean, Sis. I am certainly entitled to some acknowledgment for the way I fished him up for you?''

He spoke with the most injured air, as if his claims to having captured some highly valued, but dangerous, wild animal, had been disputed.

''Don't I tell you you shall have all the money you want as soon as I am married? Don't you go and break up this whole thing now by your greediness.''

''Greediness!'' he repeated, more injured than ever. ''If I had had as many rings and bracelets and watches given me as you, I wouldn't talk of greediness in others.''

But they made peace before reaching home, each recognizing the necessity of keeping up amicable relations with the other. The peace was of short duration, however. Miss Sadie, dressing for a drive with her lover the next day, missed a pair of heavy gold bracelets, his gift, from her toilet table. She stormed down stairs to the sitting-room, where young Dick held sole possession.

''My bracelets!'' she gasped.

''What's the matter with them?'' he asked, with ill-assumed indifference.

''They're gone—stolen.''

''Chinaman took 'em?'' the brother suggested.

''No, he didn't,'' she protested. ''I'll not stand this, Dick. I want my bracelets back.''

''Oh, bother your bracelets! Tell the old codger the Chinaman took them, and make him bring you some more.'' And picking up his hat, he left the house.

Philip Dufresne, having settled matters with the lessees of

his mother's house, had insisted on Margaret's active assistance in putting the same in order. Upon Mrs. Dufresne's
arrival she took Margaret away from her lodgings at once,
much to the surprise of Miss Sadie Briscoe, who heard of it
through brother Dick. This young gentleman had been
assiduous in his attentions to the Arizonian of late, and, visiting him almost daily, had seen and heard of the friend who
had attended so constantly on Margaret.

"The Dufresnes?" Miss Sadie asked between surprise
and envy. "Miss Benson's friends? Why, you said she
had no friends. The Dufresne's are immensely wealthy,
and the Philip Dufresne of whom I know is a tall, handsome,
dark-eyed man. But that old maid need not try for him.
He could marry the handsomest girl in San Francisco."

"Miss Benson is not the woman to 'try for' any man,"
Mr. Kendal protested, so sharply that Miss Sadie fell from
one surprise into another. Altogether this had been an uncomfortable interview. The Chinaman had been accused of
stealing the bracelets, and duly discharged from service; but
the lover had failed to bring her a new pair since.

In her new-found home, all that tender kindness could
suggest was done to make Margaret forget the past few
years of her life. In her solicitude, Mrs. Dufresne spared
herself neither fatigue nor trouble, insisting on visiting
theaters, concerts, opera—places of amusement to which
Margaret had long been a stranger. Philip's eyes always
lighted up with a strange flash when she declared, however,
that to her no place seemed so pleasant as her present home
—that she was never quite happy away from it. The place

was worthy her admiration—grand old trees shutting it in
from the street, while a terrace, bright with conservatory and
gay-blooming flowers, overlooked the blue lake, and a
smooth lawn sloped down to the water's edge.

Mrs. Dufresne had always had a mother's fondness for
Margaret, and her affection had not changed. But Philip
Dufresne would not be satisfied with a sister's love from the
girl. Margaret's nature was too transparently truthful to
conceal from Philip's eye the sore spot in her heart; but
Philip knew that time would heal what he hoped had been
only a bruise—never a wound.

Fourth of July, 187–, was to be celebrated with unwonted
splendor; and Mrs. Dufresne was not too fashionable to insist that they celebrate the day by viewing the procession to
take place in San Francisco.   Philip was instructed to secure
a front room cn the line of march, their plan being to cross
the bay in the morning, watch the procession, take lunch,
and return to Oakland some time in the afternoon.   To
Mrs. Dufresne's chagrin, Margaret wore a sombre black
dress on the morning of the Fourth, though, as Philip had
predicted, there had been divers dresses for her among those
sent from Paris.   Margaret's face was paler than it had been
for some time.

"Are you sick, child?" she asked Margaret, in great
alarm.   "Had we better stay at home?"

But Margaret insisted that she wore the black dress only
because it would surely be cold in San Francisco on the
Fourth of July; and they set out for the boat, where they
were joined by more friends.   It was a merry party that

proceeded to the city together, and just enough to fill both windows in the room. Philip left the ladies to themselves, when he had seen them all comfortably seated—Margaret alone insisting that she wanted no seat by the window, but preferred standing behind Mrs. Dufresne's chair, and looking over her shoulder. Perhaps it was as well that Philip had left the room—Margaret could not have hidden from his keen eyes the tears that coursed slowly down her cheeks and fell on the bouquet of white roses she held in her hand. Shout after shout went up from the street as the long, showy train passed by; band after band clashed out its music—loud martial strains, or gay rollicking airs. To Margaret alone the music was playing only dead-marches and funeral hymns; for she was burying her dead to-day—deep out of sight—for ever and for aye. And as her tears fell faster, the white roses in her hand drooped and withered, as her head was bent over them, for she had decreed that the sorrow and the tears should be buried with them to-day, where eye nor memory could ever rest on them again.

Strangely enough, on the boat homeward bound, Philip's eye fell first of all on the white roses in her hand. They were out on the guards together, and he was trying to shelter her from the cold wind that blew on the bay.

"What a sorry bouquet to carry to Oakland," he suggested.

"It is not going there. I was only waiting to reach the middle of the bay, so that it would not drift back to San Francisco." And, turning, she flung the flowers into the water.

"Let us go in," she said; and she laid her hand on his arm, with a touch that thrilled him strangely, when he looked hastily into her smiling face.

The cold wind that blew on the bay did not reach the shore. The closing day was warm and balmy in beautiful Oakland, and Margaret came to the dinner-table in white, with scarlet flowers at her throat and in her hair. Mrs. Dufresne was delighted with this change from her morning's costume, and Philip's eyes spoke volumes of thanks. After dinner, when she had sung Mrs. Dufresne's favorite airs, Margaret passed quietly out to the moonlit veranda, and Philip was soon by her side.

"Will you walk with me?" he asked. And she silently laid her hand on his arm.

The lake beneath them glittered in the moonlight, the air was heavy with the odor of jasmine and heliotrope; from the open windows floated the soft strains that Mrs. Dufresne was calling forth from the grand piano, and all around seemed harmony and peace.

Philip's step grew slower.

"Margaret, you will give me my answer now—this night."

She bent her head, but the moonlight betrayed the flush on her face:

"And it is—yes!"

She did not release the trembling hand he had seized, and he drew her to his bosom and held her in a close embrace.

"My darling," he murmured, "it was so long to wait."

"You knew my heart, Philip," she answered softly.

"As true and faithful a heart as ever beat in woman's breast," he said, earnestly. Then he drew her into the house. He knew how his mother longed to clasp her to her breast as her daughter.

Days of busy preparation followed for Mrs. Dufresne, who often declared, in comic despair, that she must apprentice her son to some trade in San Francisco to keep him away from under her feet in Oakland.

Margaret did not forget her old friend, Mrs. Ward; many a lovely bouquet of Oakland flowers graced her center-table. Mr. Kendal was married, and young Mrs. Kendal, in answer to a protest against her extravagance, had said that, "as she had married the old fellow for his money, she wanted the pleasure of spending it."

Philip Dufresne had always liked the honest-hearted miner, and did not lose sight of him altogether. Soon after his own quiet wedding he brought distressing news to Margaret about their old friend. He was greatly harassed in mind and pocket by the pranks of his worthless brother-in-law, for the young gentleman had carried his operations into strange territory after appropriating as much of his father's funds as he could lay hands on. Strangers were not as lenient as his father and his brother-in-law, and it required large sums to cover the boy's criminal acts and save the family ·from disgrace. Mr. Kendal looked disheartened, Philip said, and had declared that a hundred such mines as the Kendal Con. could not keep his wife and her brother in pocket-money.

Sitting by the window one bright summer morning gazing

idly down the well-kept walk, Margaret was startled to see their old friend enter the gate. She hastened out to meet him, extending both her hands. He looked so forlorn and wretched that it made her heart ache.

"Welcome, Mr. Kendal!" she cried cordially, and at the sound of her voice he looked wistfully up into her face.

"Oh, Margaret—Miss Benson—Mrs. Dufresne—what a blind fool I have been! I deserve all my trials. I am not fit to be a white man—I'm worse than an Indian."

She smiled in spite of herself at his favorite form of self-revilement; but she brought him into the parlor and seated him by the window, speaking to him cheerfully to dispel his gloom.

"It's no use," he said; "I have come to bid you good-bye. You are the only friends I ever had here—you and your husband."

He was going back to Arizona, he went on to say, for he was almost beggared, and was of no more use to himself or his young wife. With empty hands he would never return to her, for there were only slights and reproaches for him in his own home, though his fortune had been sacrificed to gratify his wife's whims and save her brother from prison. His fingers strayed nervously through his grizzled hair, while he spoke, and idly plucked at the tangled beard, and altogether he was the picture of a man who saw only desolation and a waste before him, where he had spent his life's best strength to build him up a blooming Eden.

Looking upon him, a great pity flooded all the woman's heart, and she knelt beside him and held the poor awkward hands in her own, speaking words of comfort and sympathy that filled the man's soul with peace, made him feel fresh hope, and called back something of his old energy.

Margaret would fain have detained him till her husband came, but Mr. Kendal said he would bid him good-bye at his office, and, softened and cheered, he went out from her presence.

Months later, Philip laid his arm tenderly around his wife's shoulder, and bade her read a paragraph he had marked in the paper.

"The body of a man supposed to be the once famous Mr. Kendal, the discoverer of the mine known by his name, was found on the Gila Desert, some ten days after a severe sand-storm had been raging there. The theory is that he had been laboring under an aberration of the brain, consequent upon great disappointment in finding mines he had meant to re-locate taken up by other parties—otherwise he would not have started across the desert without other water supply than a small canteen, which was found by his side empty."

Margaret's head sank on her husband's shoulder, and he turned to kiss away the tears that hung on her dark lashes.

"O faithful heart!" he said; "most tender of women and truest of wives—I thank God that you are mine."

THAT RANCH OF HIS.

THAT RANCH OF HIS.

SHE sat in the open door, her folded hands resting idly in her lap, her eyes fixed absently on the distant mountains. It was the kitchen door, and it led directly out on the wide, desolate plain. No garden surrounded the little house; no tree was there to throw its lengthened shadow in the evening's sun. But the purple lights and crimson tints on the mountain's side filled the heart of the lonely woman with pure delight. These mountains are so beautiful, more particularly to those who see them first in spring-time, and when their own hearts are rich in hope and happiness. To such they will always be fair, even when the summer's sun has scorched the verdure that clothed them with beauty, and hope has died in the slow-beating heart.

The silent woman in the doorway turned her eyes at last from the deepening shadows, and bent her head over her clasped hands. There was no use denying the fact that they ached—ached with hard, unaccustomed work; and when she raised her face again, a harsh look had crept into it, for in those few moments she had once more lived through the last months of her young existence. Not that any dread tragedy had suddenly laid waste her young life, or a great disappointment had crushed her heart at one fell blow. Everything had come in so natural a manner; and perhaps, she thought, it was the doom of all women to find less of happiness in married life than they had anticipated; though months ago when she had first seen John Marston in the fire-lit parlors of her uncle's house, he had seemed to her the perfection of all that was handsome, noble, and desirable in man. He was seated among a number of older men, who were attentively listening to stories about California.

"And how large might your ranch be, Mr. Marston?" one of them had asked him.

"I have two hundred acres in wheat," was the reply.

"Do you keep much stock?" was further asked.

"No; it is not a stock-ranch. Four horses can readily do the plowing, and I do not want to choke up the place with barns and stables."

The young girl had listened in surprise.

"Why, Mr. Marston, you talk as though you allowed yourself hardly room enough for a dwelling-house," she said.

"Indeed, there is only a very small house on it, built of wood, as most houses in the country are, in California."

"Ah! I see," she laughed—"'a little vine-clad hut'; true-love-in-a-cottage style."

"Well"—he hesitated a moment, stroking his flowing beard, then continued boldly, fixing his gray eyes full on the girl's sparkling face—"the vines are not grown yet, but can soon be planted."

Those present considered this the conventional Californian style of asking for a lady's hand in marriage: he obtained it, at least, and they were married in less than three months from that date. Then came their journey to

California and through California, till their own home was reached. In May California wears her bridal robes, and Selma's soul was filled with joy as they passed through towns where every house was surrounded by its own choicely planted grounds; and villas and country seats literally hidden in masses of gleaming flowers and graceful foliage, while the strawberries in the field vied in brilliancy of color and abundance with the cherries on the trees. Then came their own distant home.

It was true, there was no vine yet to cover the naked little house; there was no garden, no orchard to be seen. But the wild flowers grew close to the kitchen door, and when Selma crossed the threshold the little blue fairy-cups seemed to look up into her face, pleading and consoling at once. In the first half-hour she had filled every glass and tumbler in the house with bunches of the many-hued, fragrant wild-flowers, and when she complained to John:

"Now, I have no more to discover," he pointed out through the window.

"Those pond lilies—you had not discovered them," he said.

She gave a little scream of delight. "O, quick, quick! How shall I get there?" she asked, in sudden surprise. This was certainly their best room; and all at once she saw that there was no door except the one that led into the kitchen.

"Go through the kitchen, and then around the house." It was the most natural advice in the world, but she followed it with lowered head. Her eyes were bent toward the ground, and she saw the tender wheat-shafts crushed beneath her feet; but she did not see how rich of promise the broad acres lay before her, the deep orange of the California poppy flaming out from the tender green.

The wheat grew close up to the edge of the water, and when its glitter flashed into her eyes, and compelled her to raise them, she found that John had not been gallant enough to follow her; and she plucked the flowers as far as she could reach them, till her feet were wet through; then she turned slowly toward the house.

"What good will those foolish things do you?" he asked, looking up from his trunk, in which he was hunting for his meerschaum pipe, the only article of luxury he had brought out with him from "the States." "Your shoes are quite wet, and to-morrow you will have a bad cold."

She bit her lips, and her head drooped a moment; but shaking back her curls quickly, she said, laughing:

"That's true. You Californians are practical people— and here comes the man with his horses, so I'll get supper now, and you shall see that I can do something useful, too. Will you show me the hen-house? I shall want some eggs for cooking."

"Hen-house!" repeated John: "I am not keeping a chicken-ranch; you know that I raise wheat."

She studied a moment.

"Very well, but we have strawberries, I suppose. I can do wonderful things with strawberries."

"Strawberries!" there was contempt in the repitition.

"How should I waste my time on such stuff? Mr. Smith

has a strawberry ranch about four miles from here; I will speak to him about a supply to-morrow."

"But, John," she persisted, "have you not always told me that California is the land of flowers and fruit? and is our ranch alone so bare of everything that is generally found on a farm?"

John was spared the answer by the man's coming to the door to call him out; and Selma looked around disconsolately a moment in the little house about which the vines were not yet growing.

At night, when they sat silently together, Selma asked suddenly: "Do you know what I miss? The barking of a dog. It gives one such a pleasant feeling of safety, out in the country, where everything is so still at night. Don't you remember old Tiger, on Uncle James's farm? When he struck up his deep bark it always seemed to me he was saying, 'Take your comfort in your cozy room, good folks, I am here to see that no danger comes near you.' And we have none, you say? I shall miss a dog very much."

"There are many things you will miss here," said matter-of-fact John, yawning; "but what should I do with a dog? When the wheat is cut there will be sheep driven onto the stubble, and then the dog would either worry the sheep or fight with the herder's dogs."

And now the wheat had been cut, the stubble field lay bleak and bare, but the sheep had not yet come.

The sun had gone down, the wind had risen, and it made Selma shiver; but she could not make up her mind to enter the dark little house and shut it out. There was something

peculiar about the wind here; it swept along swiftly, close
above the surface of the ground, but never rising to any
great height above it.   It was sure to come with the sinking
of the sun, if it did not set in before; and when Selma was
alone, as she mostly was, it sang such strange, weird lays
around the lonely place, that she often joined in, ''to keep
from crying her eyes out.''   It was not a rude, boisterous
wind, to shake doors and rattle windows, or blow the smoke
down the chimney; but it ''keened'' at every window, and
begged and moaned for admission at the single door; and
when its prayer was not granted, it rushed suddenly away,
and the place grew so still then that Selma often wished she
had opened both door and window to let it in.

Selma had closed her eyes wearily a moment.

''How many years longer of this weary life?'' she asked;
''and then comes death—death on a pale horse—ah! there
he comes already.''   Selma had been brought up a Presbyterian, and while she strained her eyes to enjoy the unusual
spectacle of a handsome vehicle drawn by two superb horses,
she murmured with a faint smile, '' Death on a pale horse,
and—and—something or other and eternal punishment following in its train.   Poor Aunt Sally!   The bible is still in
the bottom of my trunk.''

The team stopped at the distant fence, the occupant descended to let down the bars that served for a gate, and then
drove straight across the field toward the house.   Selma had
risen, and the gentleman sprung quickly to the ground when
he saw the lithe, graceful figure standing by the doorway.

'' Mr. Marston is not at home?''   He spoke with the

slight accent which Spaniards seldom banish from their English.

"He will not return until late, I fear. If I can deliver any message you may choose to leave, I shall do so with much pleasure." It was so long since she had spoken to a stranger that she viewed this one with some interest; more so because he was the first Spaniard she had seen who was not a vaquero or a sheep-herder.

But the gentleman extended his hand deprecatingly.

"O no, Señora; how could I trouble a lady so? I will come some other time. If you would kindly tell me where I could find a vaquero? I cannot stop to put up the bars again; my horses will not stand on the way home."

And to corroborate his statement the black horse snorted impatiently, while the white one stamped the ground. Selma had quite lost herself a moment—the horses were splendid; and she repeated absently, "Vaquero? There is none. We keep no servant about the place."

"How?" asked the Spaniard, quickly. "All alone? Ah! I beg pardon, Señora, a thousand times."

Selma had recovered herself, and returned his adieux with a haughty bow; but his last look rested on a face flushed with anger or emotion.

When John came home, earlier than she had looked for him, she met him more affectionately than for some time past; she had spent the interim wondering whether it had sounded like a complaint: "There is no servant on the place."

"We have had a visitor, John—a tall Spaniard, with pale

green face and dark green eyes; and oh, such magnificent horses as he had!—one coal black, the other snow white. He wanted to see you; who can he be?"

"Well, I must say," laughed John, "for a man who has such an opinion of his good looks as Don Ramon Aliso, that is not a very flattering description.   But I recognize him by his horses.   He is our proprietor.   He has another ranch at San Diego, where he has been for some time; that is the reason you had not yet seen him.   I suppose he came to see about the sheep that are to come on the stubble here."

"What did you say?" Selma questioned, with pardonable curiosity.   "Don Ramon who?—our proprietor? Has he bought us?" she laughed;   "and does he own us now?"

"At least, the land we live on," he answered, in his cool, deliberate way, "and all the other land as far as you can see from here."

Selma had turned pale to the very lips.

"I don't understand you, John Marston"; a sudden hoarse tone in her voice would have struck anyone but her somewhat phlegmatic husband.   "Speak plainly.   Are you bankrupt?   Have I made a poor man of you so soon by my ignorance of household management and ranch affairs? Have you been obliged to sell your ranch?"

"Obliged to sell?" he repeated as he turned slowly towards her.   "Why, what stuff you talk.   It never belonged to me.   I should have to be a man of considerable means to buy land at seventy-five and a hundred dollars an acre, as they hold it here.   Later, if I have good crops for two or three years longer, we will go further south, where they don't ask a man's whole fortune for an acre of land. Or it may be that I can buy some of this, after a while; Don Ramon is head and ears in debt, like all Spaniards. His American friends will take good care that he shall not remain a wealthy Spaniard long; and if the land ever goes at sheriff's sale, I may get a piece cheap. And it is good land," he went on, musing to himself, "particularly for wheat." With that he lighted his pipe, and made himself comfortable in the large rocking-chair.

On Selma's cheeks there flamed a dark red spot, that contrasted ominously with the pallor just now covering her face.

Before John left the house next morning, he wanted to charge her with a message for Don Ramon, in case he should return.

"I beg of you to hunt him up yourself," she interrupted him impatiently, "I cannot bear the man."

"But, Selma, how unreasonable you are. Don Ramon is the best fellow in the world, and all his tenants will tell you so. If ever the crops fail, he does not stand on his share of wheat, but lets us have the whole harvest for seed, and never presses for his money. I tell you there are not many landlords like him to be found."

Selma was silent, pressing her lips together till they were white, and seemed hardly to hear what John said.

Again, in the course of the day, she had a visitor—the pastor of the Presbyterian flock of the neighboring town. A slim figure, delicate face, faultless dress, and gold eye-glasses had earned for the Rev. Mr. McBetts the name of the "dandy minister." He was a well-meaning man, however; in point of education far in advance of most of his church members, and never tired of gathering new sheep to his fold. Perhaps Selma had not succeeded in fixing a meek and patient expression on her face after a sleepless night, during which a thousand hard, indignant thoughts had chased each other through her brain; and perhaps her demeanor was not as lamb-like as a minister might have thought proper. At all events, on returning home, Mr. McBetts called straightway for his sister Almira. She was something of an old maid, but loved her brother with her whole heart, and the rest of mankind as much as she could.

"I need your assistance," he said to her. "That man Marston has brought home a jewel of a wife, and she must join our congregation. It is just what we need; she plays both piano and organ, sings like an angel—I can tell from her face—and has the air of a duchess; but that has nothing to do with it," he corrected himself. "There is something, however, I cannot fathom; you must come with me and find out for yourself. The woman is unhappy about something, I know."

Almira propped her pointed chin with her pointed index finger. "H'm—I don't quite like that; it sounds too much like the beginning of a romance, and we have had enough of that sort of thing, the Lord knows. It isn't quite a month since the graceless Greenwich went off with that worthless fellow, leaving her helpless child to the tender mercies of her husband. You used to think, too, that the poor woman was unhappy—the minx, with her silly airs and graces!"

"Well, well, wait till you have seen Mrs. Marston." A light flush had suffused the young man's face; but he knew that a serious word from him would silence his sister's sharp tongue.

She saw Mrs. Marston the very next day; and when the horse's head had hardly been turned away from Marston's door, Almira broke out with ill-concealed triumph:

"I know it all; I knew I should if I could see her myself for just five minutes. But you are right, she is not that kind of a woman, at all."

"Well?" asked her brother, with more of interest than curiosity.

"Well," she repeated, "cannot you see that she is terribly disappointed? Whether he deceived her, or whether she deceived herself, I have not yet determined, but she is terribly unhappy. You see what a haughty piece she is; see her taper fingers and her dainty ways; fancy that she came to California as the mistress of a large ranch, well fixed, and instead she sits helpless and alone on that cheerless piece of land. O, she need not try to fool me; she thinks she told me nothing; she would suffer the rack before she'd complain, but I can look right through her pride."

"Poor woman!" said the brother compassionately.

"Yes," assented the sister, carelessly; "but she's coming to church next Sunday, and she'll play the organ, she says. I am going to take her home from church with us to dinner, just to show that stupid Mrs. Henderson that her reign is over. She'll turn yellow with envy."

Her brother hardly heard the words; she was not so bad

on the whole; her charity reached as far as her tongue, he used to say in her vindication; no living thing within her circle suffered hunger or cold, but she had a chronic dislike for young, pretty women.

The following Sunday was perfect, and Selma, after having played the organ and sung "like an angel," to the satisfaction and pleasure of both brother and sister, was assisted into the minister's carriage by Almira, while that lady herself afterwards clambered into John Marston's less elegant vehicle.

The home of the McBetts, Casa Laguna, lay at a short distance from the hastily built-up little town; and the waving of trees—groups of silver-shafted birch, the spreading sycamore, and somber cypress—and the sight of green lawn were balm to Selma's spirit and drink to her thirsty soul; it soothed and calmed her more than the sermon or the hymns had been able to do.   She drew a deep breath as they entered the gateway.

"How like entering Paradise this seems to me," she said, "after living these long months on that wretchedly bare, dry stretch of land.   It was not so bad in the spring, but now it is horrible; I shall go mad, I believe"; her face was aflame; the blue eyes flashed and her clear voice trembled, but she recovered herself when she saw the young man's eyes rest with tender pity on her face.

A hoarse cry far above them gave him the welcome means of turning the conversation.

"Look at it," he said; "that is the bird of prey from which these mountains take their name—Gabilan Range.

You may travel the mountain the whole day through, and its monotonous cry will fall on your ears just like that—always far off, never changing or coming nearer, no matter how long you follow it. The man, an American, to whom the land on that mountain belongs is never called anything but "Señor Gabilan" by the Spanish people. Perhaps they think him of rather a grasping disposition—I don't know. But I am told that no Spaniard shakes hands with him; they open and shut their own hand quickly, like this, while addressing him, just as the hawk is known to fasten his talons on his prey."

We must presume that the reverend gentleman told the story merely to draw Selma's thoughts away from herself; otherwise it would hardly have been fair in him to speak of Americans with grasping disposition without mentioning his own honored progenitor. He had said to Selma, when she went into raptures at the first distant glimpse of Casa Laguna, that their place seemed so much more home-like, because it had been under cultivation longer than any other American residence in the valley, as his father had come in possession of it, by a lucky chance, at quite an early day.

Perhaps the dear old gentleman had never told his son what that "lucky chance" was.

More than ten years before, and when all the land from the Salinas valley to the coast was still in the possession of a few Spaniards, a party of Americans passed through the country to see what could be made of it. "A party of Americans traveling through the country," they were warmly welcomed and hospitably entertained at the different

ranchos which lay thinly scattered, extending for leagues together over hill and plain.   One old Spaniard, who boasted
of his descent from the Hidalgos, thought his establishment
—an ancient adobe in which his fathers had lived before him
—not luxurious enough for the comfort of *los Americanos*,
and rode across country to Monterey, to procure the means
of furnishing entertainment for his guests that would not dis-
honor his ancient name.   Even at that time there were
Americans in Monterey who knew well the value of the lands
so loosely held by these "greasers," whose trusting nature,
improvident ways, and childlike simplicity in business matters, were alike taken advantage of by the keen Yankee.   It
was an old story, how, after a few paltry sums of money received from his American friend, the poor greaser would
suddenly find himself a beggar before his own door, and his
leagues of land transferred—with all the formalities which
the American law (a sealed book to him) requires—to the
man who had so kindly advanced him money.   So in the
case of poor old Don Domingo Sanchez.   One of the party
whom he had so lavishly entertained, the good Mr. McBetts,
had bought the mortgage of the man who had furnished the
money to the Don for his entertainment; and with the greatest equanimity he took possession of the entire ranch, the
memorable old adobe house included.   Señor Domingo
Sanchez died later, in Monterey, the gray old city by the
sea, which so much resembled these poor old Dons—fallen
in state and fortune, but unbroken, both, in their pride.

The day after this pleasant visit to Casa Laguna, Selma
had all her good humor destroyed at one stroke when she

saw the Spaniard with the pale green face and dark green eyes enter the house. Her face grew more flushed than it had become from the kitchen fire over which she was bending, when it darted through her brain that again he saw how she was without a servant on the place. She shook her curls back quickly from her face, and met him haughtily on the threshold.

"I beg a thousand pardons," he said humbly, when he saw the peculiar flash in her dark blue eyes, "but this has always been a favorite spot of the ranch with me, and before Mr. Marston had a wife I often came here."

"Which you had an unquestioned right to do," was the ungracious reply. "So far as I understand, this land and all the rest belongs to you, pretty much.

He had stepped back to the open door. "All of it," he affirmed; "from the mountains to the group of trees you see yonder; and from the end of the mountain chain to the south as far as you can see."

He had lifted his hand and the noonday rays were caught in the glittering ruby on his finger, and as he moved his hand hither and thither, drops of transparent blood seemed trickling over Selma's light cotton dress. She laid her hand over her eyes a moment.

"It dazzles one so," she said; and when she removed her hand, she saw the devouring gaze of the Spaniard fastened on her face; and the sun that painted golden rings on her hair seemed to kindle a flickering fire in his deep-set eyes.

When the Rev. Mr. McBetts with his sister came, later in

the day, Selma had an insane idea of imploring Almira to take her away with her.   She felt as if she had been exposed to a scorching fire, and that safety and relief could only be found in the atmosphere of this cold, practical nature.   She grew irritable at the thought that the hated name of the Spaniard must again be mentioned between John and herself, and the impulse was strong on her to leave the lone little house forever.

"I wish we could have taken her with us," said the brother, as he cast a lingering look back from the buggy to the kitchen door, where Selma stood wistfully looking after them.   "She needed comfort and companionship to-day, if ever in her life, I know."

"And who should have gotten Mr. Marston's supper?" asked the sister.   "They don't even keep a Chinaman to do the housework.   It's a lonesome place, to be sure; but there is work enough to do to make her forget it."

Soon after, the oft-announced sheep were at last driven on the stubble; and then it was less lonesome; for Selma watched the herd and herders many an idle hour.   She had never in her life seen so many sheep, though her Uncle James was called a large farmer in Missouri, and had owned some fifty field-hands before the war.   .

The vaqueros claimed her attention above all things. "It's as good as a circus," she said, laughing, to John, "to watch them.   And I'm not a bit afraid of them, though they might stand models for Italian banditti."

It is said of the Spaniards—the Mexicans, rather—that they excel in the management and care of sheep; and it seemed almost superfluous that Don Ramon should give such close attention to this band. Yet hardly a day passed that he did not visit them, though he did not always leave his buggy or dismount from his horse; and he seldom approached John Marston's door.

One night when the wind had been sobbing louder than ever at door and window, Selma was startled by a knock and the unexpected appearance of Don Ramon on the threshold. There was no invitation extended him to enter; she only said curtly, "Mr. Marston is not at home."

"I know it," he answered; but added hastily, when he saw the sudden flash he so dreaded in her eyes, "it is he who sent me."

"You are welcome," she said more gently. She read in his eyes that he wanted to say, "*Pobrecita!* It is wrong to leave a delicate woman alone in this wilderness." But aloud he said:

"The wind that you hear howling without heralds the rain; and Mr. Marston, with more of my tenants, has repaired to the river, where the water dammed itself last year. They have taken a number of my laborers with them; and Mr. Marston has requested me to say that it might be late before he could return. I shall stay here till he comes; but can seat myself on the bench outside if I am in your way here."

Her generous heart smote her as though she had accused a fellow-being of wrong.

"No, certainly not," she said, "I am very glad of your company."

She offered him refreshment, knowing that he must have

been out in the saddle a long time, but he declined as usual; Don Ramon had never tasted meat nor drink in John Marston's house.   But when he found her thus tractable and in good humor, he ventured one step farther.   Would she not sing for him, as she often did when she was all alone?

A quick glance from the haughty eyes cautioned him, and he added in explanation:

"I know of your singing from my vaqueros; the rascals have really æsthetic tastes, though their rough looks may detract from my assertion."

Without more ado Selma sang—not for him or to him though, for she had soon forgotten that any one was listening to her.   She sang song after song, her eyes straying out through the uncurtained window, where the fire of the vaqueros was burning, and the Gabilan Mountains, rose in dim outlines against the dark sky when the fire grew low. And when she sang of the woman who had forfeited honor and home to follow her false lover, the door was suddenly opened and John Marston stood on the threshold, wet through and shaking the water off his hat—for the first rain of the season had set in, and the two people in the narrow little room had known nothing of it.

Selma sprang to meet him.

"How long you have been, John! it has been so still and lonesome."

"What! has Don Ramon entertained you so poorly?" he asked.

"Don Ramon!" she repeated; "ah! yes; I had forgotten—"

"That he was here?" laughed John. "My dear friend," he turned to the Spaniard, "what conquests you may make among the rest of the sex I don't know. This lady has never been smitten. First she describes you as a tall Spaniard with light green face and dark green eyes; next she declares she can't bear the sight of you; and now she has even forgotten that you are in the same room with her."

His own boisterous mirth prevented him from noting that the others did not join in his merriment. The Spaniard had risen and stood stiff and rigid, his olive face blanched, his lips compressed; while Selma so busied herself in getting supper for her husband that she did not even take time to shake back from her face the heavy curls that almost concealed it.

The next was the first rainy day of the season, and the herders and vaqueros were much in the neighborhood of the house; for though the sheep were scattered over many hundred acres outside of John Marston's place, the herders' headquarters had always been near his house. John Marston himself was standing in his door, looking idly on, when a vaquero dashed up to tell him that the water had again dammed itself in the river, and that Don Ramon requested Mr. Marston to engineer the clearing away of the obstruction. Drawing on his rubber boots and throwing his waterproof over his shoulders, he started out at once.

Shortly after, Selma came to the door, water-bucket in hand, and looked disconsolately into the rain. The artesian well was two hundred yards away, and the black mud ankledeep. There was not a splinter of dry wood in the house,

either, and bread to bake and shirts to iron. She was just
debating within herself the propriety of throwing the bucket
as far as she could send it, and herself on the floor for a good
cry, when she heard the heavy splash of a horse's feet from
behind the house.

"Ah! John has thought of his delinquencies and has come
back. Good John—'' mentally patting his broad shoulders.

She was giving John too much credit, however: it was
Pedro, the fiercest-looking brigand of them all, who made a
sudden dash around the corner. In her trepidation she had
commenced the journey to the well, and now stood helpless,
one slipper on her foot, the other imbedded in the tough
black loam. In the twinkling of an eye Pedro had sprung
from his horse, lifted her light as a feather back into the
kitchen, and placed the bucket, filled, beside her. Before
she could express her thanks, half a dozen other vaqueros
had made their appearance in answer to his shrill call, and
after a brief consultation they all galloped to the fence where
it was nearest the house. Without dismounting, they each
fastened their lariat around the top board of the fence, gave
a long pull, a strong pull, a pull altogether, and off came
the board with a crash. The maneuver was repeated till
they had sufficient planking, which they hauled to the house
by winding the lariat around each separate load, and fasten-
ing the end to the saddle-horn. Then they made a pave-
ment of it in front of the kitchen door, and laid a dry walk
to the well—much to Selma's astonishment and fright; what
would John and Don Ramon say to see expensive fencing
destroyed in that way? She expressed this fear when she

thanked Pedro for his attention; but the vaquero, lifting his shabby hat with the *grandezza* that the most ragged of them can assume, said courteously:

"O, Señora, the Padrone would tear down the entire fencing of the whole Sandia Rancho before he would allow the Señora to place her foot on the cold, wet ground."

And never did Selma have to set her foot on the cold, wet ground again. To Mr. John Marston's great joy, this ferocious Indian-faced fellow suddenly developed all the best traits of a well-trained house servant; and not a drop of water or stick of kindling-wood did John have to provide while the sheep were on the stubble.

Selma's church attendance had ceased with the setting in of the rain, for there was only a little open wagon on the ranch. Sister Almira was subject to neuralgia, and would not venture across country in wet weather, so that the young minister had to make his visits alone. Selma had not yet joined the church; and after meeting the Spaniard at the Marstons' house once or twice he expressed his apprehension lest Selma should join the Catholics.

"It would not be for your husband's best interests, my dear Mrs. Marston," he advised her. "The Catholics have no influence whatever in this part of the country, and the congregation is composed almost entirely of the Spanish and low Irish population. And besides, what lady would want to be seen of a Sunday entering the old barn which they had turned into a church?"

He did not understand, as did the Spaniard, the sudden flash in Selma's eye, and he heard only a very pardonable affectation of Christian humility in the answer that came a few moments later:

"God knows that I think the lowliest place devoted to His worship too good for a poor erring mortal like myself to enter; and my conscience tells me that I am not fit to become a member of any religious congregation."

Satisfied that Selma did not mean to become a Catholic, he trusted to luck—"God's own good time," he said—for the rest.

Whenever the Spaniard met the young man at John Marston's, his eyes followed him as the eyes of the panther follow his prey; and he always maintained on such occasions that he neither spoke nor understood a word of English.

For John Marston these were busy times. Down by the river Don Ramon had leased to him one hundred acres more, at a really trifling rate. The land lay in rather an inconvenient location, and so far from the house that he had built himself a little shanty on it to shelter him through the night: when the rain was incessant, roads were too heavy to travel in the dark. But the prospects were fair for a good crop. "And then," he said, knocking the ashes out of his pipe, "we will go farther south, where they raise olives and oranges, and all the fancy things that cost so much money, and that you women so hanker after."

Selma's pale face grew still whiter as he said it, and her voice was broke by a sob as she answered, "Yes, John, certainly."

John's natural phlegm must have grown into positive obtuseness of late, or he most certainly would have noticed the change in Selma's manner and appearance. There was a restlessness in her eyes that made them gleam out darkly from the slender white face, and her voice was harsh and tender by turns, as though she were never in the same frame of mind two minutes together. Perhaps that she felt more lonesome than ever; for the sheep had been driven back into the mountains, and when she looked from the window now at night she saw only impenetrable darkness, where the fire of the vaqueros had lately been shining. Since the rains had ceased, the wind had found its way back to the lone little house, and came rushing up to the door again, where it cried and moaned to be let in. The new grass had clothed mountain and plain with robes of hopeful green, and the meadow-lark climbed upward on its waves of song.

But in Selma's heart there was neither hope nor spring nor sunshine. It was as if the storms of winter, that had raged and torn through the mountain-clefts, had found an abiding echo in her breast. And often, when at the close of day a pale shadow moved by like a phantom where those brigand vaqueros had broken away the fence of the ranch, she clasped her hands to her heart and implored wildly and incoherently, "Lead us not into temptation, but deliver us from evil; for Death comes riding on a pale horse, and hell and eternal punishment follow in his wake."

And one night the phantom moved close up to the lone little house lying all unguarded on the open plain, and the shadow grew dark on the threshcld of John Marston's home. With a fainting heart Selma passed across it. "It has been no home to me," she said with a shiver; "the dreary, desolate place where no living being gave me love or sympathy—save one.''

Before her stood Don Ramon's light carriage—the same in which she had seen him first, many months ago—and the horses she had so admired stamped and pawed the ground, as though counseling dispatch. The Spaniard's arms were outstretched to lift her into the vehicle, but with sudden passion he motioned her back.

''Not with that shawl on you—the wedding-gift of John Marston! Throw back hat and shawl, and all your finery, into the house. I bade you wear your meanest dress; Ramon Aliso can himself afford to dress you.''

As in a dream, she turned back to the house to fling from her the offending shawl; but the long silken fringe twined stubbornly around her fingers, the door escaped her grasp, and the wind hurled itself wildly into the room, filling all the house with sobs and wailing.

''Hasten, love, hasten,'' came in dulcet tones from the carriage, and with compressed lips Selma turned forever from John Marston's dishonored home.

''Let the dark night and the wild winds take possession,'' she muttered; ''he will not suffer as I have suffered, for he has never loved me, and has no heart to break.''

The next moment soft furs were wrapped about her, and strong arms held her in a close embrace, while the horses dashed on, as if conscious that they must bear to a place of safety a costly stolen treasure. She struggled to free herself, moaning bitterly:

'' Oh, the sin and the shame of it all! Had I a mother

with whom to take refuge, or a brother to give me a home, it would never have come to this. But now—lost! lost! lost!"

He spoke to her soothingly, as one speaks a child to rest. "Do not speak so wildly. You are my only love, and in a year's time you shall be my wife, for divorces can be obtained for money among *los Americanos;* and if all should fail you would still be my only love, and mistress of all my estate your whole life long."

She uttered a scream, and pressed closer to him.

"We are pursued! I will never live through the disgrace and the scandal—"

Again he spoke soothingly:

"It is only Pedro, the vaquero—who so admires you, and who would stab that clumsy gringo to death before he would let him get possession of you again. Be tranquil, love, we are not pursued."

Who, then, is the man with set, white face, on sweat-reeking horse, following in dread silence the carriage tracks that lead from his very door? Hour after hour passes by, and when the Spaniard, accompanied by his grim bodyguard, draws up in his elegant vehicle before the door of the little hotel in a distant town, the worn-out horse of the pursuing rider breaks down beneath him; and as Don Ramon is about to lift his half-fainting companion out of the buggy, a heavy hand is laid on his shoulder.

"Draw your pistol, accursed villain," said John Marston, in a low voice still as death, "and let that woman find her way into the house alone."

The face that the Spaniard turned to him was pale and unmoved as his own; only a slight quiver of the thin nostril spoke of the passion raging within him.   Pedro had quickly approached his master; he let Selma's inanimate form glide into his arms, and turned with flaming eyes to his enemy.

"You have no pistol?   Then I will throw away mine too!"   John Marston flung his heavy weapon across the street.   "Now come on, with your fists!   Ha!   Put that knife away, cowardly Spanish dog—"   He threw himself forward to wrest it from his antagonist's grasp; but he was blind with fury, and the next moment he fell back—a deep gash in his forehead, running upward till it made its way into the heavy masses of his tawny hair.

A dozen men sprang from the bar-room of the hotel, each more anxious than the other to see who and how many had been killed.   Among them was the sheriff of the county—a Spaniard—and to him Don Ramon explained, in a few whispered words, the state of affairs.   Then that official turned indignantly to the waiting crowd.

"Just to think, *amigos*, what a dangerous man that gringo is; he actually attacked my friend Don Ramon with a pistol—here is the weapon now.   Fortunately Don Ramon managed to strike it out of his hand; and in falling, during the tussle, the man must have hurt himself.   It is my duty, at all events, to place him in safe custody, where he can do no more harm."

So John Marston, wounded, bleeding and insensible, was placed in safe custody where he could do no more harm; while within the next half-hour Don Ramon Aliso, with fresh horses, was speeding toward the nearest railroad depot, bearing with him his stolen treasure.

Charity covereth a multitude of sins; so do big diamonds; and plenty of both are to be found in San Francisco. At a charity ball they can be seen in perfection—both diamonds and charity; for all sorts of people are admitted for sweet charity's sake, and to swell the receipts for the night in dollars and cents.

We go late to such a ball, of course, and study with wonder and delight the magnificent dresses there—the papers will tell us in the morning who was inside of them. At this particular ball is a lady conspicuous for dress and diamonds. The heavy satin of her dress flames in the color of the California poppy; and diamonds shake and glitter on bosom, hair and fingers every time she moves. It is a ponderous frame to display dry goods and jewelry on, and to cover the frame so thoroughly must have cost large sums of money. But that's what she has her money for, people say; she has no one to leave it to when she dies. Poor, wealthy, vulgar Mrs. Merritt! Ever since her immense wealth—realized from the opportune sale of swamp lands mortgaged to her worthless, departed husband—had fallen into her enormous hands, it had been the one cry of her really good heart—"Alone in the world, with no one to leave my money to!"

However, she was not alone at the ball to-night; beside her was a figure the entire reverse and opposite of the worthy matron. A delicate lavender silk fell gracefully around the slender form, and a single rose was half hidden among the heavy gold-brown curls. There was an expression of weariness on the pale, oval face that was not well suited to the gay scene; and the haughtily curved lips responded only in monosyllables to the volubility of the mammoth woman.

A small circle had formed about Mrs. Merritt, and she is discussing her domestic and financial affairs freely with the five hundred friends.

"Yes; I have some one now to leave my money to, for I have legally adopted her—dear little chick—and I'd like to see the first one of you young scamps make love to her for her money. She's had her own troubles, poor child, and she so hates and despises men that I run no risk of having my money squandered by a graceless, ne'er-do-well of a husband."

"You are perfectly right, Mrs. Merritt, to guard both your treasures well;" it was a handsome, rakish-looking individual who spoke. "But would you not introduce a fellow if he vowed and declared he had no dark designs on either? Come, now—for old acquaintance sake—let me beg your fair *protege* for the next dance."

"She'll not dance to-night, Harry Underwood. My little chick has a pretty hard head of her own, in spite of her gentle eyes; and she has declared that she will not dance. Perhaps, too, I have spoiled her just a little; but she is the dearest child, for all that, and really loves me, for all my rough ways. You may believe me that I cherish her as the apple of my eye."

The loving look she cast over to her companion seemed suddenly frozen in her eyes.

"What ails the child?" she cried in alarm. "Are you sick? Away from here, all of you; don't you see she can not breathe here?"

With her stout fists she thrust back the throng of the curious who had gathered at the cry of "fainting woman." The straining eyes of her companion were fixed on the farther end of the room, and the pale lips breathed but a single word into the woman's ear.

"Nonsense, child!" she exclaimed impatiently, "you are dreaming again. Do put that fickle Spaniard out of your mind at last. Come, we will go to one of the sitting-rooms and I will order champagne."

But the pale lips approached her ear again.

"No—no, aunt, I am not mistaken. It is Ramon; see, he is coming this way."

It was, perhaps, the uncommon stature of the woman that drew the looks of the Spaniard toward her, as she stood upright, with craned neck, to scrutinize him. From her his glance glided to the form beside her, and with a few quick strides he had reached them—just in time to catch the fainting woman in his arms.

"Make room there," he cried sharply; "this lady has fainted from the heat—stand aside, please."

The music striking up at this moment, there was no difficulty in leaving the hall unobserved; the Spaniard laid his burden on the lounge in a small sitting-room, and bent anxiously over her. The woman in orange satin could bridle tongue and temper no longer.

"So you are the delectable Ramon, about whom the

poor thing has been breaking her heart—and you hunting
fresh pastures in the meantime, no doubt. O, a fine set
you are—Spaniards and Americans alike, don't I know you
—ugh!   And that poor creature driven out of her house by
the avaricious landlord, and not a stitch of anything but
what she had on her. What should have become of the
unfortunate child if I had not found her that very day—you
—you heartless deceiver!"

Her feelings had gotten so much the better of her that
she overlooked entirely the possibility of "her chick's"
needing any assistance to recover from her swoon, and only
when Ramon had bathed her temples, and Selma had
opened her eyes, was she recalled to the needs of the
present. Ramon kneeled beside the lounge and chafed
the cold little hands as he asked, with trembling
voice:

"You do not believe what this woman says? Surely,
you knew that I had not willfully deserted you, my life, my
angel?   Those rascally Americans had me seized and
imprisoned suddenly and without warning, when it came
time to foreclose the mortgage on the Sandia Rancho, so
that I could make no effort to redeem it.   The wounding of
John Marston furnished the pretext for my arrest—though
John Marston has never been heard of since. From the
moment I regained my liberty I searched for you—O, my
love, I need not tell you with what eagerness and anxiety.
My heart broke in the hopeless search; I neither slept nor
rested—I sought everywhere—and have found you at last,
never to part with you again.   For we start to San Diego

to-morrow, to my rancho there. I am still a wealthy man, though half my land is lost.''

'' Start to San Diego to-morrow, indeed!'' mocked Mrs. Merritt, her broad face flushed, her arms akimbo, ''and take my child without so much as saying, ' By your leave.' Do you know that I have adopted her, and left her all my money—''

In the ball-room, meanwhile, there was a commotion of a different kind. At the entrance door appeared a fresh arrival, viewed rather critically by the smiling ushers. By the widest stretch of charity, his corduroys and heavy boots could not be construed into full-dress, though the man was a gentleman, and handsome enough, in spite of a fiery scar that crossed his forehead and buried itself under the masses of his tawny hair. He had evidently been sold an admission ticket, so what could they do but admit him?—especially as the quantity of wine he had already taken augured that he would take a good deal more. A titter ran through the crowd near the door, as he turned apologetically to one of the gentlemen in regulation dress.

'' So much light here,'' he said, ''and so many handsome ladies—it's bewildering to a fellow. Could you not introduce me? Came in from San Joaquin yesterday, and sold my wheat this morning. Would not some of the ladies take a glass of wine with me? No offense—I am a stranger, you see, and don't know the rules of the place.''

The ushers had one after the other edged themselves away, and one of '' the many handsome ladies '' turned to her companion.

"It's the Hoosier from San Joaquin; my husband once pointed him out to me. He burrows in the San Joaquin Valley all the year round, comes to town only when the harvest is in, spends the money he gets in a week's time, and never goes back till he has had at least one broken head to pay for. Watch now, and you will see him pick a quarrel with some one in a very short time. But I do think the managers ought to have taken his pistol from him."

Very likely they had not seen it; they were not watching him as closely as these ladies, who discovered the little weapon only as, passing through the crowd, his coat was for an instant displaced by some one jostling against him.

Pushing on, he came directly in front of one of the little sitting-rooms, which are so cozy to enjoy a quiet supper and harmonious conversation in. In this room, however, there was loud talking, and the occupants seemed engaged in anything but harmonious conversation. A woman's sharp, vixenish voice attracted him.

"What's going on here?" he asked, recklessly peering in. "Anything I can take a hand in?" He was still at the gaming table with his thoughts. "God's Death!" he shouted suddenly, his eyes clear, and his senses sobered in a moment. "That accursed greaser again? I'll give you no odds against me this time, you damned Spaniard. I know I'm going to hell, but you shall go there first—" and before the man could rise from his kneeling position, John Marston's hand had sent a bullet crashing through his brain. The sight of blood maddened him all the more.

"That woman there!" he screamed, turning fiercely to

the prostrate figure on the lounge; but the arms of the gigantic woman were clasped about him, he could neither shake her off nor use his pistol, and the weapon was wrested from him before the strong arms freed him from their unwelcome embrace.

Policemen were on the spot; again, as on that night so many months ago, John Marston was taken into safe custody, to prevent him from doing more harm, and to be held till the Spaniard should appear against him at the bar. It was a vain precaution. Don Ramon Aliso had gone before a higher bar, and poor Mrs. Merritt, with her kind heart and her vulgar ways, had to find some one else to leave her money to; for Selma did not survive the shock of that dreadful night.

THE STORY OF A GARDEN.

THE STORY OF A GARDEN.

Never was garden more unintentionally started, and never did one prove greater source of pleasure. One of the row of detached cottages, which my elder brother had built for the purpose of letting to tenants, was occupied during one summer by a younger brother with his family, who purposed returning to the States at the close of the following winter. The town lies in the midst of the Salinas plains, and as these cottages were pretty much on the outskirts, the surroundings were flat and dreary enough. George, however, had the foresight to plant trees—little snips of eucalyptus, about six inches high—one row along the outer edge of the sidewalk, another row inside the white paling fence.

To make the glaringly new place a little more homelike during my sister-in-law's sojourn in California, I had a dozen or two of plants sent up by a San Francisco florist, and set out in the little front yard of the cottage—fuchsias, a few double geraniums, pelargonias, pansies—common enough flowers, which would entail but small loss by their death or destruction, after having served their purpose.

It so chanced, one day about Christmas time, while on a visit there with mother, that my little nephew brought me two small twigs of honeysuckle—little sprigs about four inches long, broken off a neighbor's vine at haphazard—not slips or shoots. It was a wet, rainy day, and I stuck them in the ground by the front porch, as children do when they play at making gardens. I went back to the city, mother remaining in Salinas till the time should come for my State-brother's departure for his old home; then I went up for a last visit, and was surprised when mother pointed out two nicely growing honeysuckle vines, and said they were the little sticks I had planted. By this time, as the winter was a wet one, the little eucalyptus had more than doubled their height; the geraniums looked as if they did not intend to die, by any means, after their brief period of usefulness; and the fuchsias were covered with the merriest, gayest bells of royal purple, deep red, and starry white. Mother had, in the meantime, set out a verbena slip here, a bunch of violets there, in the little front yard, and began to cast longing glances at the much larger space in the rear of the house, which stood covered with weeds a foot or two high. I, too, found myself often on the front porch, watching the almost visible growth of the scant collection of plants; and finally, before the day came on which we were all to leave the little cottage, and my bachelor brother to his solitary fate, we had concluded not to abandon either, but to refurnish the cottage and install mother as housekeeper for brother, while I was to spend there such brief periods of my existence as I could pass without breathing the air of San Francisco.

And now we commenced growing a garden. I haunted the florists' shops and fancy nurseries in and about the city, brought and sent home all the flowers I could see or think of—had many a batch of worn-out, gnarled old plants palmed off on me as ''sturdy growers,'' and many a "goose" flung at my devoted head by my big brother, be-because I could not tell a healthy, thrifty flower from one that had been forced into temporary bloom and beauty by the gardener's art. To my unspeakable joy I was one day presented with a bundle of a hundred rose cuttings, and on carrying these to Salinas in person, my brother's interest in the garden was at last fully aroused. The ground back of the house had ceased to be a wilderness; the soil had been turned, beds laid off and all sorts of seeds sown. On a piece of ground next our garden proper, and in the immediate vicinity of an artesian well, George laid all the rose cuttings in rows, close together, the object being to give them as much water as possible through the summer, to make roots, so that they could be transplanted in the fall. A little, rude paling fence was built around the patch, and, as it had just about the right dimensions for a grave, the neighbors' children got to calling it our graveyard. As it was still early in the year, we continued to plant, mother and I, all the slips, seeds, and flowers we could buy, beg, or borrow. I dare say the seeding and planting was not always done strictly according to rule; and my brother, who understands something of gardening, no doubt often had his patience sorely tried by the lack of system and knowledge we displayed. But what matter, so long as everything grew and thrived and flourished? Every small bit of geranium that was broken by accident was stuck in the ground and grew to be a bush. Every little twig of fuchsia, every fragment of petunia, heliotrope, pink, showed the same accommodating disposition. No soil but that of California can boast of

such clinging love as its children bear it. Fling away the
bit of heliotrope in your hand, drop the spray of fuchsia on
the ground at your feet, throw but a cup of water upon it,
and you will be surprised, some odd morning, to find a
blooming bush at your door. The sand of San Francisco,
or the black adobe of Salinas, will make the same generous
return for the smallest amount of labor.

When June came I thought our garden was splendid.
There had been a sollya planted by the front porch on one
side of the hall door, and a climbing-rose (cloth-of-gold) on
the other; the bases of the pillars at the outer ends of the
porch were already covered by the honeysuckle. I had
found at a nursery two aquilegias, dark brown and dark
blue, with buds on them, and had transplanted them into the
front yard; and never did flowers look so lovely as these
simple, graceful plants, old-fashioned, but handsomer far
than many of the costlier, newer kinds. The roses in the
"graveyard" *would* bloom, no matter how often we broke
off the buds; and the stock (gilliflowers) which we had
sown early in the year, blossomed out in the richest colors
and most delightful fragrance, and continued so to bloom for
the next three years. A little slip of heliotrope had been
set out by the steps at the front door, no one thinking that
the hop-o'-my-thumb would ever do more than fill out its
little corner. By fall, it had grown to be two feet, was covered with flowers all that winter, and the next spring shaded,
under its then stately height, countless little plants sprung up
from the seed. These were transplanted to different parts of
the garden, and some of them proved really choice varieties,

with clusters larger and finer than the parent flower could ever boast of. The roses in the "graveyard," which had been marked whenever they had shown their color by their buds, were transplanted after the first rains in the fall, and commenced blooming almost immediately; and a tiny slip of a passion-vine, set out about the same time, a calla lily of three small, delicate leaves, and a diminutive yellow jasmine, entered on a race for the championship in speed and endurance. How their strength held out, all through the winter, is a marvel to me. With what pride I picked my daily bouquet in the year-old garden, I need not say; and some of the railroad officials can testify to the huge bunches of flowers I used to bring with me to San Francisco.

If I had thought the garden splendid in June, when it was only six months old, how much more so did it seem to me the June following, when it was just eighteen months old. I had been absent for some time, and when I neared the well-known cottages, I was surprised by a dark-green shimmer along the whole road. The eucalyptus trees had made good use of their leisure, and had grown a full head taller than my big brother. As the whole length of the block belonged to him, he had had the double row of trees extended all the way down and around the corner, though there was no building on the lower half of the block, only the white picket fence enclosing the lot. I could hardly realize that this was the bare, bald-looking place I had once so detested, as I stopped before our own particular cottage. Honeysuckle vines were twining tenderly about the corner pillars of the porch, and drawing their network across to the next support; they were covered with bunches of white, creamy tubes, and the air was heavy with their perfume. The climbing-rose had reached the height of the lattice-work on its upward journey, and its yellowish flowers formed a most effective contrast to the sky-blue of the sollya blossoms, trained up on the other side of the porch. The beds were edged variously with dark-blue violets and pink daisies, above which bloomed salvias, euphorbias, lantanas, tube-roses, forget-me-nots, carnations, white lilies, Japan lilies, iris, primroses, ranunculus, lilies-of-the-valley, pansies, anemones, dahlias, and roses—white, red, pink, yellow, crimson, cream —in the wildest profusion. On the porch, on either side of the hall door, stood a Turk's-head cactus, with large, trumpet-shaped, rose-clored blossoms; and above, on the doorposts, hung two cages, "Yakob's" on one side, "Jimmy's" on the other. At the corner of the house I could get a look into the garden at the back, and was fairly dazzled by the bright colors in the sun. But the sun had destroyed quite a number of plants, mother said, particularly her hydrangeas, and she was going to have trees in the garden to shade her plants. As she is quite an independent old lady, she had determined to trouble no one, but raise her own trees. A little box filled with earth, and two bits' worth of eucalyptus-tree seed, was all she wanted, and in an incredibly short time she had a miniature forest on hand, which she distributed to suit herself.

Every well-regulated garden has its own toad, I believe; and I discovered ours, one day, in the "wood-house." This is an institution where garden implements, kindling-wood, disabled chairs, broken-nosed pitchers, and the like are kept; and, while rummaging here for something, my hand suddenly touched some alarmingly cold object. A bound and a scream was the natural result, and when mother came and threw open the door, we beheld for the first time our toad—a tender little thing, not over an inch or two long or broad. He looked gravely into my face, surprised and displeased at the fuss I had made about it, and then demurely hopped away. After this we saw him frequently, generally seated behind the yellow jasmine on the "half round" bed, but just as often perched on the top of an old stone jug in the wood-house. But he croaked when he felt like it, and it meant neither sunshine or rain, so far as I could discover.

About this time I visited San José, and there, at a pottery, saw a garden urn which I knew would look perfectly lovely in our garden. It stood about a yard high from the ground, could be taken in two pieces, and was to cost five dollars. I had it sent home; but, somehow, George never liked the thing, though he had it painted a bronze-green at my request. I lugged it into the front yard, underneath a eucalyptus tree, with an immediate background of pink-blooming double geranium. In it I planted a heliotrope (they grew like weeds all over the garden), surrounded by a wreath of some drooping little vines, which hung over the rim of the urn. This whole arrangement I mounted on an empty candle-box, around which I planted the periwinkle with its far-reaching arms, to hide the box and make believe it was a pedestal. Placed at the head of the broad walk or alley formed by the two houses, and viewed from the bottom of the garden, I thought the effect was charming. But my brother thought differently; and when I came to Salinas again, the box pedestal had been chopped into kindling-wood, and the urn, in two pieces, was idly rolling around the yard. The heliotrope had died, George said, and the periwinkle would not grow. I quietly gathered up the urn, dragged it to the front porch, filled it with earth, and planted a beautiful pink pelargonium in it, surrounded by a wreath of blue lobelias. I watched it and tended it, and when I left, it was under the impression that this was the prettiest piece of furniture in the whole establishment. On my return I could see neither the urn nor the plants in it, and immediately commenced a "still hunt" for both. I found the urn at last, drew it out of its hiding-place, rolled it to the front porch once more, and commenced operations. I took the largest of the Turk's-head cactus, and, as I could not handle the thing on account of the long thorns, broke the pot to pieces and managed to slide the plant into the urn. Then I carefully gathered up the fragments of the big flower-pot, put them where I had found the urn, and considered a good day's work done. I had beaten my brother—the cactus was too much for him, and, as far as I know, the urn stands on the front porch to this day.

Soon after, another equally bitter but equally wordless war was waged between us. The garden was now so grown up—so choked up, in fact—that many things which had been planted in the first place to make a quick growth, could be well spared. Among these, first and foremost, a vine called water-ivy by some, German ivy by others. It grows rapidly, has a pretty, glossy, dark-green leaf, and is the favorite resort of a large, hairy, black caterpillar. Partly on this account, and partly because it dies down in winter and leaves a mass of tough, black, string-like lines clinging to the trellis, I had always hated it, and wanted George to root it out, as there were so many prettier vines in the garden—English ivy, woodbine, passion vine, ivy geranium, smilax, clyanthus and running roses. George, on the other hand, hated my beautiful sollya, because the resinous matter, which exudes from it with the sun, always caught the dust and adhered as a black mass to the flooring of the porch. But the plant was graceful and the flower lovely, and I would not pull it up. Neither would he pull up the water-ivy. At last I commenced on this myself; but it was so tough, and so spread out and rooted in, that I made but little headway, and went to San Francisco before I could fairly finish the task. When I came back my sollya had disappeared, root and branch, and that horrid water-ivy was still in its place. The porch was so thickly covered with vines now that the sollya was really not missed; but I had to get even with my flint-headed brother. After much labor, I succeeded in dragging the objectionable ivy out of the ground, threw the whole thing over the fence, and took my departure for the city, well satisfied with my efforts at ridding the garden of a nuisance. Returning within a week or two, behold!—the water-ivy, replanted in its old corner. Without a word I dug it up, and threw it over the fence on the other side and felt quite triumphant when its former

place was vacant on my next visit.   Months later, I chanced
into the vacant lot below, which had been set out with roses
and evergreens, when what should I see but that detestable
water-ivy, growing as if nothing had happened it, in a far
corner of the lot.   I ran back to the house, found a hatchet,
pulled up the plant, hacked it into little pieces, and
threw it, by bits, into the street.   That was the last of
the water-ivy.

 Amid these ''wars, and rumors of wars,'' fair June had
come once more—two years and six months, to a day, since
I had unintentionally started a garden by sticking a little
twig of honeysuckle into the ground.   Verily, a goodly
showing was here, for a garden that had been neither
planned, nor laid out, nor sub-drained, sub-soiled, nor anything else that Eastern people think indispensable for growing a garden.   George met me at the depot, after several
month's absence; and long before I could see the row of
cottages, I saw the trees waving high above them.   Turning into the street, we entered an avenue of tall, stately
trees, swayed by the noonday breeze, and shading garden,
sidewalk, street and cottages.   The skimp little things that
had been objects of my scorn two years before, now commanded my respect and veneration, for there is nothing so
impressive and solemn to me as the rustling of the wind in
the trees.   From out between the paling-fence, and above
it, great round clusters of double geranium—pink, rose,
scarlet—thrust themselves into the faces of the passers-by;
for all these plants, with the exception of a few white and
salmon-flowered ones, had been banished to the fence, on

account of their impudently forward growth. Some of the leaves were the size of a large palm-leaf fan, the stems were as large round as my arm, and one of the scarlet double kind was actually making its way from the fence to the roof of the house. The cloth-of-gold climbing-rose at the front porch was climbing over the roof, and the heliotrope—the old original one, in the corner by the steps—was eight feet high, though it had been wilted down by the unusually severe weather of the past winter. The honeysuckle, which we had once so cherished and protected, had taken possession of the better part of the porch and house, and mother made daily attacks on it with carving-knife and garden-shears, to keep it from forcing its way inside. The jasmine was twelve feet high, the passion-vine an impenetrable wall, and the calla lily grew all over the garden; it had been separated into fifty different bushes, and they bloomed from the first of January to the last of December. A dozen gladiola bulbs which had been placed in the ground, made the garden look like a dry goods store show-window; and when it came time to take up the bulbs we filled baskets with them, and then had to pull up as weeds the blades that sprang from the countless small ones left in the earth. Hyacinth, tulip and other bulbs increase in the same proportion; and the flowers seem to retain their bloom longer here than they do in the Eastern States.

One of the homely German proverbs says that " our appetite grows with the eating." The more garden we had the more we wanted. The only free space left in the yard,

about twenty feet square, on which fronted the wood-house
and the back porch, was now traversed by rude benches,
rising one above the other like steps, completely covered
with flowers growing in pots; and the bees of all Monterey
County gathered right there, as if they thought these
flowers, being in pots, must excel those in the ground.
The side-wall of the wood-house had been trellised all the
way up, and here a separate fuchsia-bed had been estab-
ished.   It was sheltered from the hottest sun as well as
from the cold that sometimes nips them in the winter-time;
and I will engage to pick a bouquet of the most variously-
colored fuchsias from that bed, any time of the year, be it
January, May or October.

Still, I don't boast of our fuchsias; I do not think that
they thrive in Salinas as they do in this horrid San Francisco; we have no plant in the garden over eight feet high,
and there is no stem there more than one inch and a half in
diameter.   But our lemon-verbena!   That is something to
boast of.   It may seem strange to Eastern folks to hear a
lemon-verbena spoken of as a shrub; this particular one,
however, is a tree.   It was a slender shoot of two feet in
height when we set it out; it is fifteen feet now, and the stem
as large around as a stout man's arm.   It is monstrous, but
has lost none of its fragrance by its vast proportions.   It
is the home of a dozen humming-birds, who build their
nests in it, and are tame enough to visit the cages of
"Yakob" and "Jimmy" on the back porch; for there
are no children with prying eyes and climbing feet to
disturb them.

"Yakob" and "Jimmy," poor fellows, had twice a very narrow escape from those feathered Apaches, the king-birds. In both cases "Yakob's" vigorous lungs had brought timely help; "Jimmy," a timid, oppressed-looking little canary, had sat huddled up in a little heap, as far back as possible in the cage, when rescued, with his head tucked under his wing. After this, the cages were hung out on the back porch, where they could be seen from the dining-room and kitchen. The birds were really fond of flowers, and enjoyed the garden as much as any other member of the family. "Yakob," a splendid singer, was spoiled by petting, and naturally grew headstrong and willful. Among other things, he insisted on coming out of his cage when-ever he felt inclined to roam through the house, and would not sing unless he had his way. He always wanted "Jimmy" for company, and together they wandered from room to room—"Yakob" leading the way, "Jimmy" humbly bringing up the rear. But they were not ungrate-ful, and "Yakob" would strike up a brisk, lively air, hopping about the floor by mother's feet, "Jimmy" sing-ing a feeble little second. We used to be very careful about closing the doors and windows when first they were allowed to leave their cages, more particularly the hall-door. This opens into the house from the front porch, and as you enter, you have George's room on the left, the parlor to the right, through which you pass into the dining-room, where the cages hang by the window.

One day I happened in the dining-room just as the birds were crossing the parlor floor and hopping up to the hall door, which stood wide open. I was afraid to startle them, as they did not know me as well as mother, so all I could do was to watch. Presently "Yakob" stood in the doorway, craned his neck to look up at the sky, shook his head, turned to "Jimmy" to say that it was not safe out there, and led the way into George's room, where they both perched, as usual, on the bouquet. After this, the door was never closed on their account, and "Yakob" even made short trips to the lemon-verbena, on different occasions, leaving "Jimmy" behind on the porch. As I said, they were really fond of flowers—devouring their own weight in mignonette, many times a day. George always brought them a handful when he came in to his meals; and if he ever neglected it, there was war in camp. "Yakob" would flutter around, scold, and work himself into a great fury; and if he happened to be shut up in his cage, I have seen him clutch the door with his little claw, shake it, and screech in the most vindictive manner, and I knew perfectly well that he meant; "Ho—let me at him! I want to peck out his eyes!" "Yakob" was afraid of nothing; but "Jimmy," as I said, was easily frightened, and had a strange horror of George's black hat. He would flutter wildly about, if the black hat approached his cage, and his little heart would beat with fear for an hour after. One day, as both cages were hanging on the back porch with the doors open, George's hat came unexpectedly around the corner, and "Jimmy," in his first fright, shot out of the cage and made for the trees. George, never thinking of the mischief he should work, started after him, tore off the fateful black hat and tried to catch "Jimmy" by throwing it over him. The frantic bird flew over the top of the house, got in among the trees on the street, and was never heard of again. "Yakob" still lives—a saddened life; he has neither sung nor left his cage since "Jimmy's" flight.

The toad, however, is still on hand. Mother had called my attention to the fact that his croaking could plainly and frequently be heard, but that he was no more to be seen. Looking around for a larger flower-pot, on one occasion, to transplant a slip that had grown into a bush, she stooped to pick up one that stood, inverted, among the flower-steps I spoke of before. With a horrified scream she dropped the crock, for under it appeared what she thought at first was a curled-up snake, but which proved, in reality, to be our little toad, grown in circumference to the size of a large saucer, and fat as a pig. He stared at mother quite as fixedly as he had once regarded me, but uttered a gratified croak as he hopped away. Can any one tell me whether he had lain under that crock for weeks and months growing fat? Surely, there was no possibility of his raising the heavy flower-pot from the ground every time he wanted to take temporary shelter under it.

Elsewhere I have spoken of the enormous size the stems of some flowers here attain. When we have lived a number of years in this state, we forget that there is anything remarkable about these things. It is only when we note the astonishment of strangers and tourists, who see them for the first time, that we are reminded of its being something extraordinary. A cousin of mine, who generally spends his furloughs in European travel, and who prides himself somewhat on the collection of rare and beautiful plants in the conservatories on the ancestral estate in the Fatherland, devoted his last furlough to a trip to this country. Driving with him through the Golden Gate Park, I expected, of course, to hear him say how much better and finer they had "all that sort of thing in Europe." But he was honest enough to express his surprise and admiration; and when I remarked casually that the lupine had been found very serviceable in keeping the sand from drifting, he looked in bewilderment at the huge, grayish-green bushes I pointed to.

"Lupines?" he said, "Do you call those lupines?" And he sprang from the carriage to convince himself, cut off one of the branches, stripped it of its leaves, and said he would send that to Alt-Jessnitz to astonish his brother.

"Then why not cut down one of the bushes and send the main stem?" I suggested.

But he only laughed and shook his head, saying that would never do—this was bad enough. It reminded me of Pat, who asked his employer to write a letter for him home to his people in Ireland. "Tell them," says he, "that we get meat three times a week in this country."

"But Pat," the man corrected him, "don't we give you meat every day?"

"True for you," was the reply; "but divil a bit would they believe it at all, at all; sure, three times a week is as much as I dare tell them."

The one regret of my life clings about this same cousin.

It so happened that I did not succeed in showing him a single heliotrope more than five or six feet in height. The previous winter had been severe; most of them had been nipped by the cold, and had not yet attained their former dimensions. We did not get time to cross the bay to Oakland; and all I could do was to give him my word that I knew of different places there where the heliotrope had clambered up to the second story of the house. As a well-bred man he could not doubt my word, but—it was *awful* hard to believe.

"You see," he said, "we have an *orangerie* at Alt-Jessnitz, too—under glass, of course, in winter-time; and the orange-trees there grow *so* high. But heliotropes——" and a surreptitious shake of the head told me that he was not convinced.

Let me say it again; "Our appetite grows with the eating." Though a thousand blossoms flashed their brilliant hues through the sun-lit garden, and filled the air with perfume, I could not help but think of other flowers which we could not grow in the grounds. Begonias, for instance, in spite of all that florists may say to the contrary, will not live in the garden through the winter. Then there are camelias, rhododendrons, gloxinias, amaryllis; and none of these were to be found in our garden.

We are all remote descendants of the monkey, I think; at least our instinct to imitate is easiest accounted for in this manner. Passing along the street one day, I saw a newly-erected green-house, built entirely of glass, covered with a coat of white paint; and the moment my eyes fell on it, I knew just what we wanted.   I rushed home out of breath, and proposed that George build a green-house.

"I've no more time or money to lay out on that garden," he grumbled.

But I was not discouraged.   I knew him to be passionately fond of begonias, and I called to his mind how many specimens of the begonia had passed in through the garden-gate, and out over the fence—dead.   I represented to him that he would keep on buying begonias, and throwing away their corpses, till the expense would reach that of a good-sized green-house, and he would curse his folly and short-sightedness at last for not having built one in time.   Feeling that my speech had made a deep impression, I knew that I could safely leave the rest to mother, and returned to San Francisco.

A month later he wrote: "Come and see the green-house; it is twelve by sixteen feet, and cost fifty dollars to build."   I went as soon as I could.   A perfect beauty was that little green-house.   It stood against the fence at the bottom of the garden; the board fence itself had been raised to form the thirteen-feet high wall, and from there the roof sloped toward the garden.   Everything about it, except this fence-wall, was window-glass, covered with a thin coat of white paint.   Thus it gleamed out magically from among flowering shrubs of oleander, magnolia, lilac, bridal-wreath and roses.   Graceful, slender trees, the trees that mother had raised in the little box, flung light, fitful shadows over it; and, altogether, the effect of the little structure was more than charming—it was enchanting, fairylike.   Inside, on either hand, and along the back wall, were shelves; and George had already filled a great portion of them with begonias—but begonias in such endless variety that the one name does not seem sufficient for all the different kinds. Being no florist, I can not call the multitudinous members of the family by name; but aside from the two principal divisions (discernible to the unprofessional eye), the flowering begonias and the foliage begonias, there must be some fifty subdivisions. The different flowers were from the deepest scarlet to the brightest coral—pure white, salmon, pearl-pink, faint red, bright red, pink, another red, another salmon—no two shades alike, but always playing in the same colors. Then there was the Rex begonia, with its grand, silver-tinted leaves; another with funny little leaves, all hairy, and mottled like a toper's nose; round, glossy leaves, and leaves with a bright rim running around them— all begonias, but no two just alike.

The floor of this grand conservatory was exactly what it had been while it was still common garden; even the white rose that climbed up the fence was still there, though capped of its longest branches. Geraniums, pinks and heliotropes that happened to stand in that part of the garden had insisted on growing till their heads struck against the lowest shelf, and they seemed stupidly staring at the changes around them. Of course the place is not heated, either winter or summer; there is no trace of fire, steam or any other artificial heat within a hundred yards of it; but the house contains all the exotics that grace the conservatories of the Eastern States—camelias, bouvardias, azaleas, gloxinias

and a hundred more.   Pretty as the glass-house looks
in the light of the sun, I think it is prettier still at night,
seen from the outside, when brilliantly lighted up within—
and a two-tallow-candle-power is sufficient for this purpose.
To see it then, when every leaf and blossom seems delicately
traced on the illuminated glass—when the trees above cast a
momentary mantle over its brightness, to let it beam out
softly again the next instant, while the wind whispers mys-
teriously among the slender leaves, and the night is made
fragrant by the breath of a thousand flowers—no one would
ever think that the garden was purely a chance one, and the
conservatory merely an afterthought.

For the third and last time let me say that '' our appetite
grows with the eating.''   Many a time when I stand, garden hose in hand, draggled and wet to the waist, like a
mermaid, I measure with my eye the distance to the farther
fence that surrounds the next cottage.   Our garden is not a
large one, and the flowers are actually crowded.   Now, I
think—and mother thinks so too—that George ought to
have that cottage moved to some other lot, so that the fence
between our grounds and the neighbor's yard could be torn
down, and the whole space turned into one large garden.
And what mother and I think will come to pass.

ST. MARY'S.

ST. MARY'S.

LONG ago, during the first year of my residence in California, I had the good fortune to find a home in the family of dear Mrs. Bissel—and long may she live in the land! It never occurred to me that I was *boarding* there; we seemed like one happy family, though there were sometimes as many as twenty-four children in the house at once. It was not in the heart of the city, and there were large grounds, with shrubs, and an occasional oak tree, surrounding the house, which gave one a charming illusion of being in the country, and which mothers with run-about children fully appreciated.

When I look back upon the happy time now, and recall the different personages who made up the household, I find that the individual who commanded and received the greatest amount of consideration was Bridget, our cook. We all bowed to her tyranny and consulted her pleasure, particularly when it was a "bad day" with her—which it was very often. On such days Mrs. Bissel herself entered the kitchen with fear and trembling; and as for one of us invading Bridget's dominion during a "spell of weather" we would just as soon have thought of thrusting our heads into the furnace at once. There was no possibility of denying that she was an excellent cook; but, considered purely as a woman, she was a terror. At the children's dinner, which took place at four o'clock, one or two of the ladies were generally present; and if it so happened that none of the legitimate mothers could conveniently attend, one or the other of the ladies would take the place. Now, a dozen or two of average San Francisco children would not consume their common dinner in unbroken silence; and whenever I happened to be the *de facto* mother, the urchins always seemed unusually animated. To see Bridget then, if it was a "bad day" with her—as it generally was—make her sudden appearance at the dining-room door, when the hubbub was greatest, the iron spoon with which she had just basted the meat swung high in air, her black eye-brows contracted to a thunder-cloud, and her eyes flashing fire, was not conducive to a child's quiet sleep at night.

"Will ye be shtill—ye murtherin' young dhivils ye? Howly Moses! but I'll put yez in the oven and roast ye alive!" And ere the shrill tones of her voice had died away, the little ones, even the most courageous boy in the crowd, would seem turned into stone with fear. Then, without a feature of her face changing, she would pile up another dish with flaky white biscuit, warm ginger-snaps, or anything else that was tempting to a child's appetite, and send it into the dining-room by the waiting-girl. As to the waiting-girl, it was always strictly enjoined upon her *never* to touch anything upon the stove, in the stove, anywhere about the stove—anything in the kitchen, in fact,—except what Bridget set down on the large table expressly for her. This she carried into the dining-room; and woe betide her if ever she discovered speck or spot on the edge of dish or platter, which Bridget had overlooked. Truth to tell it happened very seldom, for Bridget was neatness itself except in her dress—she said she had no time to waste on that. Mrs. Bissel, to give her time, made the attempt once or twice to furnish her with an assistant. But they all went the same way, generally on the third day, flying through the kitchen door, with a soup-ladle, or stove-lid, a toasting-fork, or anything else that came handy to Bridget, flying after them.

Once, when she had a particularly "bad day," poor Mr. Bissel, just returned from a journey—during which, perhaps, the recollection of these bad days had grown fainter—innocently brought out the blacking-brushes in the kitchen, and started in to polish his boots. He didn't reach the polishing point, however; for, while he turned for a drop of water to moisten the paste with, brushes, boots, and all took a sudden spin out through the open door and across the porch into the yard. His wife had always tried to inculcate lessons of patience and forbearance; and there was merely a blank, noncomprehensive expression on his face for a moment; but then, turning with a sudden "Well, I never—" he would certainly have added something stronger, had it not been that a glance at the well-filled range reminded him it was nearly dinner-time, and that Bridget was ruling goddess of the roast. Another instance of how men are slaves to their appetites.

As there was a stable and carriage-house on the grounds, one of the families boarding with us kept their coachman there, John Hand; and to him we soon assigned the *rôle* of liberator. Bridget was not bad looking, and *could* be amiable. John Hand seemed a hopeful subject, and we took turns at dinning Bridget's perfections into his willing ears.

Particularly on "bad days" did we follow this pursuit with avidity, extolling her art and economy in cooking, the spotless purity of her kitchen domain, her beauty, her thrifty ways, and the swift retribution she had visited, in the shape of a milk-and-water douche-bath, on the head of the milkman when he once tried to supply our numerous family with diluted cream, and short measure at that. Such a wife must make the fortune and happiness of any man, we argued to John Hand.

Mrs. Bissel shook her head at our plottings and endeavors. One day, when Bridget was having an outrageously "bad day," and we were working up John's affection for her in a corresponding degree, she said, "You will never succeed. Poor Bridget has her own troubles, and it is not all temper with her." She hinted at something that Bridget had once confided to her, in regard to "a foine young man back in Ireland," who was poor like herself, which was the reason that "the two of them couldn't get married." After Bridget's departure from the old soil, her mother had written something about the transfer of the "foine" young man's affections to the daughter of a wealthy farmer, and Bridget, receiving no assurance from him to the contrary, was trying to school herself to the belief that Tommy was faithless. It was hard, of course, that we should have to suffer for the perfidy of this man; but we tried hard enough to make another man pay the penalty, to little avail, as the sequel will show. In fact knowing Mrs. Bissel as well as I did, I had often had a glimmer of an idea that it was not altogether on account of Bridget's proficiency in the art of cooking that her mistress had so much patience with her; and to myself I said, '' Well, Bridget is certainly more lenient with Mrs. Bissel than with the rest of us—a sign that she appreciates, at least.'' But the same evening, at dinner, I touched Mrs. Bissel lightly on the arm and whispered to her that the tomato salad had just a faint flavor of coal-oil, and had better be removed from the table.

'' For goodness sake,'' she whispered back, '' don't say a word, or Bridget will never let me come into the kitchen again. I trimmed my lamp at the kitchen table, and she told me then to clear out, but I would not do it.''

The tomato salad was not pressed on the diners, and Mrs. Bissel luckily escaped a reprimand from her cook.

One morning a most distressing circumstance occurred— distressing as unlooked for, as we all had a clear conscience and knew that for the last month none of us had ventured into the kitchen to ask Bridget's permission to heat a flat-iron on the range, or draw a cup of hot water from the boiler (we generally got more of that than we prayed for, anyhow)—a number of distressing circumstances I should have said; for not only were the biscuit streaked with yellow and burnt to a crisp, but the steak was tough and cold, the coffee resembled dish-water, and no muffins, buckwheat or corn-cakes were visible to the eye or discernible to the sense of smell. Had Mrs. Bissel not been a strong, vigorous woman, she must have sunk beneath the cross-fire of injured looks and impatient questions directed to her—or against her, rather. Had she dared to disobey Bridget, or talked back to her? Had she spoken a single rash, cross word to her, and brought disaster on the whole household? She held up her hands to stay our imprecations. She vowed she had behaved in the most exemplary manner; but Bridget had had a letter from home last night, a very disturbing—or rather, important letter—and it had unsettled her nerves. There was no more said on the subject, as we saw the uneasy glance Mrs. Bissel directed toward the kitchen-door. The gentlemen were quickly through with their breakfast and hurried down town, while the ladies were feeding on the anticipation of "hearing all about it."

With one accord we all assembled in a small room, well out of Bridget's way, after breakfast, and there we heard all about it, sure enough. The mother had written that a brother of her deceased husband had died and left them all his money—"shtacks and poiles of it," Bridget said—as much as two or three thousand dollars. At the same time Tommy had written, after a long, long silence, to say that his heart was breaking to see his beloved Bridget once more, and that she might expect him now, at an early day. That the girl would marry him as soon as he set foot on land and chose to have her, he seemed to have no doubt—no more than Bridget had herself. John Hand was desperate, and went so far as to hint that if the accommodating uncle had not died at so opportune a time, Tommy would never have allowed his heart to break for Bridget. But he got a fine dressing-down for his pains, and Bridget would never speak a word to him after.

Tommy came; Bridget invested all her savings in a black silk dress, a black velvet hat (with a feather, of course), and a gay cashmere shawl. That she was supremely happy I need not more particularly state; suffice it to say that we got burnt saleratus biscuit more than once, instead of light muffins, and that she went so far as to set a flatiron on the stove for me with her own hands one day. They were to be married in church, as a matter of course; and the Sunday just before, when the last bans were to be published, I went to St. Mary's, and took my seat in a quiet nook, where I had the whole church before me.

It was a day perfect and lovely, as days are only in California. There was an added gleam of brightness in the sun because it was Sunday morning, just as I fancy that there is a peculiarly sad tone in Sunday afternoon's sun. The soft, golden air floated in through the upper portion of the tall, gothic windows, and the sombre dome of the church seemed gradually to become filled with the warm light of the sweet May morning. In low, thrilling cadences the notes of the organ fluttered and wavered through the lofty building, the priest sprinkled the cleansing water right and left, and "*Asperges me, Domine*" came in beseeching tones from the balconied organ-loft.

When I raised my head again, I saw John Hand's square shoulders somewhere in front of me, and I wished honestly that it might be his name that was to be coupled with Bridget's, and not black-eyed, slender Tom's, for I could not divest myself of the thought that only Bridget's little fortune had drawn him to her side again. Soon the " preaching priest " of the day mounted the chancel, and among those whose names were published as about to enter the state of holy matrimony were Bridget O'Neil's and Thomas Finly's. Next, our prayers were requested for the repose of the souls of those who had died during the week, and whose death was brought to the notice of the Reverend Father; and then, after the preliminary cough and throat-clearing of his congregation, he began his short sermon. I have forgotten the words of the text, or where it could be found in the Bible, but it was a lesson on renunciation; and involuntarily, as the sermon proceeded, I let my eyes rove in search of John Hand. He sat with his shoulders bent and his head bowed, a homely picture of sadness; he really loved the vixenish thing who was so ready to marry her fickle.lover of long ago, and the thought came to me then that we had been guilty of cruel wrong to the honest-hearted fellow.

The sermon progressed; John's head drooped lower and lower, and when the sermon was over and the officiating priest had again approached the altar, I noticed that the poor fellow was kneeling, his face covered with his hands, and great, silent sobs shaking his broad shoulders. Poor John! Not for you alone was that sermon preached; the pale young priest at the altar, whose gentle voice echoes with subdued yet sonorous ring through the church, has struggled, battled, and renounced; the white-haired woman kneeling humbly at the shrine of Mary has felt the sorrow and the triumphs of the Christian soul; and the tall, fair girl in the balcony above, whose pure notes are so clearly distinct above all other voices, carries '' Renunciation '' traced on the white forehead and written in the depths of her dark, sad eyes. And as the organ peals through the arched space, and the full choir answers the chant of the priest, the lower wing of the window beneath which John Hand kneels is blown gently open by the summer wind, a narrow strip of sunshine falls across his auburn hair, and the glint of something white and silver, flashing in the light, is for an instant seen above his head. It is a dove that has found its way in through the open window, and flies swiftly to the altar, where it rests among the heavy shadows beneath the vaulted ceiling, folding its wings peacefully, as though it had come to stay.

Bridget's marriage did not turn out well; it soon became known that Tom, though not dissipated, was often away from home, and that Bridget was fretting her life out. Whether it was really this, or whether her more than human "infirmity of temper" had been but the symptoms of disease lurking in her system, I can not say; but Mrs. Bissel told us one day, with tears in her eyes, that she had been to see Bridget, and that the poor thing could not long survive. She regained all her old vigor of disposition, however, before her death, and Tommy found that every cent Bridget could claim had been transferred to her mother before her death.

It was a rainy, blustering day, when Father Gallagher, at St. Mary's, requested our prayers for the repose of the soul of Bridget Finly. Tom was in church, occupying almost the same seat that John Hand had once filled; and I fancied that the wretch had come there merely to have the pleasure of hearing his wife's name read out among those of the dead. But somehow, when the organ thundered through the spacious church, poorly filled with people to-day, he seemed to shrink within himself; and pretty soon I saw him on his knees, his head bowed, his face covered. Just then an angry gust blew full against the tall window, and as the lightly fastened shutter blew open, heavy drops of cold, bleak rain fell on the bowed head, and the wind tugged viciously at the black curls which had once been poor Bridget's pride and delight.

MODERN MONTEREY.

MODERN MONTEREY.

RUSKIN recently spoke of the resemblance existing between a duck and a snake, implying, perhaps, relationship at some long-passed day. Ducks and snakes are both stupid animals, and have no souls. A bird, however, has a soul, and I could easily believe it to be related to the human family, if it were only for having in common the one trait—the irresistible desire to flit when the spring-time comes. No matter how soberly and sincerely I say to myself all through the winter, "I shall not want to go anywhere next summer; that will be a saving, and I can get me an elegant summer suit." But when the spring-time comes, I find that that part of my soul which is related to the bird grows very restless, and before the summer is far in the land I have forgotten all about the elegant suit, and am flitting somewhere.

This year it was to Monterey. It was not the first time my steps had turned that way. I had been there many times before, and I have learned to love the old place, which holds so much of interest to the American people. Historical associations alone, however, have never yet made any place pleasant or desirable to live in; but in Monterey nature has done much, though art and improvement, until quite recently, very little, to make the town and the surrounding country attractive.

In regard to its earlier history the main difficulty is to

know where to begin to speak of it. That Juan Rodriguez Cabrillo must have passed the harbor in his cruise of 1542; that Viscayno landed here, and took possession for the Spanish king in 1602; that Father Junipero Serra reached Monterey in 1770, with the good ship *San Antonio*, and on the second of June celebrated the first mass under the trees—we have all heard and read so often that I am afraid of being "choked off" by the editor if I attempt to say it again. Still, there is some excuse for lingering a moment over the arrival of the good priest Junipero Serra, for he built the beautiful Mission of San Carlos, in Carmel, the lovely little valley with its stretch of shining white beach, and its remnants of mission garden and old orchards. And, besides, the very tree under which the altar was erected for the serving of the mass is still spreading its broad shadow over the earth, and the tree still standing there is proof that the whole story is true, if even it had not passed into history as a fact. He came ashore; upon first landing, brought thirty-eight out of the fifty of the ship's crew, monks and sailors, with him; and, after declaring the land the property of the King of Spain, took spiritual possession of the realm for his church. The ground must have undergone considerable change since then, for where the ugly wooden cross stands to-day, marking the spot where this first mass was said, a little run, or gulch, has washed its way deep into the soil, and the slope by the tree, where the worshipers would naturally have knelt, is so narrow that thirty-eight people could not possibly have crowded around, unless some of them had descended into this gulch, a proceeding neither dignified nor practicable, either then or now. The tree from which the bell was suspended that bright June morning has toppled over, and the trunk is now lying prone in the tiny stream it had so long overhung.

Monterey itself should be viewed afoot. This advice is not an insinuation against the state of the streets, though the truth is that every street has a gully running through the center. The streets are wide enough, however, and one can drive either to the right or the left of the ravine, and, as my brother philosophically remarks, these gulches will be of considerable help in building the sewers. Some of the older streets run in any and every direction that happens to suit; the newer ones run due east and west, north and south. Monterey has grown of late, in both size and importance; but the newly erected American residences, I am glad to say, have nothing of the rectangular, hard-cornered look about them which new American houses are apt to have. A spirit of veneration for the traditional quaintness of the old capital seems to have mercifully guided the hand of the designing architect, and the result is that the modern features of the town blend harmoniously with what was already there when the Americans came. And surely, what they found there could not have been so utterly despicable. The place had been the residence of the Spanish governors for fifty years, and of the Mexican governors for twenty-five. To be sure, we know how far removed from the center of civilization California was in those days; still, there were men of character and distinction among the long line of governors, priests, generals, who once dwelt here—men whose mark it is neither easy nor altogether desirable to efface.

Many of the *adobe* houses, solid two-storied buildings, lie in the midst of large gardens, surrounded by high walls built of *adobe*, or the chalk-stone found in the vicinity. When built of chalk-stone, the upper portion is frequently of hard-packed earth, overgrown and covered with shrubs and weeds; when raised of *adobes* alone, they are always finished with a layer or two of red tiles, and above, and out from behind these gray walls, with their red edge, crowd the green foliage of tree and bush, and the tender pink and golden yellow of apple-blossom and the cloth-of-gold rose. The gate is grated, permitting a broad view of the garden, and a glimpse of the interior of the dwelling, if the hall-door happens to be open, for the gate is always just opposite the front door of the house. A number of houses are but one story high, and they are the coziest of all, the generous veranda promising shade and coolness for the summer-time, the heavy walls and deep fireplaces insuring warmth and comfort for the winter months. Many of the less preten-tious houses have no fireplace at all, except the apology that serves for culinary purposes. The climate is so mild that there is no suffering from actual cold—it is only the uncomfortable sensation creeping over one on a long, rainy day that needs to be banished by looking at a cheerful fire.

Quite a number of the wealthy prominent Americans lately removed to Monterey have bought some of the better preserved of the old *adobe* structures and have con-verted them into desirable and attractive homesteads; for, no matter how indolent and non-progressive the Spanish population may have been, there is one element in this sleepy old place which never stood still—the plants and flowers of field and garden. They took no holiday, summer or winter, these thousands of roses, lilies, vines and trees; they kept right on growing, growing, growing, till they have covered houses, fences, ruins, with a tangle of scarlet, gold and purple blossoms. In the garden of a Madame Bonifacio (I beg pardon for growing personal—I do not know the lady, but I want other tourists to enjoy what I saw), there is a trellis over the walk, from the hall-door to the gate. The entire trellis is covered with a rose crowded with blossoms, yellowish in color, the size of a breakfast-saucer. The stem of this rose is a tree, as large round as the neck of an ordinary-sized man. This must be seen to be believed, I know; but it's there.

Pretty well back, on something of an eminence, stands Colton Hall, named after the first American *alcalde* under the military administration of General Riley. It was originally designed as both a town-hall and a school-house, and answers the latter purpose still. No one will ever go into raptures over its architectural beauties, though the building is quite large, built of the handsome light chalk-stone, and well finished. Here the first California Constitution was framed, in September, 1849; it is really the cradle of our State laws—and a good sound cradle it looks to be, even to this day. Beside it stands the jail (ominous juxtaposition), built of imported stone. The cause of the distinction enjoyed by the jail (to be erected of imported stone, when native chalk-rock was good enough for the town-hall) was in reality a bad augury for Monterey; for, during the time the government had its seat here, these stones were sent for to build a dry-dock with. As soon as it was decided that the Legislature and the State Government should be removed to San José, this project was abandoned, the stones were used to build the jail with, and, soon after, Monterey entered upon the long sleep from which it is only just awaking.

Closer in is a long, two-story, shaky *adobe* building, bearing every mark of old age about it, without having yet advanced to the dignity of a ruin. This is the Presidio of Spanish times, the *cuartel* of the Mexican *régime*, and the soldiers' quarters of the beginning of our own Government. It lies in the heart of the town, abandoned and deserted, save for a room or two in the lower story, where otherwise homeless wanderers at intervals take up their abode. The fort itself, and the *casamata*—the place where the powder and shot were stored, and the cannon were kept—are out on the hill, to the west of the town; and, as I had a great curiosity to inspect these relics close by, we wended our way through the busy streets, and were soon ascending the hill. On the lower terrace, overlooking the Bay of Monterey, stand the remains of thick *adobe* walls, with a heavy, blackened log protruding here and there from the heaps of *débris*. This is the *casamata*. No other traces of older fortifications are visible on this plateau; but back of this, on the summit of the hill, there is still a solitary cannon, pointing its warning finger at the bay. Steep as the climb was, we mounted to the rampart and descended into the interior. The earthworks had been star-shaped. From the main road at the foot of the hill, I had often noticed a low roof, barely visible above the outer walls. Now I had the gratification of seeing it near by, at last, and found that it was the block-house—the last resort of the garrison, had the outworks ever been taken. The sturdy old thing looked defiant even now, with its notched loop-holes and impenetrable timbers; but out of the low entrance-door hung wisps of hay and bundles of straw, showing that it had degenerated into a mere storehouse for the abundant grain that now grows around it. A little farther back, but well protected by the cannon of the fort in former times, are the ruins of the soldiers' barracks, with no signs of life about them, save that a lizard glides swiftly by over fallen logs and decaying timbers. The officers' quarters were in better condition, and we mounted the stairs that led, on the outside, to the upper story. Messieurs the officers had been comfortably fixed, as usual, I'll warrant; large, well lighted rooms, fireplaces, and the most magnificent view imaginable. Standing on the rude balcony, which the landing of the stairs forms in front of the house, one gets a wide look across bay and city. Over these placid waters there the *Savannah* came gliding, on the second of July, in 1846; and on the seventh of the same month the stars and stripes were raised by Commodore Sloat, right here in front of us, over the old Mexican *casamata*, and yonder in the town, over that rambling, two-story *adobe* house I spoke of before. The Mexican people were well enough satisfied to accept the

Americans and their rule, so far as I could learn from Don Rosario Duarte, who came with Commodore Dupont on the *Cyane*, as an American marine, though a Spaniard by birth; but their rulers were wide apart and divided in their opinions on this point. Governor Pio Pico, in his little speech, anathematizes the "hordes of Yankee immigrants who have already begun to flock into the country, and whose progress cannot be arrested."

"Already," he exclaims, "the wagons of this perfidious people have scaled the well-nigh inaccessible summit of the Sierra Nevada, crossed the entire continent, and penetrated to the fruitful valley of the Sacramento. What that astounding people will next undertake, I cannot say; but in whatever enterprise they do embark they will be sure to prove successful." Thank you, friend Pio Pico, we have endeavored to verify your kind predictions. Don Mariano Guadaloupe Vallejo showed a great deal more "savey" on this occasion. He said: "Why should we shrink from incorporating ourselves with the freest and happiest nation in the world, destined soon to be the most wealthy and powerful? Why should we go abroad for protection when this great nation is our adjoining neighbor? When we join our fortunes to hers, we shall not become subjects, but fellow-citizens, possessing all the rights of the people of the United States, and choosing our own federal and local rulers."

The only thing in the way of treasure that our soldiers got in the city of Monterey at the time of its bloodless capture were one hundred and fifty pieces of ordnance—

cannons, large and small—which are at present decorating street corners and serving as hitching-posts. They are stuck in the ground, without much attention to "heads or tails," and remind one—I don't mean to cast reflections—of the bravado of most Mexican military: ferocious of aspect, but utterly harmless and incapable of doing serious injury. The heaviest two pieces are "planted" in front of the Monterey Whaling Company's office, near the fort, as if they had proved too heavy for further hauling. Next to this house (the Whaling Company's) stands a red brick building, of many memories. It was built, very early, by Mr. Dickenson, one of the party who came in 1846, just ahead of the Donners, and barely escaping their horrible fate. He had with him his wife and two daughters, young ladies who were greatly sought after, and much courted and flattered. The boldest admirer they ever had, however, was an enormous grizzly, who forced his way into their room one night and insisted on making them a friendly call anyhow, no matter how strongly they objected. Young ladies had lungs in those days as well as now, and I can imagine how their cries and screams rang through that old brick house. One of the young ladies, married long since, lately presented a brick from the wall of this building to the Society of Pioneers.

The surroundings of Monterey could not well be more beautiful if they had been gotten up to order. Hills, gently rising, the chain broken here and there by a more abrupt peak, environ the city, crowned with dark pines and the more famous cypress of Monterey (*Cupressus macrocarpa*).

The Lomalto is a bald peak, with a lower peak, more gently sloping, for its neighbor. The whole was formerly called the Cerro San Carlos—for to this Holy Charles seems to have been assigned the guardianship of Monterey and the Carmel Mission. To the right, or west of us, as we stand facing the bay, is the hill bearing the remains of the old fort, beyond which winds the road to Point Pinos and the light-house; to the left of us, east, lies a forest of pine and live-oak, and above the trees waves the flag from the tower of the new Hotel del Monte. Before us the bay lies calm and blue, and away across, on a light day, even without the aid of a glass, can be seen the town of Santa Cruz, an indistinct white gleam on the mountain side.

And now, having devoted the whole morning to historical researches—which led to the discovery of an owl, a mole and several lizards among the ruins of the fort—let us follow the waving of the flag, which beckons us out of the "dark forest-green." A short mile from the heart of the town lies the new hotel, over which these crazy, sleepy old Montereyans are fairly going wild. There are two roads by which to reach the place, one along the sea-shore, while the other, a longer drive, takes us by the handsome Catholic church, across one or two narrow lagoons, and past the ancient, as well as modern, graveyard. Whichever way we drive, we enter directly into the forest—not "grove," as these horrid people call it, but veritable, venerable, old-fashioned forest. Pines (*Pinus insignis*), trying their best to reach the stars, are intermingled with live-oaks of singularly tall, straight growth (*Quercus agrifolia*). There is nothing gnarled or stunted about them; no bleak wind has ever crippled their growth, or distorted the solid trunk into weird, repulsive shapes. Evenly the long, low-hanging branches spread on every side, giving shade and protection to hundreds of flowers and ferns. A thick carpet of native grasses serves them for bed, and the poison-oak, the bane and pest of most California country resorts, is conspicuous only by its entire absence.

The horses seem to check their speed of their own accord as they enter this solemn forest dome, and I am just about to make myself ridiculous, by the suggestion that they are listening to the peculiar, low, soothing whisper that the wind breathes through the tree tops, when a cry of surprise cuts off my brilliant remark. A fairy castle has just risen out of the ground, or dropped from the skies, and rests airily among the trees in the distance. I was afraid to breathe when I saw it first, for fear of dispelling the vision; but, as we approach, the thing assumes more solid lines, a more substantial shape, and I find that we are right in front of the much-talked-of new hotel.

Who planned the place, or laid it out, in the common parlance of mortals, I don't know. I don't know what it cost, and don't want to know. Don't, for pity's sake, let us destroy the few æsthetically romantic impressions that are graciously vouchsafed us in this land of dollars and cents. Let us enjoy the rare pleasure of ranging around and through the place without giving heed to the fact that the architect's rule and the carpenter's square were employed in its construction. For the information of those prosaic beings who must have feet and inches, let me say that the building is very nearly three hundred and seventy-five feet long, three stories high in some parts, four in others. The whole, on closer inspection, seems a happy mixture of forest chateau, Italian villa, and old English country seat, though they call it, I believe, Queen Anne or East-lake style. Outside are the spacious verandas of the Italian villla, inside are the wide halls and generous fireplaces of the English manor-house. Outside, the lofty forest, the blue waters of Lake Como, *vulgo Laguna Segunda*, blinking through the distance, form incomparable scenery. Inside, the broad staircases, the many-shaped windows, each framing in a sylvan view, the variously arrayed rooms in the different towers, the manifold entrances and exits, always leading into the forest-green, make the house picturesque. Now, I don't really know whether interiors can be picturesque—I don't know whether artists allow that term; but I insist that "picturesque" is the only correct word to apply to the inside of that building.

A drive is to be constructed from the east of Monterey, along the beach, by the whaling station, all the way around Point Pinos and the light-house, along Moss Beach, to Cypress Point, to the old Mission, and across the country, back again to the hotel. A Cliff House is to be built on the highest, most wildly romantic spot near Point Cypress—a resort for the people at the hotel and for "citizens at large." The fact is, that if any one undertakes the entire drive in one day they will want some kind of a resort on the way. There is also a race-course near the hotel, and all the walks and drives, near and far, are being constructed of gravel brought from Soledad. Of this large tract of land, small tracts will be sold to people who wish to establish a permanent summer residence in the country. Some of the land in the vicinity of the hotel has been divided off for this purpose also, and so near to it that people who are afraid of the drudgery of housekeeping can take their meals at the hotel.

California enterprise, by the way, was never better illustrated than in the erection of this hotel. On the fifteenth of January, of this year, the giants of the forest held undisputed possession of the ground which the house now covers. On the first of February the architect arrived with his force of men. At the time of the present writing (May 15th) there are over three hundred men still at work in the house and on grounds; and on the third of June, before this paper is laid before the reader, the hotel will be thrown open to the public.

It was a day of rare enjoyment that I spent there; and as I, like the cook, Frederika, in *Old Mam'selle's Secret*, always think of others, I gathered what I could of the many wild flowers growing there, for the benefit of those who take an interest in our California flora, and brought them home to Dr. Behr, who has kindly given me the botanical names of the different varieties my basket held. They are the *Aquilegia, Viola aurea, Orthocarpus, Castilleja, Convolvulus, Collinsie, Eschscholtzia*, and others, which I had carelessly so mutilated as to be unrecognizable. The backward season has been more severely felt by the butterflies than the flowers, and there was not so great a variety as there should be. But among those who have their home and being there the Doctor mentions these: *Anthocharis sara*, the *Melitæa*, *Cœnongrepha Californica*.   And *àpropos* of the Doctor, he is really heaping coals of fire on my head, for I once cut · very deeply into his scientist heart.   When it came time for my usual spring-flitting, several years ago, he said to me:

" Toward the south, where you are going now, there is a blue butterfly which has not yet been classified.   If you bring me a specimen of this butterfly it shall be named after you, I promise."

It must be admitted that the Doctor understands a woman's nature at least as well as that of a rattle-snake or a tarantula-hawk.   He did not say, " Madame, I expect you to devote a few spare moments to the advancement of science in our new country."   He simply stimulated my activity by promising that my name should ride down to prosperity on the back of a blue butterfly.   Well, I stopped at San Luis Obispo, climbed the height of the Santa Lucia Mountain, and almost the first thing I saw was a magnificent blue butterfly. My escort captured it, after some trouble.   It was cruelly impaled on a pin, which I stuck, for better security, into the log upon which I had sat down for a rest.   On my return to the city I hastened to Dr. Behr, told him where I had found the blue butterfly, and described it most minutely.   The Doctor rubbed his hands in high glee.

" The description is correct," he said, nodding; " it must be the right thing.   The whole tribe shall be called by your name now.   But where is the specimen?   Let me have it."

" What, the butterfly? " I asked.   " Oh, that's on the

top of the Santa Lucia Mountain. I came away and forgot it there."

You should have seen the Doctor's face! Out loud he said nothing, but I'd give something pretty to know what his private opinion was just then of women in general and myself in particular.

No Monterey trip is complete without a visit to the old Mission. A lovely spot, this narrow Carmelo Valley, leading to the sea, or the bay rather, which takes its name, I suppose, from the Carmel River emptying within it. It is a pity that these old places are allowed to go to decay. This building here, at least, might be preserved, if not restored, as it is built of stone—the light-yellow chalk-stone of the country. The roof has most all fallen, but the architecture and construction of the old building would disgrace no builder of the present day. It has the slightly Moorish tone which I imagine I can discover in all these places built by the Spanish *padres.*

The bells are gone from out of the towers, but the delicately wrought cross on one still points to heaven. Of the twelve arches which originally spanned the nave, some are quite solid, and could easily support a roof; and if the whole were restored, it would be one of the grandest monuments we could bequeath to grateful generations coming after us.

No wonder Father Junipero Serro loved the spot so well that he wanted to be laid to rest here, where he had performed so important a part of his life's labor. The land was rich with the grain he had sown, and the docile Indians who trimmed his vines in the Mission garden loved him, perhaps more devotedly than their newly given God, for they could not see Him, while the good *padre* provided for them as a father does for his children. But now comes the knotty point, over which there has been so much contention. That the *padre* was buried inside of the old church, there seems to be no doubt. The question is, what became of his bones? Long after the mission system "had outlived its usefulness," the bishops of San Luis, Los Angeles, and San Juan Bautista, came in solemn state to remove the sacred remains to a place not so dilapidated as the Mission church had become. To their consternation, they found nothing to remove; and, though the story was hushed up as much as possible, all sorts of rumors went flying among the superstitious Catholics of Spanish and Indian blood, as to what had become of the good father's bones. Having some curiosity on the subject myself, I once more sought my oracle, Don Rosario Duarte, and asked what he thought had become of this pious man's ashes.

"That," he said, "I can tell you. My mother-in-law, who died ten years since, at an advanced age, has told me a hundred times of the deputation of high officials and humble monks who came all the way out from Spain to carry back with them the bones and ashes of Father Junipero Serro. There are still three of the old Mission Indians living here in town. One of them, a woman named Yumesa, will corroborate my statement, for she claims that she can recollect how every one of the *caballeros* and *monjes* comprising this deputation looked."

I tried my best to find Yumesa, not because I doubted

Don Rosario's word, but because I wanted to see what a real, live Mission Indian looked like. I failed to discover her; but of the thousands who will flock to Monterey in the course of this summer, I hope that some one may make it a special task to find and interview Yumesa.